QUEST

Quest
by
Paul Anthony

The right of Paul Anthony to be identified as the author of this work has been asserted by him in accordance with the Copyright, Designs and Patents Act of 1988. Any similarity to actual persons, living or dead, or actual events, is purely coincidental.

~

First Published 2023

Copyright © Paul Anthony

All Rights Reserved.

Cover Image © Dan Gordon Promotions

Published by

Paul Anthony Associates UK

http://paul-anthony.org/

By the same author

~

In the 'Boyd' Crime Thrillers…

The Fragile Peace

Bushfire

The Legacy of the Ninth

Bell, Book, and Candle

Threat Level One

White Eagle

The Sultan and the Crucifix

Thimbles

The Journey

*

In the 'Davies King' Crime Thrillers…

The Conchenta Conundrum.

Moonlight Shadows

Behead the Serpent

Breakwater

Harbour Lights

~

By the same author

~

In the Thriller and Suspense Thrillers…

Nebulous

Septimus

Sapphire

Quest

*

In Autobiography, true crime, and nonfiction…

Authorship Demystified

Strike! Strike! Strike!

Scougal

*

In Poetry and Anthologies…

Sunset

Scribbles with Chocolate

Uncuffed

Coptales

Chiari Warriors

*

In Children's book (with Meg Johnston)…

Monsters, Gnomes and Fairies (In My Garden)

~

To Margaret - Thank you, for never doubting me.
To Paul, Barrie and Vikki - You only get one chance at life.
Live it well, live it in peace, and live it with love for one another.
To my special friends - Thank you, you are special.

~

With thanks to Margaret Scougal, Pauline Livingstone and Patricia Henderson for editing and advising on my works over many years.

~

... Paul Anthony

The pen paused, restrained only by the tragic circumstances of life, but when replenished and complete, moved on, gliding relentlessly, fuelled by the unique independence of the writer's mind...

*For Margaret: my sounding board,
my unequivocal love, te amo.*

~

*The most resilient undercover operatives are those who fight battles we know nothing about. Such trailblazers engage in covert risk-taking investigations of unimaginable intricacy. They are the unknown and unspoken of who have chosen their path in life and walk it with a silent pride.
It is their quest in life.*

~

In honour of... Red Alpha Six...

~

INTRODUCTION
~

This is the story of Sam Quest, a man from the streets of Northern England. Of medium build, with carefully combed, long dark brown hair that rested on his ears and spread towards his collar, he stood five feet ten inches tall and favoured a black leather jacket, dark-coloured trousers or jeans, and a roll-neck sweater. He was a lover of casual clothing and did not possess a suit or tie. Even Sam's lifestyle, in his adult years, was easy-going.

Sam joined the police and became a detective in Carlisle. He developed a reputation as a good thief-taker despite serving only four years. It was said that he was a natural who quietly got on with the job. Indeed, some of his colleagues, for he had few friends, reckoned he was endowed with a sixth sense: an instinct that empowered him to make a correct judgment or decision without conscious use or mental activation of the normal intellectual processes. He had a nose for crooks and an uncanny ability to successfully profile people as good, bad, or ugly within minutes of first contact. Despite this, he was not renown for shelving individuals into lifelong compartments that would remain locked forever. His mind and attitude were flexible, subtle, and constantly evolving as he progressed through life. It was said that he lacked compassion for his fellow man, could not be swayed by an emotive response, and occasionally enjoyed challenging authority.

The young man had lived an isolated life following the death of his mother who had died from heart failure. She bequeathed Sam an alcoholic father who took his own life twelve months later leaving his son to fend for himself as a teenager. Sam Quest experienced a hard time, was occasionally bullied at school, and tended to shun retaliation preferring to hide in the shadows until the dust had settled. Yet he was blessed with good memory and the capacity to exercise revenge when he chose to. When he exacted revenge, there was no hiding place for those whom he considered his enemies. His brain appeared to be wired differently from others that he worked with.

There was no adequate explanation in the minds of many but perhaps isolation and early independence had taught him more about street life than others in his peer group. He'd learnt the hard way and had carried a heavy burden for most of his life, from the gutter up. Yet he possessed a streak of determination that had not gone unnoticed by those who had recruited him and trained him to his present level.

What did astonish many was the day Police Constable Quest topped the final examination at training school. Only a few years later did people realise that he was possessed of a memory that was beyond comparison with others of his ilk. His powers of retention were unique and often a source of either jealousy or admiration dependent upon the individual sitting in judgement. Those who loved him wanted to emulate him. Those who hated him harboured a fit of juvenile jealousy that was common amongst his rivals in the police force of the day.

Yet despite such admirable capabilities, and whilst in his early twenties, things changed.

Such things that you are about to read never happen. Do they? Or is apparent fiction sometimes close to the truth?

~

Author's Abbreviations for the reader

~

Asset = Source/Informant/Origin of Intelligence

C I D = Criminal Investigation Department

DG = Director General

Europa = Quest (codename)

FSB = Foreign Intelligence Service based in Russia

Jackdaw Three Three = Naval Intelligence

Jupiter = Rafferty (codename)

Mr Blue = The Chief of M15

Mr Green = The Chief of M16

Mr Black = The Chief of 'Black Ops'. (Rafferty)

NCA = National Crime Agency

Pearls = Class A drugs

Red Alpha (Six) = MI5 Surveillance Team/Call signs (numerical)

~

Chapter One

~

During the night
Botchergate, Carlisle
Some years ago.

The hushed black dark of the night exploded into a riotous frenzy of amber and red flashing lights when the sudden scream of an anxious burglar alarm invaded the environment. Long, loud and piercing, the siren alarm indicated that somewhere in the labyrinth of streets that formed Carlisle city centre, a building's security system had been interfered with. Broken electronic contacts and hidden sensors had detected movement inside premises that were locked and secure. An alarm had been triggered and the electronic reaction to the unauthorised opening of doors and windows was underway. It was loud and clear with flashing lights, a wailing siren, and a telephone auto-dialler that had transmitted a pre-recorded 'phone message to the local police.

But what had caused the alarm? Was it a cat clawing at a door in an isolated alley at the back of somewhere, a drop in temperature when the weather changed, the removal of a roof slate, a door forced by a jemmy, a brick thrown through a window, or a fault in the electrical network that fed the city?

Bill Barnes would be the first to know as he sprinted from St Nicholas into Botchergate with his combat boots pounding on the pavement and his police duty tactical belt bouncing from his torso. Made of durable nylon, the belt was overloaded with his, radio, torch, taser, handcuffs, and an overabundance of equipment he might need in the course of his duties as a city cop.

'The gun shop at the top of Botchergate next to the hotel,' splurged across the radio net. 'Alarm sounding! 1096 location!'

'Bottom of Botchergate gaining ground!' shouted Bill as he stepped into the roadway to dodge a swaying drunk. 'Thirty seconds!'

'Crime car attending from Hardwicke Circus,' radioed Sam Quest as he swung his vehicle into Georgian Way and slammed the accelerator to the floor. 'One minute!'

'All units attend!' from Control.

In nearby Court Square, a car engine burst into life.

At the gun shop, the burglar stepped over the broken glass that had showered the pavement, reached inside, and retrieved the brick that had smashed the window. He raked the sides of the window with the brick causing the smaller shards of glass to dislodge and fall to the ground then he hoisted himself safely through the space and landed on his feet inside the shop. Removing a pair of heavy-duty bolt cutters from his jacket, he cut the security chain on an open display rack and helped himself to three semi-automatic rifles.

A Ford saloon hurtled out of Court Square and screeched to a standstill outside the gun shop. The driver jumped from the vehicle and threw an overgrown sledgehammer through the open window. There was a clatter when it hit the floor. A canvas holdall followed and landed next to the burglar's chosen tool.

The intruder picked up the sledgehammer and heaved it against a metal cabinet that was fixed to the wall.

The cabinet bulged. The sledgehammer swung again and buckled one corner loosening it from its holding. A third blow took out the cabinet that crashed to the floor. A further blow to the back of the cabinet found the weakest segment and ripped the metal apart.

A hand reached inside the inadequate cupboard and withdrew a score of pre-loaded detachable box magazines. The first magazine witnessed itself loaded into a semi-automatic rifle. The others found their way into the holdall. Each magazine was capable of discharging thirty rounds.

The burglar dashed to the window and handed the ill-gotten gains to his accomplice.

'Now! Quickly!' yelled the driver who opened the rear door of the Ford and threw the rifles and bag of ammunition into the passenger compartment.

The burglar climbed through the window and launched himself into the rear passenger compartment of the Ford.

Taking off at speed, the driver wrestled with the steering wheel whilst his thieving co-conspirator rolled in the back with three stolen rifles and a bag of ammunition for company.

'Move it!' screamed from the back seat.

'Hang on tight!' from the driver.

It was all over in one minute.

Bill Barnes sprinted towards the scene radioing, 'It's a smash and grab. A dark blue Ford has just left the scene and is heading towards me at speed.'

Barnes moved into the middle of Botchergate, withdrew his baton, and threw it at the oncoming vehicle before diving to the offside of the road and narrowly missing the getaway car.

There was an explosion of glass when the policeman's baton made contact. The Ford's windscreen disintegrated; its driver lost control, and the vehicle mounted the pavement before colliding with a lamp standard.

Forcing the gearstick into reverse, the getaway driver realised that the front bumper of the car was badly tangled with the lamp standard. Their horns were locked in deadly combat and the lamp standard was winning. The rear wheels spun and burnt a tread pattern into Botchergate, but the escape was over.

Jumping from the car, the driver was immediately taken down by the brute force of Bill Barnes who smothered him as the two men fell to the ground and Bill overpowered his adversary.

Sam Quest thundered into the fray, slid the around the Crescent, and roared to the scene of the collision. Snatching the handbrake, Sam slewed the unliveried crime car to a standstill an inch from the rear of the burglar's getaway vehicle.

'At scene! Engaging!' radioed Sam. 'Assistance required! Armed suspect at the scene! Trigger! Trigger! Trigger!'

Slithering from the rear of the Ford, the burglar landed on the tarmac dragging a semi-automatic rifle with him. He regained his feet and drew the rifle level with Sam as the detective sprang from the crime car to confront the suspect.

'Back off or I'll shoot!' threatened the gunman pulling the rifle into his shoulder.

'Give it up,' shouted Sam.

There was a snap from a pair of handcuffs when Bill Barnes secured the driver and rolled him towards the front of the Ford and into a safer place where he took cover from the gun threat.

Bill's prisoner kicked out, caught the policeman in the stomach, and attempted to run off but Barnes clung to his leg and brought him down again,

The gunman stepped back, raised his rifle, hugged it into his shoulder, and threatened, 'Get down! Get out of the way or I'll kill you!'

Sam ignored the order, threw himself at the gunman's feet, and pushed him backwards. Caught off balance, the gunslinger momentarily lost control and the rifle pointed skywards at the precise moment he pulled the trigger.

A score of bullets ripped through the air when the gunman kept firing and the smell of cordite mixed with fear filled the nostrils of Sam Quest and Bill Barnes.

Window upon window from the surrounding shops caved in as the loose cannon's bullets smashed into the glass in a frenzy of uncontrolled mayhem. Fragments of glass exploded on the ground. The walls were peppered with bullets that gradually grew closer to Quest's head as the gunman tried to regain control.

The struggle on the ground continued with the gunfire exploding around Sam's ears. The constant staccato noise pounded in his skull as the barrel of the gun lowered to eye level and shell casings ejected from the weapon.

Unable to line up his target, the gunman repeatedly struck Sam about the head and shoulders with the rifle butt as the sound of approaching police sirens grew louder.

'You're nicked,' yelled Sam as the two men rolled along the gutter struggling to overpower each other.

The gunman rammed the rifle butt into Sam's face. There was another clatter when Sam dislodged the rifle from his enemy's grip and it fell onto the pavement.

A well-formed fist smashed into Sam's face blackening his eye and cutting the skin close to the tear trough. Blood spurted from his face before Sam felt another blow to the nose followed by a knee into his groin.

Sam caved in, hadn't the strength to continue, and felt the gunman thumping his head repeatedly. The feeling of the fist hammering his skull blended with the echoing sound of the bullets still fresh in Sam's brain. Gradually, he began to drift into unconsciousness as blood escaped from his face and streamed into a pool in the gutter.

Moments later, half the police team on duty arrived in Botchergate to see the gunman regain both his feet and his rifle.

Two officers equipped with pistols stepped forward and instructed the gunman to drop the weapon.

There was no response other than the rifle drawing a bead on the firearms officers, a finger curling around the trigger, and the first hint of a squeeze of the firing mechanism.

A hail of gunfire from two Heckler and Koch police pistols floored the gunman and took him to his last breath.

He died on the streets where he had delivered his evil doings. A police boot approached, kicked his rifle away, and then stood watching the final seconds of the gunman's life.

An ambulance arrived with its siren blaring and blue lights flashing from the roof. Two paramedics assessed the situation before loading Sam into the rear of the vehicle voicing, 'One dead and this one alive. Casualty! Accident and emergency! We can stop the bleeding but it's a head injury too. I also see heavy bruising. Come on! Let's go!'

The rear doors closed and the ambulance took off with its siren blaring and lights flashing as Bill Barnes helped drag the remaining prisoner into a police van and a tarpaulin was lowered to cover the gunman's body.

A sergeant arrived at the scene and took control with the top brass following minutes later to scrutinise events. The keyholder for the gun shop was called and a scene of crime examiner was called out to secure forensic evidence and take photographs of the plot. A duty detective took over the initial investigation as the Ford was extricated from the lamp standard and impounded by the police. Suddenly, the lights went out in Botchergate when the electricity circuit embedded inside the lamp standard fused and an electronic effect knocked out all the other lights on the street.

Three hours later, the Ford was reported stolen, and Sam Quest was lying in a hospital bed having made his statement to Jack Wishart, the late duty detective, who confirmed the criminal arrested by Bill Barnes would be held overnight and charged with burglary, firearm offences, and various other offences later that day.

'Sorry, Mr Quest!' explained Dr Adams, the accident and emergency consultant. 'You were badly beaten about the head, face, and shoulders. An x-ray reveals no damage to either your skull or your limbs, but I will not discharge you until you have rested properly, I am satisfied that your eyesight is good, and nothing further is amiss.'

'Nothing was broken, good! Thank you, Doctor. If I Can have my things, I'll get out of your hair and go home.'

'No, Mr Quest! I also want to test your hearing once your brain has calmed down. Your body needs time to recover from the trauma of blood loss and body shock. You will stay here overnight until we are completely satisfied with your condition.'

'Are you sure? Do you have to do that?' challenged Sam.

'I want to see your vital signs improve and I'm anxious we check your eyes again before you are free to go.'

'Oh! It's just that I have a lot to do, Doctor.'

'It's not a game, Mr Quest,' argued Dr Adams. 'Just because you are a police officer does not mean that you get special treatment and are released sooner than other patients. You can walk out of this hospital now and there's nothing I can do to stop you. But if you collapse in Casualty Drive don't expect a round of applause from the staff on duty when they carry you back in. The nurses have enough to do with patients who need care without worrying about those with your curious attitude. Now, are we on the same playing field, Mr Quest? Do you understand what I'm saying to you?'

'Perfectly,' nodded Sam shrugging his shoulders. 'I fully understand, Doctor. Thank you for keeping me on the right path.' Turning to the detective present, Sam said, 'I'll catch up with you tomorrow, Jack. I'm done. The job is too much for me. I can't take a battering like that and carry on being a cop. I haven't got the balls.'

'You could find them if you tried,' suggested Jack. 'You survived. Why don't you man up for God's sake?'

'It's the only part of my body that swine didn't hit. I'm aching all over. No, Jack, I've done my bit. I'm not spilling any more blood on the city streets. It's over.'

'It's not the best way to go, Sam. You know what the alpha males in the nick will say, they'll say you were a bag of tripe. Or something like that.'

'I don't care,' replied Sam. 'I've done my time.'

'Time? I think it's high time you left, Detective Constable Wishart,' intervened Dr Adams. 'Words of comfort and rest are needed now. Since you can offer neither to Mr Quest, please vacate the premises immediately.'

Jack Wishart placed Sam's statement in his briefcase, shook hands, and left the cubicle.

Settling down into the bed, Sam asked the doctor, 'Is there a phone I can use, sir? I'd like to call a friend.'

'Of course, I'll have the trolley phone brought shortly.'

Half an hour later, Sam dialled a number and waited. A voice answered with, 'Jupiter!'

'Quest!' replied Sam. 'We're on. I'm in the Cumberland Infirmary, Carlisle, Accident and Emergency Department under the care of Doctor Nigel Adams. He has diagnosed me with head and shoulder injuries following an incident last night when I dealt with an armed robber! Shots fired and I'm lucky to be alive. Heavy bruising and some muscle discomfort are apparent. My head is full of the noise of a gun constantly discharging! I also have a cut eye, facial bruising, and blood loss. That said, no broken bones and they tell me that it's just a question of time before I'm discharged. Mind you, I feel a headache or two is on the way and I expect a couple of nightmares will follow. I've rehearsed them all.'

There was silence before Jupiter replied, 'It sounds perfect, Quest. Are you happy to proceed as planned?'

'Yes! I'm ready, boss.'

'I am not your boss, Quest and never will be. You are your own boss. Don't ever call me boss again. Understood?'

'Yes! Sorry! Just habit.'

'Good! You know what to do, Quest.'

'I'll be there,' replied Sam who ended the call and snuggled beneath the sheets. 'I'll have a nap before my first nightmare.'

Out in the city streets, life went on. The lamp standards were resurrected. An alarm sounded in a factory on an industrial estate, a 999 call was received when an incident of domestic abuse was reported, and a man was found in a drunk and incapable condition at the bottom of Botchergate.

Sam touched his cheeks and felt how sore and tender they were. Despite the medication, his head pounded, and his shoulders ached incessantly. His mind wandered to the barrel of a gun pointed at him with the shell casings ejecting left, right and centre as his mind tried to comprehend it all. He lay back and studied the ceiling as the night duty staff quietly went about their business in the ward.

'What have I done?' he thought. 'What the hell have I done? That's my holiday plans scuppered for the next few years. Maybe the rest of my life too. I need to can the kayak, I reckon. I can't see myself paddling down the river for a while. All because of one crazy night and a phone call lead me to change my life forever.'

~

Chapter Two

~

Dawn, the following day.
Piccadilly,
London.

      Rolling lawns and tall trees beautify Green Park: one of the eight Royal Parks situated in Central London. It is the home of the Bomber Command Memorial which commemorates the crews of RAF Bomber Command who embarked on missions during the Second World War. Close by witness the Commonwealth Memorial Gates and the inscription thereon which reads: 'In memory of the five million volunteers from the Indian sub-continent, Africa and the Caribbean who fought with Britain in the two World Wars.' Deeper inside the park one can also find the Canada Memorial. The Canada Memorial remembers the one million Canadians who served with British forces during the two World Wars. The narrow walkway, dividing the memorial in two, faces the direction of the Canadian port of Halifax in Nova Scotia, from where many Canadian service personnel sailed for Europe. The bronze leaves embedded in the granite are maple: the national symbol of Canada.
      With such remembrances on display, one might be forgiven for thinking that the world was at peace. The situation, however, is often different for those planning conflicts.
      Piccadilly is a road in the City of Westminster, London. It runs parallel to Green Park and is situated to the south of Mayfair, between Hyde Park Corner in the west, and Piccadilly Circus in the east. As part of the A4, it connects Central London to Hammersmith, Earl's Court, Heathrow Airport and the M4 motorway westward. Piccadilly is just under one mile long and is one of the widest highways in London. The street has existed since at least medieval times, but in approximately 1611, Mr Robert Baker acquired land in the area and began making and selling piccadills. Baker improved the area, built his home, and extended his workspace. The manufacture

of piccadills increased and eventually lent its name to the street now globally recognised as Piccadilly. A piccadill, historically, is a large broad collar of lace that became fashionable in the early seventeenth century.

In a side street adjoining Piccadilly, and close to the Japanese Embassy, a white pickup van fitted with a cherry picker drew up. Two men wearing dark overalls got out of the passenger side of the vehicle. The word 'security' was printed on the back of their coveralls.

Manhandling equipment from the pickup, the duo cordoned off the base of a lamp standard with cones and a traffic barrier. They signalled to the van and the driver swung into Piccadilly and parked close to the lamp standard. One of the men then occupied the platform whilst the other activated the cherry picker. Once at the correct height, the operator began fitting a new camera system to the lamp standard. The camera system consisted of multiple lenses that were part of a CCTV system. Linking the system to the lamp standard's electrical network, he adjusted the angle of the camera lenses so that the system covered Green Park.

Traffic reduced speed due to the hazardous activity, but pedestrians ignored the work and carried on regardless. It was a public display of fitting a new security system for the Royal Park.

The team began testing the system. Interested bystanders could see how the lenses pointed towards the park and away from the nearby buildings to their rear.

Music played from the van's cabin as a bus drove further along Piccadilly and dropped off its passengers.

Inside the platform, the workman removed a dust cap from the rear of one of the cameras. Only he could see that the camera had two lenses. One lens pointed forward to Green Park whilst the other lens was pointed from the rear of the camera at the front door of the travel agents. The camera was fitted with a tiny wide-angled lens that could not be seen at the rear. The front of the camera, however, clearly possessed a visible lens that was pointed at the park. Dark in colour, the cover lens blended into the body of the system and pointed at the front door of the travel agents. All the other lenses pointed into the park.

'All in order,' voiced the operator of the cherry picker.

'Bring me down,' from the platform.

The cherry picker lowered, returned itself to the body of the pickup, and waited for the team to finish their duties. They loaded the cones and barriers into the pickup and drove away.

In another part of London, eager hands manipulated a computer keyboard whilst the camera system began to record the comings and goings of all those who visited both Green Park and the Novikov travel agents in Piccadilly.

~

Chapter Three
~

Carleton Hall, Penrith
Cumbria
Three Months later

The name 'Carleton' originates from the days of the Anglo-Saxons. 'Carle' means farmer or peasant whilst 'ton and tun' both signify a village. Carleton village itself is a small line of houses along one side of the A686 road that forms part of the boundary of Penrith's built-up area. Carleton was once a prosperous hamlet, and the local Cross Keys Pub was a stopping-off point for travellers and the centre of activity in the area.

In modern times, the presence of Carleton Hall dominates the former village which has been engulfed by progress and the growth of the town of Penrith. Standing on land close to the River Eamont, the property was first owned by a family named Carleton who were prominent in the area at the time of the Norman Conquest. They owned the building until 1707 when it was purchased by John Pattison who was an Attorney at law in Penrith. Upon his death, he left the property to his son, Christopher, who died without issue. The Pattinson estate then devolved to his three sisters, the eldest of whom received Carleton Hall as her share. She was married to a Mr Simpson of Penrith. He rebuilt part of the Mansion, added stables and out-buildings, and laid out the gardens and grounds resembling what is present today.

But time marches on and Carleton Hall was first recorded as a grade 11 listed building on 24 April 1951. On this date, Carleton Hall became the police headquarters for what is now Cumbria Constabulary.

It was to police headquarters that Sam Quest was taken in the rear seat of a taxi he had hired that morning. The vehicle drove through the underpass beneath the A66 highway and dropped Sam off outside the main entrance.

The detective entered the reception area, completed the security procedure, and was escorted to the office of George Edwards: Cumbria's Chief Constable.

In his late fifties and of stocky build, Edwards carried a slight paunch that was visible despite his tight-fitting uniform. His attire complimented a receding hairline and a thin grey moustache. He was entertaining a guest when the intercom on his desk buzzed and his secretary announced, 'Detective Constable Quest is here, Chief Constable! He has an appointment with you.'

'Ahh! Quest! Yes, show him in,' replied the Chief.

Sam strolled in wearing a black leather blazer, a roll-neck sweater, dark denim jeans, and a pair of black suede shoes offset by a black balaclava that had been rolled down to lay across the crown of his head.

'Morning, sir,' offered Sam who reached out and accepted a handshake from the Chief.

'Take a seat, Detective Constable,' gestured Edwards as he considered Sam's attire in a disapproving manner. 'How are you today? I presume you have recovered somewhat and are ready to push on with the matter in hand?'

'I'm much better, thank you, sir,' replied the detective who nodded at a dark-suited gentleman standing by a window overlooking the lawns of Carleton Hall. 'And yes, I'm ready.'

'Are you sure?' asked the Chief who lifted a document from his desk, waved it in front of Sam, and said, 'I see you have been diagnosed with PTSD, Post-traumatic stress disorder. In the police service, it is often caused by involvement in incidents with firearms, shootings, knives, extreme violence, bombs, explosions, fatal road accidents, child deaths, cot deaths, deaths involving limb severance and decapitation, suicide, and dealing with death regularly. On average an operational police officer can expect to deal with eighty-five incidents as described above in a thirty-year operational career.

- 27 -

You are here today because I am told you wish to jump out of the frying pan into the fire. It all seems rather stupid to me. Do you not agree that the decision that awaits you is something that you ought not to rush into?'

'I'm not rushing into anything, sir. I'm aware of what lies ahead and have prepared myself accordingly.'

'In that case, I have to be sure that you have been fully briefed as to the next stage of your career,' explained the Chief.

'I understand. We've been planning this for some months now. I just needed the best way out and the opportunity arose when those two broke into the gun shop and I ended up in the hospital.'

Edwards nodded sympathetically and ventured, 'Constable Bill Barnes received a commendation for his work that night, Quest. I don't understand why you refused to accept yours. Very strange! Am I to take it that you have considered the proposition that if you sign these papers today your current colleagues will be talking about you in a way perhaps not anticipated by yourself?'

'Others in my department know why I am here today, sir,' replied Sam. 'I've told them I'm resigning because I can't stand the heat. I lost my bottle when that gunman tried to kill me. I couldn't bear being assaulted again. I told them I had no intention of spending my life in and out of the hospital doing this crazy stupid job. I've had enough. I'm not strong enough either mentally or physically to do the job properly. That's what I said.'

'And did they believe you?'

'Yes!' concluded Sam. 'Otherwise, I would not be sitting opposite you at this desk today. Plus, I found five white feathers in my locker this morning. You know what that means, don't you?'

'I certainly do,' replied the Chief. 'It's a widely recognised symbol of cowardice. In a short period. you've switched from hero to coward. They've taken an obvious dislike to you, Quest. Do you know who it was?'

'I think so but I'll keep that to myself if you don't mind, sir. Without knowing it, whoever put the white feathers there may have done me a favour. If all goes to plan, I'll remain a coward for some time. Hopefully, I'll soon be the unwanted man by next week.'

'And the forgotten man shortly thereafter,' proposed the Chief. 'Are you sure you want to proceed?'

'Absolutely!'

Turning to his guest, Chief Constable Edwards said, 'Is there anything you wish to add at this stage, Bernard?'

Emerging from the shadow of the curtains, Bernard Rafferty engaged the detective with, 'I'm pleased to meet you at last, Quest.'

'I recognise your voice,' replied Sam. 'Have we met before?'

'You know me as Jupiter.'

'Ah!' shrugged Sam. 'Jupiter! The Roman God! If memory serves me well, Jupiter struck down his enemies with bolts of lightning and eagles were his sacred birds. How am I doing so far?'

Rafferty's facial expression remained solid and unchanged when he responded, 'To date, you have followed the briefing perfectly and the Security Service are pleased with your progress. Logan is looking forward to your next meeting. However, I should tell you that Jupiter is only my codename. I'd love to strike down our enemies with bolts of thunder but, alas, technology has thus far not taken us along that path.'

'A question of time?' suggested Sam.

'If time is crucial then welcome to my dedicated team of sacred eagles,' replied Rafferty shaking Sam's hand. 'You will remember from your studies that in Greek and Roman mythology, the eagle was Jupiter's bird of choice and served as his messenger.'

'Which is what you want me to do,' declared Sam. 'You want me to be someone that resembles a personal messenger for the Security Service?'

'I detect a thin slice of humour in your response, Quest, but you seem to have grasped part of your brief well and to the point.'

'You mentioned a dedicated team. My brief suggests that if you are Jupiter then I must be one of the moons that orbit you.'

'Which one would you like?'

'Europa!' declared Sam. 'One of the sixty-nine moons orbiting the planet Jupiter. Am I one of many?'

Rafferty allowed a thin smile to crease his cheeks, denied an answer, but replied, 'The fact that you can compare the briefing with elements of the solar system, as well as Greek and Roman mythology, tells me you are aware of what is required. Sadly, the work ahead is much more realistic than folklore and fantasy. However, I suggest we clear the paperwork up before we go any further.'

'I agree,' replied Sam. 'I'm aware of the content. Where do I sign?'

'Here and here,' signalled the Chief Constable pointing to two distinct piles of paper on his desk. He laid a hand on one set and said, 'These papers, when signed by yourself, will be lodged in your file here at police headquarters. They will signify to anyone who reads your personal file that you resigned from Cumbria Police on this date because of injuries sustained on duty that affected your mental health and your ability to continue effectively in the role of a police constable. A medical certificate will show that after the assault upon you, the condition of PTSD was diagnosed, and you were declared unfit for duty. They will also see a handwritten note from me indicating that you were regarded as something of a deserter and had received five white feathers from your colleagues. I'm going to write you up as a coward, Constable Quest.' Glancing at Rafferty, Edwards said, 'That is what you wanted, is it not?'

Straight-faced, Rafferty nodded positively.

The Chief Constable then gestured to the other pile of papers and continued, 'Your signature on these papers authorises your covert transfer as a detective to a section of the Security Service that Mr Rafferty oversees. You will continue to receive your police salary and contributions to your pension. That said, for security reasons, your salary will not be paid into your bank account. Rather, it will be paid into an account administered by Mr Rafferty of which I have no knowledge. Indeed, I have very little knowledge of what Mr Rafferty does. Nor would I wish to do so. In basic terms, Quest, you are about to formally resign from the police when the truth of the matter is that you are merely transferring into a long-term undercover position. Such arrangements are unique and extremely rare. You ought not to confuse the role asked of you with that of a surveillance officer attached to one of the many different operational squads in the police service. The kind of undercover work you are about to embark on is much more complex than that.'

'I'm sure it is, sir.'

'Once you sign, Quest, there is no going back.'

'Could I borrow your pen, sir?' pleaded Sam.

Edwards handed his pen over and watched as Detective Constable Sam Quest resigned and recommenced his career under the guidance and governance of Bernard Rafferty.

'Good luck, Mr Quest,' stated the Chief Constable. 'I will secure the police papers. Mr Rafferty will take the papers relevant to your new job to London with him where they will be secured in the Security Service. I only hope that in the years ahead you will one day be able to afford a suit and tie and conduct yourself in a manner befitting an individual who works for Her Majesty's Government.'

'Thank you,' smiled Sam.

'Mr Rafferty,' declared Edwards. 'I deliver to you Samuel Quest, as discussed.'

'Sam, sir,' intervened the detective. 'I was christened Sam and that's what it says on the papers I have just signed. Did you read them, Mr Edwards?'

With a scornful glance at Sam, the Chief Constable turned to the MI5 man and stated, 'Yours, Mr Rafferty, I believe. I give you Sam Quest, as requested.'

'Accepted,' replied Rafferty.

Sam laid the Chief's pen on the desk and stood back.

'Follow me, Quest,' rasped Rafferty.

Moments later, the office door closed leaving Edwards alone and Quest and Rafferty heading out of the building to a location that Edwards neither knew nor cared to know.

The Chief drummed his fingers on the table before leafing through Quest's file. Eventually, Edwards unwrapped some of the papers and read the notes that had been handwritten in the margins of his some of his training reports.

'*A good memory surely born from many hours of revision,*' was written in black ink on his initial course report. '*Determined, occasionally arrogant, possibly deceitful,*' in another report. '*Possessing the ability to blend into the background,*' scribed in the margin of his surveillance course.

The Chief thumbed the sheets of his recruitment papers looking for answers to the questions fermenting in his mind. If British Intelligence wanted him, was it because he harboured a history of extreme right-wing political views? Or was he so far to the left that he was a member of the Communist Party? I suppose such people can be turned to work in the interests of the United Kingdom. Or is Sam Quest a Muslim of the Islamic faith? Or perhaps a Jew? It would make sense for them to recruit him and infiltrate him into a mosque somewhere if that be the case. Yet written boldly for all to see were the words, *no religion, no politics.*

'What was all that about?' the Chief asked himself. 'Quest was outstanding in his surveillance course and then topped his crime course. Suddenly, he's snapped up by British Intelligence as if he was a pot of gold that had been mistakenly dropped in the gutter by one of the richest people in the world.

There's nothing in these reports that portrays him as valuable. He recently failed a basic firearms course that over ninety per cent of officers passed with ease.'

Chuckling, Edwards thought, 'I hope they don't want him to be a sniper. They're going to be disappointed.'

Edwards turned another page and continued, 'He doesn't even possess any linguistic abilities. Such remarks made by course instructors are commonplace. Why is he gold dust? There's nothing glorious about Sam Quest that I can see. He's just a scruffy lout that never had any loyalty to us. I asked why they wanted him and was told I don't need to know. The next thing is they recruit him behind my back, and we're all done and dusted. Still, Quest is finished. He will soon be the forgotten man of Cumbria Police. Good riddance! I don't like people who jump ship whether they've got PTSD or otherwise. Hero to zero in ten seconds flat. Well, he certainly wasn't a hero that night. Barnes and the firearms officers yes. Quest no! Now, which instructor remarked that he was possibly deceitful?'

Chief Constable Edwards turned the pages, fingered the relevant scribble, and thought, 'Ah! Inspector Daniels! I must remember Inspector Daniels since he can dissect an underling's personality. A good man is Daniels. A man who can spot deceit in officers like Quest.'

Removing a fountain pen from a fancy wooden pen holder on his desk, Chief Constable Edwards took a piece of A4-sized paper and wrote a note for Quest's file. The note began with '*Not fit for purpose,*' and ended with, '*A good example of cowardice in the face of adversity amalgamated with a chronic case of post-traumatic stress.*'

Edwards secured the papers in a document bag muttering, 'If Rafferty is Jupiter and Quest is a sacred eagle nicknamed Europa then who the hell am I in the pecking order?'

~

Chapter Four
~

The Fort
Scotland
Three months later.

Situated between Nairn and Fraserburgh, the eighteenth-century castle stood resolute and proud on the Moray Firth coast of northern Scotland. About an hour's drive from Aberdeen, Inverness, and the Cairngorms, the stronghold enjoyed both an isolated position and easy access to much larger communities. The fort, as it was affectionately known, was a training ground for operatives attached to British Intelligence.

Bernard Rafferty entered the library and nodded to the two men present. Tall, lean, and muscular about the shoulders and chest, he cut a good figure with a tanned complexion and a flat stomach born from a regime of regular exercise and keeping fit. He removed a bottle of brandy and three glasses from an oak cabinet.

'Quest, we meet again. How are you?'

'Good, sir!' replied Sam. 'And you?'

'Likewise! I'm pleased with your progress. My colleague tells me you are ready. Isn't that right, Logan?'

'Sam Quest is as ready as I can make him, sir,' replied the barrel-chested six-foot-tall Logan. 'We've somehow managed to cram six months of training into three months of hard work.' Logan smoothed his military-style thick moustache, looked Sam up and down, smiled, and continued, 'He's as fit as a fiddle from a month running up and down the mountains of the Cairngorms and as wily as an old fox from learning his craft on the streets of Aberdeen and Inverness. He'll do. Quest makes the grade, sir.'

Gesturing his interest, Rafferty uncorked the brandy and began pouring the contents into three large balloon glasses whilst saying, 'Quest! As you know Mr Logan here is a retired Regimental Sergeant Major in the Royal Regiment of Scotland. The regiment and its forebears are older than the walls of this castle. Like yourself, he was specially selected some years ago to train my team of operatives in various techniques.'

'I presumed he was military from the outset, sir,' replied Sam. 'Even from the day of our first meeting when he suggested I might be interested in a special type of policing.'

'Well, I did tell you were being trained by the best,' chuckled Logan who accepted a glass from Rafferty.

'You are a man of mystery, Logan,' suggested Sam.

'In what way?'

'After all these weeks, I still don't know your first name. You've always been Logan and nothing else.'

'Good! Logan, it is and Logan it will continue to be. I'm pushing into my late fifties, Sam. When I decide to leave it will be quietly without fanfare and as Logan. Only Logan! That is all you need to know of me.'

'Yet you know everything about me.'

'It is the way of this life,' replied Logan raising his glass. 'You'll get used to it, Sam.'

'A problem for you, Quest,' remarked Rafferty. 'What is the difference between surveillance, counter-surveillance, and anti-surveillance? What relevance does it have to your brief?'

'A quiz!' countered Sam ith a smile. 'Brandy and quiz night at the fort. Not something I expected.'

'Challenge noted,' replied the straight-faced Rafferty. 'An answer is required. How sharp is your mind?'

'Surveillance will take place when I am tasked to gather information about a person or group who are of interest to us,' responded Sam. 'It may include observation using electronic equipment, such as closed-circuit television, or interception of electronically transmitted information like internet traffic, postal interception, or phone calls. Whenever appropriate I will call you and request the deployment of specific technology and devices. You will consider that request and action it where it is appropriate to do so. Jupiter has the final decision on what technologies to use because you have a much broader and in-depth knowledge of what is available.'

Rafferty studied Quest as his student continued, 'We use surveillance to prevent or detect crime, espionage, or terrorism. It's often a two-way process because we know that some organised crime syndicates often use surveillance to plan and commit crimes. Indeed, some businesses gather intelligence on their competitors, suppliers, or customers.'

'Go on,' gestured Rafferty. 'How would you choose to follow a target, Quest?'

'On foot. I would be directly behind the subject or situated to their left or right and their rear. I might even choose to be ahead of the subject,' declared Quest donning a pair of spectacles which he removed form his jacket pocket. 'As you know, these glasses enable me to see behind as well to the front and there's always reflections in the windows if we're in the right environment.'

'Quest has worn them well,' added Logan.

Rafferty nodded and continued, 'And whilst driving?'

'I'd follow in an identical manner but if there were a team of us present, I'd use the box system, place the subject in the centre of the box, and react to their movements.'

'Anything else?' probed Rafferty.

'That's the tip of the iceberg but there's also drone coverage and...'

'Enough!' interrupted Rafferty raising his hand. 'I just wanted to see your reaction to my questions. I want that knowledge embedded in your brain every time you move. What about counter-surveillance, Quest.'

'Counter-surveillance is a method I will use to help me recognise that I may be under surveillance. It's the practice of avoiding surveillance or making surveillance difficult for those who may be following me. There may be occasions when I know I am being followed and take no action because it suits me to do so. But if I need to dodge my followers, I'll use the counter measures that Sergeant-Major Logan taught me on the streets of Aberdeen and Inverness. I intend to ensure my safety and the security of our operations. I'll use anti-surveillance methods to allow me to do the things I need to do when I know that I am under surveillance myself.'

Rafferty glanced at Logan who acknowledged with, 'The man knows the theory as well as the practice, sir.'

'Good!' replied Rafferty who handed Quest a brandy. He raised his glass and said, 'Congratulations, Quest.'

'At last! I'll drink to that,' added Logan. 'Well done, Sam. It has been an adventure training you. I wish you well in the months ahead.'

The two men took a sip of brandy apiece before Sam reluctantly followed suit and then queried, 'Just a point, sir. I have no legend, no false story, no made-up biography that I can recount to anyone I meet who may suspect me of being a police officer. Is that the next thing we do before I am allowed to fly with the eagles?'

'You'll be engaged in undercover work relevant to drugs importation, serious crime organisation, and matters of national importance referred to me by higher authority,' explained Rafferty. 'I will shortly give you a telephone number that will connect you to the Jupiter office. It lies within our operations centre and in my absence, it may be answered by one of my team. However, Quest, you will report directly to me and only me. In addition, you will only take instruction from me and no one else. Is that understood?'

'Yes,' replied Sam. 'But what about my legend? Surely, I need to set up a false background for my safety?'

'Your life is your legend, Quest. Don't hide your past. Anyone who decides to check you out will find that you are a former disgraced cop who packed in before he got the sack. Your cop pals have written you off as a failure and a coward. One violent incident knocked you down. You couldn't hack it anymore. But since you left Cumbria, Quest, Logan has updated your computerised career papers. Your Chief Constable Edwards referred to it as your personal file. It's all been computerised since you left the job. It's the technology you know. It has its advantages for some and disadvantages for others. You now have a criminal record relative to supplying drugs since leaving the police and you are suspected of continuing to supply Class A drugs. You're flagged to one man in the National Crime Agency. The criminal record is in your name and if anyone ever interrogates that name on the Police National Computer, they will be flagged directly to Commander Logan at the NCA.'

'I thought you were military,' queried Quest.

'I am a man of many means,' replied a deadpan Logan. 'As you said a short time ago: a man of mystery.'

'And a good man with a computer,' revealed Rafferty. 'People we are interested in, and putting you against, may well decide to do a background enquiry into you. Let them do it. You left the police because you weren't up to the job. Now you hate the cops. Don't forget that.'

'Will that work?'

'Organised crime syndicates check people out. They won't expect to find someone who freely admits to being an ex-cop and they'll find one of their kind in Carlisle who'll know the ins and outs of the city detectives. Some of the crooks will have heard about you on the grapevine. Criminals swop notes about cops. I'm sure you've heard that before.'

'Yes, I have.'

'Remember, Quest, when you left you expected to be branded a coward who wanted out of the kitchen. It was too hot. Your colleagues even gave you five white feathers so that you would remember them. A mark of respect? I think not. Now you are not just a coward, you are the forgotten man.

Your past is your legend along with a delicate twist of drug abuse just to give some flavour to those who may become suspicious of you. It's one less thing to worry about. Understood?'

Nodding, Sam asked, 'How long does this go on?'

'It's a five-year cycle,' revealed Rafferty. 'When five years is up we'll re-evaluate the operation, submit you to psychological assessment as part of our standard procedure, and then come to terms with the future thereafter. Don't worry, Quest. We'll look after you. Your salary will be paid into a bank account maintained by my service. You won't see a penny enter your account until your time with us is over. At which time the account will be assigned to you. There will be no withdrawals and you will receive five years' salary.'

'A lump sum?' probed Sam, slightly confused. He opened his mouth to ask another question.

Rafferty cut him off with, 'After all, you've lost your job, resigned, hit the pavement with nothing to show for it, and you are a proven coward. You're out of work. You are a penniless nobody, Quest. Just as we planned.'

'How will I make ends meet?'

'From hand to mouth until you get your feet under the table,' explained Rafferty. 'I want people to see that you are penniless. It's part of your legend. When the time is right, you'll be provided with a second-hand car and a debit card in your name. The account relevant to the card will never run out of money but the total balance will always be low and match your disposition in life. You'll see how it works out as we progress.'

'Of course, I will,' shrugged Sam.

'Tell me, Quest. One last question! How will you know when you are making progress?'

'When I find a weakness inside the target organisation. A weakness or frailty that we can exploit and turn to our advantage. Will that do, Mr Rafferty or is this still part of an unofficial examination? Is quiz night still live?'

'It will do for now.'

'I beg to differ, Mr Rafferty, but I note that the training I have undertaken presumes that the target is beyond reproach, cannot be tackled by normal methods of policing, and is highly professional in what they do.'

'That is correct, Quest.'

'What if they turn out to be less than proficient at what they do? They may be first-timers in the world of crime. In my experience, some criminals are never as good as they think they are. They gain a reputation amongst their peer group because they've not been caught, not because they are above the law. Often, it's because of police resources. There aren't enough police officers on the job to control crime effectively. It's a political thing. Successive governments don't want to spend too much money on the police service. Just enough. And they don't want the police to become so big and powerful that democracy is threatened by a police or military-style coup like we occasionally see in other countries. Some crooks are lucky. They manage to stay under the radar for a long time before we hook onto them. Don't you agree?'

Rafferty grinned, handed a business card over, and said, 'Power! Politics! And still challenging authority, I see. Why am I not surprised? Memorise the number on the card, Quest, because the recipient of the call will indicate you have phoned a bookmaker. You have an account with a bookie now. Horses, dogs, anything goes! My office is the bookmaker. It is the Jupiter office as far as our organisation is concerned. The people working there have high-level security clearance and work directly with me. They will look upon you as an asset and not know your identity. Is that clear?'

'Yes! I suppose it is. I'll take your word for it.'

'Good! If you are interrupted by the enemy when you ring or think you are being listened to, just revert to placing a bet on a horse. If your bet is on a race that is fifteen, thirty or forty-five minutes after the hour, then we will know that you are not secure. If your bet is on a race that takes place on the hour, we will know that you are safe to speak. Your call will be diverted to me wherever I am within seconds if need be. Don't try to check the telephone number on the card because it doesn't exist. It has no history and no subscribers. Bear in mind, you have been selected for a specific job. This matter is between you and me and no one else. Logan here is the only other person in the team you may physically meet. I will deploy him to cover you when needed or when we learn of something detrimental to your safety.'

'It's like being a spy,' chuckled Sam.

'Because you are a spy, Quest. My spy. Unique and unknown and it will stay that way. Your codename is Europa, by the way. Not that I expect you to use it but that will be how you are referred to by members of my team. Just for your information, Quest.'

'Europa! Back to Jupiter's moons. Great! In that case, Jupiter, when does the fun begin?'

'Now!' declared Rafferty removing a document from a briefcase. 'Read this. It's the briefing for the job ahead.'

The Moray Firth heaved as Sam read his brief. The sea crashed into the ancient brickwork, pounded the fort's masonry, and then withdrew to recover its strength.'

'Do you know anything about ships, Quest?'

'They float on water and if I wasn't here, I'd be on holiday in a kayak in the waters off the Algarve coast,' explained Sam as he read the document. 'That was my plan until this started.'

'How about Liverpool instead of Portugal?' probed Rafferty. 'Ever been there?'

'No! Not all.'

'Liverpool has a long history of smuggling drugs and firearms, Quest. It's one of the oldest ports in the country and, as an example, was a key location in the 1919-1921 Irish War of Independence. The Irish Republican Army smuggled many of its weapons out of Liverpool in their fight against the British army. That said, Quest, we're more interested in what is being smuggled into Liverpool at present. Ever worked in a dockland environment, Quest?'

'No! Never!'

'Not to worry. You soon will. You mentioned kayak.'

'I did.'

'That might come in handy. The target is a ship called the Ankara Queen. I want to know all about the ship, its crew, its cargo, everything. You'll be on your own and you know how to contact us. Take your time. Build the case. Make it happen.'

'And if there's no case to make?' challenged Quest.

'Oh, but there is. There certainly is. If the intelligence from M16 is right then we're talking millions of pounds, Quest. Millions! Submerge yourself in that document. I want you on the inside, whatever it takes and however long it takes.'

'Millions of pounds! Ever thought I might change sides?'

'Read the brief, Quest. You can challenge authority all you want but beware that the hand that feeds you can also bite.'

'The Ankara Queen,' smiled Sam as he glanced at the man he knew as Jupiter. He thumbed through the file and added, 'Looks like happy reading, Mr Rafferty.'

The weeks idled by as Sam moved into lodgings in Liverpool and began the slow process of infiltrating the dockland community.

While walking the streets, Sam spent his first few nights sleeping in a shop doorway and using a broken cardboard box to provide a degree of warmth. A week later, he was begging in the main thoroughfares leading to the docks. Constantly moved on by police and shopkeepers, he soon became a familiar figure scrounging for cups of coffee and a scrap of food, or a pound or two. Within the month, he signed on and claimed unemployment benefits. Job hunting took over his life and a succession of low-paid opportunities came his way. He frequented a couple of local bookmakers and placed a bet on a

- 42 -

horse race. It was a good win that was known in the gambling community and celebrated on the street by himself with a bottle of vodka that he shared with the down and outs. It was also an opportunity for the Jupiter office to push some money Sam's way. The gambling win covered the other cash that Sam received from Logan on behalf of Jupiter. In a relatively short space of time, the locals picked up on Sam Quest. The win helped him move into a flat in Vauxhall. Taking possession of a second-hand light blue Ford Fiesta, he gradually became a familiar face around the pubs and cafés located in the Bootle Dock area. When the opportunity arose, he successfully applied for a part-time job in a pub and began to watch and report on the individuals connected to the Ankara Queen and the berth at which he reckoned it would one day arrive.

Then there was the woman who occasionally wandered into his life. She was tall, attractive, and appealed to him. He'd only met her a handful of times in the Rope and Anchor whilst he'd been working. But each time she was with a bunch of girls from an office somewhere in the docklands, she stood out in his eyes. Talking, chatting, perhaps the odd funny quip that was a nervous joke, but night by night, day by day, every time they met, they grew a little closer. Yet they were far apart. There was no relationship to speak of, just a man and woman drawn to each other in an inexplicable way that was known only to themselves. Was life tugging at the heartstrings or was it just a coincidence that there was a growing bond between them? The girls gossiped and decided that the new man on the block was tall, dark and handsome. Worthy of chasing perhaps, or just a matter of female taste? The regulars thought the woman was beautiful. Was that all that was needed to light the fire? There was no way of cementing that relationship. Or would it be a friendship? Sam learnt that she worked in an office in the Regent Road area and went by the name of Jenny.

'Jenny!' thought Sam. 'Who is she and where is she from? Single, married, in a relationship or what, I wish I knew more about her.'

Nothing was going wrong for Sam Quest. Everything was as perfect as it could be. He felt neither danger nor isolation, yet he still had not found a way into the organisation. But life was a breeze. Always a breeze when strolling by the Mersey at night, looking, watching, and following the brief.

In the busy highways of central London, a cobbled street introduced Faversham Mews and a row of classical houses built in the early 19th century when George IV was Prince Regent. Within one of the houses, on the ground floor, a Mr Black presided over a meeting between himself, a Mr Blue and a Mr Green. No one else was present, not even a secretary to take notes. The chairman, Mr Black, was Bernard Rafferty who was in charge of 'black operations' for MI5: the Security Service. Mr Blue was the Director General of the same service whilst Mr Green was the Chief of MI6: the Secret Intelligence Service.

Once Bernard had poured coffee for the secret trio, the meeting began.

Mr Blue rubbed worry from his tired eyes and declared, 'Misha, gentlemen! Operation Misha! It keeps me awake at night because we are no further forward than we were twelve months ago. I'm constantly looking for inspiration, but it's a rare commodity. Have either of you come up with any ideas since our last meeting?'

'I hope Operation Europa will provide a breakthrough,' suggested Rafferty. 'I don't see any other viable alternative. Operation Misha is known only to the three of us. If we open the book on this one and involve the government and other agencies, we might never solve the puzzle because Misha will close down without us making a scratch.'

'The answer must be staring us in the face,' suggested Mr Green. 'The problem is which face.'

'I support the need to keep the lid on this one. When the time comes to inform the government and other agencies then we will do so. Meanwhile, we are the gatekeepers. Can we expect progress, Bernard?' enquired Mr Blue.

'Yes! Our asset is positioned to take advantage of the situation. I expect progress to be made within the next few weeks. The initial target is known. It's just a waiting game until a situation arises where entry can be made.'

'I see,' mused the MI5 man. 'I had hoped for quicker progress but have learnt to be patient when I must.'

'Patience is one thing,' interjected Mr Green from MI6. 'Security is quite another and that is my primary concern.'

'Oh, our asset is safe at the moment,' revealed Rafferty.

'I wasn't thinking of his security,' snapped the MI6 officer. 'I was thinking of the security of Operation Misha and your asset is part of that operation even though he doesn't know it. The operation must be deniable at all costs. No one, I repeat no one, needs to know what the true target of our operation is. What is said between us remains between the three of us here at Faversham Mews. Is that quite clear?'

Both Rafferty and Blue nodded in agreement.

'The asset thinks it's drugs,' continued Green. 'Let him think that until it's time to move up a notch. Can you confirm that there is no link to either of our organisations other than the physical presence of yourself and Logan?'

'I can!' replied Rafferty.

'Not one piece of paper! Not one digital record!'

'I can assure you both that we are in total control of our asset,' declared Rafferty. 'And the operation remains deniable.'

'I see,' replied Green.

Mr Blue, the MI5 man, merely nodded his acceptance.

'Trust me,' suggested Rafferty as he engaged both men. 'Europa is the asset's codename and you may hear it from me in telephone calls between us. The asset trusts me, gentleman. Now you must trust me.'

'God help him,' muttered Blue. 'He has no idea of the dangers ahead. He thinks he's been recruited for one job when that job is purely a lead into another.'

'There is no God,' suggested Green. 'He's not on the payroll. Our asset is on his own.'

'He has our support,' declared Blue.

'He is potentially our weakest link if he transfers his loyalties to the enemy,' suggested Green. 'Such things are always possible. The asset is not one of us. He is an apprentice, as far as I am concerned. I trust you have selected well, Bernard. Woe betide you if you have failed us.'

'I have faith in the man.'

'Have you considered that if he becomes threatened to a severe degree, he may not be able to take the heat anymore?'

'There are now four in the chain but only three of us are dedicated beyond understanding to Operation Misha and the task ahead,' voiced Rafferty. 'We have an operation within an operation simply because we can transport Operation Europa to outside organisations whilst securing Operation Misha as our primary concern. However, gentlemen, may I suggest you both look to your security before criticising the security aspects of my operation.'

'Your operation?' queried Mr Blue angrily. 'Not ours?'

'Well, as I understand from you, sir,' replied Rafferty. 'This is one of the most important operations that has been undertaken since the end of the Cold War. We are about to find out if there are any leaks in our organisation, and other organisations that serve the nation.'

'There are always leaks,' replied the MI5 boss. 'Usually, a slight twist is all we need to prevent a major link. Our eyes are always open.'

'It took me long enough to select our asset from those I was monitoring. I have faith in the man. To succeed, we must trust each other and right now, none of us knows who Misha is. Let's watch the dice roll and see where it takes us.'

'The dice!' replied Green. 'I don't like gambling. But I take your point.'

'Where did the original information come from regarding Misha?' enquired Rafferty.

There was no reply, but Rafferty persevered with 'Mr Green! Mr Blue? One of you must know surely?'

The wind outside grew in intensity and rattled the ground-floor windows slightly as Blue, Green and Black continued their conversation in the quintessential elegance of Faversham Mews.

~

Chapter Five

~

The Rope and Anchor
The Docks, Bootle, Liverpool
Three weeks later.

A breeze whipped through the building when a terrified customer tugged the pub door open and ran for his life as a wooden stool sailed through the air and ricocheted from the bar into the optics. The apparatus exploded, dislodged half a dozen bottles of spirits, and drenched the barman who was on his knees behind the bar hiding from the mayhem in the pub.

Another stool followed suit but crashed into one of the Irish bruisers who was squaring up to his arch-enemy in the spit and sawdust area of the shabbiest pub in town. Both men were tall, muscular, tattooed about the arms, and bore facial scars and marks from other conflicts. They were hard-looking men in their late twenties and early thirties the like of which Alex, the barman, had feared from the moment they had entered the licensed premises.

'Sean O'Leary! Be stopping that now or I'll be having to put you flat on yer arse!' shouted Patrick who was obliged to duck low when the heavily built ginger-haired Sean threw a haymaker at him and then picked up a broken bottle from the bar.

Brandishing the jagged edges of the bottle at Patrick, Sean stumbled forward, jabbed into thin air, and promptly felt the full weight of a stool crash down onto his back when Sam Quest ventured into the fray and downed him.

Patrick O'Malley glanced at Sam, stepped back and was about to kick Sean in the stomach when the front door of the pub burst open and succumbed to the entrance of another dozen Irish labourers who were up for a fight whatever the circumstances.

Malek Osman, an overweight middle-aged man wearing a dark suit and carrying a briefcase, looked aghast and muttered, 'Let's get out of here. I don't need this.'

Within minutes, the whole pub was alive with fighting men swinging, punching, and kicking each other as if their very lives depended upon it.

Sam ducked down, sneaked around the corner of the bar, and bumped into Alex who had managed to retrieve the telephone and was dialling 999 from his hiding place.

Osman gripped tight his briefcase and made for the front door. Cut down by a salvo of fists, he fell to the ground where he rolled himself into a ball. He dropped his briefcase which slid towards the bar and, in the melee that followed, he lost sight of his most valued possession.

Sam snatched the briefcase, glanced towards Malek Osman, and tried to unlock the combination lock by the sheer force of pressure. He failed and pushed it back towards a gathering of kicking feet.

'What are you doing?' snapped Alex. 'You thieving bastard! You've no right to do that. It's not yours!'

'No! But you're right. I am a thieving bastard. The damn thing is locked.'

The mob stamped on Osman's legs, trampled him, and then ventured onwards into the heart of the pub where Sean and Patrick were again squared up to each other.

'You okay, Mr Osman?' shouted a dishevelled Sam.

'Get me out of here,' mouthed Malek, his voice almost inaudible in the noise now echoing from the pub walls.

A bottle flew and clattered into the wall as the fighting grew in intensity and a swishing noise in the bar yielded the production of a long-bladed knife in the hands of a drunken Irishman.

Whoosh! The blade tore through the atmosphere and narrowly missed someone's torso.

A terrified Malek crawled into the comfort zone behind the bar and pleaded, 'You! Sam or whatever your name is. Get me out of here. Now!'

'Where's the key for the back door?' shouted Sam.

'That way,' pointed Alex banging the phone on its cradle. 'I got through. The police are on their way.'

Malek glanced at Alex and snapped, 'The cops! That's all I need. Get me up. I can't stand up. Get me on my feet. My briefcase?'

A look of panic filled Malek's face when he searched for his briefcase.

'Here!' yelled Sam kicking the briefcase towards Malek who stooped, picked it up, and gathered it to his chest as if it were a new-born child.

As bottles and glasses soared through the air in a mindless moment of utter madness, Sam ignored the fighting and dragged Malek towards the back door of the Rope and Anchor whilst Alex curled into a ball and buried himself inside the bar counter.

Negotiating the rear passageway out of the pub, Sam hauled his newfound Turkish friend to the back door, propped him up against the wall, and then reached for the door handle.

'It's locked,' revealed Sam. 'There's no key here.'

'We're trapped,' shrieked Malek. 'What now? Don't go back. It's pandemonium and they'll lynch me if they find out who I am.'

'Don't I know it,' replied Sam. 'Watch out!'

Taking a step back, Sam launched a shoulder charge at the pub's rear door. The door creaked and wheezed but hardly moved an inch. Sam tried again and then put his foot to the centre of the door before the wood splintered, surrendered, and crumpled to the floor.

'Come on,' shouted Sam. 'On your feet!'

Crawling on all fours, Malek felt pain in his lower limbs. His thighs were on fire and his legs were sore. He clung to Sam and used his body as leverage to regain his feet.

'Up!' yelled Sam as the Turk eventually planted both feet firmly on the ground.

The door at the end of the corridor behind them burst open and the sound of brawling men invaded Sam's ears when Sean O'Leary began running towards them.

'Out of my way!' shouted the Irishman.

Sam grabbed a nearby stool and threw it at O'Leary before grabbing Malek by the collar of his jacket and hauling him into the pub's yard. Overweight and unfit, Malek bounced from the walls when Sam struggled momentarily before manhandling him down the passageway.

O'Leary felt the full force of the stool in his face, grabbed his broken nose, squealed, and fell to the floor with the noise of chaos in the background and Sam determined to get Malek out of the pub.

Malek was in the rear yard amongst the empty beer barrels and unwanted gas canisters that had seen their day. He tried the gateway to freedom as the first hint of a police siren sounded in the distance.

The gate was locked.

'The cops are coming. Quick! Help me! I can't climb that wall with these legs the way they are,' wailed Malek.

'Oh yes, you can,' replied Sam who bent down and shouldered Malek up the wall until he reached head height. At that point, Sam relocated himself and pushed Malek by the buttocks until the Turk was at the top of the wall.

'Leave the briefcase,' yelled Sam. 'It's slowing you down. Drop it!'

'No way,' replied Malek. 'Never!'

'Then drop down on the other side,' shrieked Sam. 'I'm coming over.'

Sean O'Leary appeared in the yard. His nose was slightly bent to one side and blood dripped constantly from a nostril and splashed his tee shirt. Dishevelled, bruised, bleeding and looking for an escape route, the heavily tattooed thug caught sight of Sam and shouted, 'I'm gonna kill you when I get hold of you. Make no mistake you horrible little cretin. I'm gunning for you. You're going down. Down! Down! Down!'

Sam ignored the threats and ran towards O'Leary who raised his fists ready to smash them into Sam.

Almost, face to face with the ginger-haired Irishman, Sam ducked, spun on his feet, turned himself around, and sprinted back towards the wall. He leapt and grabbed the top wall coping leaving the Irishman standing open-mouthed at the antics on display.

From the top of the wall, Sam waved at the mop of hair that was O'Leary and shouted, 'See ya!'

Dropping to the other side, Sam dragged Malek with him.

The sound of sirens filled the air as a host of blue flashing lights neared the pub and Sam hoisted Malek onto his shoulder and bundled him along the street. They turned into an alleyway where Sam yanked Malek onto the pavement and took a deep breath saying, 'It's not just your legs that are heavy. You weigh a ton.'

Malek struggled to his feet whereupon Sam caught his arm and guided him along the lane heading inland and away from the immediate area of the docks. As they did so, Sam noticed how important the briefcase was to Malek. It was as if the briefcase was glued to his body. They were inseparable.

Back at the Rope and Anchor, Merseyside's finest burst through the front door of the pub in numbers and shouted, 'Stand still! This is the police! Stand still!'

Patrick ignored the cops and threw himself through the front window of the pub in an escape bid. The resultant glass and the drunken Irishman landed at the feet of a police dog handler who held Patrick at bay until his colleagues handcuffed him.

The battle inside the pub raged on as the police fought to gain control and save the pub from further damage.

Alex popped his head above the parapet, realised they were all still fighting, and dropped down behind the bar again.

Outside, Sam helped Malek along the alleyways and then turned into the street where he stepped onto the roadway and flagged down a taxi.

'Where to?' probed Sam turning to Malek. 'Your shout.'

'Crosby! Take me to Crosby,' ordered Malek, his head throbbing, his legs thundering, and his thighs bruised and burning with pain.

'You heard the man,' cried Sam into the driver's face, 'Crosby! Quick as you can.'

'Whereabouts!' asked the taxi driver.

Pulling a wad of banknotes from his jeans pocket, Sam thrust them at the driver and said, 'Just Crosby. Now shut up and drive!'

The taxi driver looked at the bundle of cash, grinned profusely, grabbed the money, and replied in a scouse accent with, 'Right then! Crosby, it is then. Let's go.'

Hustling the cumbersome overweight Malek into the rear of the taxi, Sam pulled the rear door closed behind them and sat back as the taxi lurched forward and another couple of police vans roared by on their way to the Rope and Anchor.

Malek looked up at Sam from his crouched position in the taxi as the vehicle travelled towards Seaforth and the apparent safety of Crosby. Within minutes, the docks were behind them and the Rope and Anchor pub was out of sight.

The dock system ran seven and a half miles from Brunswick Dock in Liverpool to Seaforth Dock on the east side of the River Mersey. Similarly, the Birkenhead Docks ran between Birkenhead and Wallasey on the west side of the Mersey. The docks boasted many terminals but one terminal was of particular interest to Sam

Quest. It was the berth capable of housing two post-Panamax container ships. They were the largest ships in the dock system and were of such a magnitude that they were too big to negotiate the Panama Canal as their size did not fit the original canal locks. The terminal of interest to Sam only berthed the largest vessels that visited the Port of Liverpool, and one was due to arrive in the next few weeks. The ships that were too big for the Panama Canal all had one thing in common and that was that they all traversed the ocean from Puerto Bolivar on the River Magdalena, Barranquilla, in Colombia. They crossed the Caribbean Sea, side-stepped Puerto Rico and Bermuda, and negotiated the North Atlantic Ocean before arriving at the Liverpool Dock system.

Through Seaforth, en route to Crosby, Sam glanced at Malek and said, 'You okay now, Mr Osman?'

Still slightly shaken, Malek replied, 'Yes! I'll be even better when I get home. How do you know my name?'

'You're a dock supervisor.'

'But you don't work on the docks,' replied Malek. 'I've only ever seen you in the Rope and Anchor.'

'That's right. I work part-time in the pub collecting glasses, tidying up and stuff. General dogsbody, they call it.'

'Ahh! I see. That pub is the main drinking hole of half the men who work in my terminal.'

'The post-Panamax one?'

'That's the one. Do you know me from the pub?'

'Yeah! But you're not a regular, Mr Osman. I've only seen you once or twice before in the Rope. You speak good English for an Albanian, sir.'

'The name is mostly Albanian but I'm Turkish. I've been here long enough to speak better English than Turkish. Why do you ask?'

'No particular reason. Just making conversation during a taxi ride. You just picked a bad day to visit the Rope and Anchor.'

'What happened back there?' enquired Malek. 'Jenny and the girls told me there was never any trouble in the pub even though it's not the smartest dump in town. But all hell broke loose.'

'Jenny? Who is Jenny?' probed Sam. 'Is she a regular at the Rope? Should I know her?'

'I don't know. She's my secretary. The Rope is just handy for all of us, that's all. What caused the fight?'

'Labourers!' revealed Sam. 'They've been working on the road system at Vauxhall near the Liver Building. Resurfacing the tarmac, I heard. They've been looking for a local for a few weeks now but everywhere they go they find a docker's pub. They chose the Rope and Anchor today with the idea of taking over the pub for themselves. Dockers out, labourers in! If you see what I mean.'

'I'd no idea,' voiced Malek.

'You wouldn't unless you'd been a regular there. You've got Irish dockers from Liverpool and Belfast and Irish labourers newly in town from Dublin. It doesn't take much to work out why they hate each other.'

'Ah! The Irish problem! I've heard about it,' admitted Malek. 'There are similar problems in Turkey.'

'But not with the Irish?' chuckled Sam.

'No!' laughed Malek. 'Censorship! For and against, and a whole lot more!'

'What made you go to the Rope today?' enquired Sam.

'I could say the end of the month!' replied Malek. 'It was payday for everyone! But it was Jenny's birthday.'

Hiding in the recess of his mind, Sam captured the image of a woman that fascinated him. She was the one called Jenny who was an occasional visitor to the Rope. She was always with a bunch of girls from the docks. Was that the same Jenny? Tall, good-looking, always short skirts, and a smile that electrified the room? Was that the girl who had a personality that seemed to key directly into his?

'It's the only time I ever go out,' continued Malek. 'Jenny suggested the Rope and Anchor but none of us knew about the feud between the labourers and the dockers.'

'You should get out more.'

'No thanks,' answered Malek. 'But thank you for getting me out of there in one piece. It could have been nasty if they'd trapped me in the pub.'

'You're a dock supervisor,' stated Sam. 'They'd have lynched you if they'd known that you were one of the bosses, and some of those labourers are mad enough to slit your throat without a thought.'

'Yeah! There were some hard men in that pub, and I saw a knife or two being flashed.'

'Well, we're both alright, that's the main thing.'

'Thanks for your quick thinking,' offered Malek.

'I think your job is to oversee the workers who load and unload materials from the ships,' said Sam. 'I'm told that unloading can be dangerous and backbreaking at times but there are a lot of administrative duties that dock supervisors do. You need a degree nowadays, don't you?'

'Yes!' nodded Malek. 'I've got a degree in logistics. My job is to write out the protocols for safety, first and foremost, and make sure everyone from the deckhands to the shift leaders and loadmasters knows what to do and where to unload the cargo. Why are you so interested in my job?'

'I'm not interested in what you do,' chuckled Sam. 'It's all about the supply chain process and it's way above my capabilities. Why do you think I'm scrimping a few pounds every week in the pub?'

'I don't know. You tell me.'

'I've been trying to get any old job on the docks for the last few weeks. I've been mooching around asking people if there were any vacancies. They told me to see the dock supervisor or a shift leader. Your name was mentioned along with a few others. As a last resort try a loadmaster, they said. Well, the shift leaders and loadmasters are no help at all because they're too busy and only employ their mates from Liverpool. Supervisors like you sit on their backside in the office so that's no good to me either.'

'You're job hunting?' enquired Malek.

'That's right.'

'I'm not surprised but you need to smarten yourself up. Look at yourself. Unshaven, unruly hair, torn jeans and a grubby sweater. And you're job hunting!'

'I get by,' replied Quest.

'You had a wad of money to pay for the taxi.'

'As you said, it's the end of the month. I just got paid today. Cash in hand. I'm not on the payroll. Like you, I didn't want to hang around to be caught by the police even though I'd done nothing wrong. I don't trust them. Jeez! Too many questions from the cops and they might have sold me to the taxman. I hate the bastards. I can't afford to pay tax on my paltry wage, and they'll bend you over backwards if it suits them.'

Malek looked away, paused, but then replied, 'Did you give the taxi driver all your wages?'

'Yeah, fool me!' replied Sam. 'It was a spur-of-the-moment thing. No brains! It's too late now. My fault, not yours. I'll get by.'

The taxi approached Crosby, stopped at a junction, and waited for the traffic lights to change to green.

Malek Osman squared his tie, ran his fingers through his dishevelled hair, and pulled a wallet from his jacket. Handing over a couple of twenty-pound notes and a business card, he said to Sam, 'What's your name?'

'Quest! Sam Quest!'

'Come and see me on Monday morning. The address is on the card. Regent Road, do you know where it is?'

'Yes, I do,' said Sam accepting the banknotes and the card. 'Thank you. At least that will get me a meal over the weekend.'

Malek leaned across to the driver as the taxi took off again and said, 'Next left, driver. Third house on the right.'

'Got that,' replied the driver who did as he was bid.

'Be sure to take this man to the city centre when you've dropped me off,' proposed Malek bunging another couple of notes into the driver's hand.

'No problem,' from the driver who pulled up outside a detached bungalow on the outskirts of Crosby.

Sat in an acre of land, the building occupied a spacious plot boasting sea views and a double garage. A dark blue Aston Martin occupied a central position in the driveway.

Opening the taxi door, Malek stepped out of the vehicle clutching his briefcase. He turned to Sam and said, 'Monday morning! I'll get you into something, but I don't know what. You helped me. I'll help you. You deserve a break. I'll see you then.'

'Can I ask you something?' voiced Sam.

'That depends! What did you have in mind?'

'You got a problem with the police like me? I wondered what it was, that's all.'

'Just like you,' replied Malek. 'I don't trust them.'

Malek was gone from the taxi. He was down the driveway clutching his dearly beloved briefcase and hobbling into the bungalow before Sam could reply.

Sliding from the rear seat, Sam stepped into the roadway, swayed gently from left to right covering the frontage of the building with his zippo, and lit a cigarette. Inside the zippo, a miniature camera took a video recording of the bungalow and the Aston Martin parked on the driveway.

Seconds later, Sam replaced the lighter in his pocket, inhaled the cigarette, and then got back into the taxi with, 'You heard the man. City centre please.'

Half an hour later, Sam entered a telephone kiosk in Lime Street, dialled a number, and asked to place a bet on a horse race due to run at five o'clock that night.

'Jupiter!' voiced Rafferty when he picked up the call.

'Quest!'

'What you got for me?' replied Rafferty.

'A zippo full of recent photographs of the docks and the dockers working the main terminals. I also have a contact on Malek Osman. He's a dock supervisor at the terminal where the big ocean-going ships berth. I'm talking Panamax shipping containers.'

'I'm interpreting Colombian ships,' responded Rafferty.

'There's one due this month. I'm watching for it and I plan to take my kayak out and see what the berths are like from the seaboard side. I want to know if any hidden drop-off points can't be seen from the dockside.'

'Good idea!'

'Osman handles all the paperwork on the ship cargoes. He sorts out what goes where, when and to whom. If there's a shipment labelled for delivery in the UK, he's the one who knows where it goes. He's a suit with a brain. When the Ankara Queen berths, Osman will be the man who knows what's on board and where it's destined for. Word is that he keeps himself to himself and has little contact with the cargo handlers, the shift leaders, or the loadmasters. He's an office man. The King of the administrators who looks after his office staff and shuffles paper to the workers.'

'An interesting supposition,' from Rafferty. 'But no evidence to support it.'

'Not yet,' argued Sam.

'If he's the lynchpin in the organisation then surely, he has people around him that he can trust as well as people he's running. Are you sure you're on the right man, Quest?'

'I have a feeling about him,' explained Sam. 'Just the sixth sense kicking in. I want more on him because he's in the right place and rings my bell. I pulled him out of a pub today when there was a battle between two sets of Irishmen. He's had a kicking and couldn't stand up. I got him out and away. Now he loves me to the extent that I've got to go and see him on Monday for a job in the dockyard.'

'I see!' noted Rafferty. 'Progress at last! What else do you know about him?'

'Five feet eight or thereabouts. I'd say forty-five to fifty with a slight paunch due to his office life. The name suggested he was Albanian but he tells me he's Turkish. He had a briefcase with him. He lost it in the mayhem. I got hold of it but didn't have enough time to break the combination lock. Malek wouldn't have gone anywhere without that briefcase. We need to know the contents.'

'An admin man, you said,' replied Rafferty. 'Probably besotted by paperwork. Keep it in mind but I'm not committing the Red Alpha team to a covert entry and search until I know more.'

'Understood! It's on the back burner for now. Might be something; might be nothing. Look, he panicked when he heard the police sirens on their way to the scrap. He wanted out of the pub because the cops were coming. He had no intention of fighting the Irish. Osman is a strange kettle of fish. He was with his office staff but didn't want anything to do with the police.'

'Maybe he's wanted,' suggested Rafferty. 'That might be the first sign of weakness in either him or the organisation. He doesn't seem to be a strong individual from what you say. I'll run a check against him. Meanwhile, try and crank open that weakness in him. Is he hiding something?'

'Could be! Yes, please, run a check against him,' agreed Quest. 'I think he's on the bottom rung of the ladder, but the important thing is I think I've found the ladder. I don't think he wants to be tied up with the police in any way, shape, or form because the less the police know about him the better.

Dodging the police might mean no more than not being questioned by them about anything. Just a gut feeling I have. Anyway, I'm presuming Malek Osman is his real name. He says he's Turkish so who knows? Just watching the comings and goings of people like him down on the docks I can tell you that every Wednesday he takes the afternoon off. I don't where he goes or what he does but I'll be on him next Wednesday now that I know where he lives.'

'Good,' replied Rafferty. 'He might take a trip to the golf course. Who knows! Logan will arrange a new motor for you. You'll get a postcard posted to you in the mail with a Lanzarote postmark. The card will show a picture of a car in the background. Use a microscope to read the number. Logan will leave the car in the multi-level car park as arranged. The keys will be on the inside of the rear tyre along with an updated zippo. Leave your old one on the rear inside tyre of your old motor. Logan will lift the old zippo and download the content. Understood?'

'Cheers! I got that,' replied Quest. 'For me, Osman is an admin man and there's always an admin man somewhere in the mix. Legally, the ship's master must report any goods arriving at a UK port to Her Majesty's Customs and Excise. He's also got to notify the authorities of any passengers who are going to disembark or crew members who will be paid off. All those things must be reported within three hours of the vessel reaching its berth. Bear that in mind if Osman becomes a realistic target. I'm guessing that if we are successful, we will need to be accurate if we ever get near a strike. That's a three-hour time slot wherein we might know what Malek Osman is up to. Where, is another question? All to play for?'

'Making a note!'

'The captain of the ship must also make a declaration using papers supplied by the International Maritime Organization. The forms must contain the ship's manifest which contains details of the entire cargo. There's a score of forms to complete by the ship's captain and they take some working out, I can tell you.'

'You're saying that Osman is the man who will know all about this side of things and may even have advised the master of the incoming ship on how to prepare them and how to word them to the extent that they get through Customs without any problem?'

'Yes, I am. That's where my instinct takes me. Maritime transport documentation is a jungle of paper whether it's an import or an export,' proposed Sam. 'And Malek Osman is the man that administers this Panamax terminal.'

'All of which suggests the man in charge of the paperwork may well be involved if he has guilty knowledge.'

'I'd say so,' replied Sam. 'I'm sure that not all dock supervisors are would-be drug tsars, but I have a hunch about Malek Osman. I can't explain it, but he feeds the loadmasters and that's where I need to concentrate next. Is it the same loadmaster every time? Who talks to the captain of the ship? Who releases the cargo on the ship? And who collects the cargo from the ship and arranges for its delivery in the UK. I think Osman handles all the paperwork and bamboozles Customs and Excise.'

'If that's the case,' replied Rafferty. 'Someone is told what to pick and where to take it.'

'Yes, someone moves the cargo we're interested in, and they are told to move it by a loadmaster who has been notified by Osman as to where the load is on the ship.'

'You might have a long way to go, Quest. The Ankara Queen was registered in Ankara, Turkey, ten years ago but its home port is Barranquilla in Colombia.'

'Another Turkish connection,' proposed Sam. I presume the Ankara Queen has come to notice before?'

'The vessel has been subject to a rummage search before under section twenty-seven of the Customs and Excise Management Act of 1979. The result was negative, but you've made a start,' decreed Rafferty.

'When was the last rummage search?'

'A couple of years ago in Southampton,' revealed Rafferty. 'But our sister service, MI6, has heard various rumours over the years pointing to the likelihood that the ship is used to smuggle drugs. Probably cocaine or heroin, maybe both, we don't know.'

'Rumours!' challenged Sam. 'Nothing concrete! Maybe the ship is clean, and the rumours are false,' offered Sam.

'Perhaps! But I doubt it. What's next on your agenda?'

'So far, I've housed him at an address in Crosby,' continued Sam. 'He lives in a big posh bungalow with an Aston Martin in the driveway. It's all on the zippo for you. I want the vehicle owner and the full history of the house in Crosby and ears on the telephone at his office in Regent Street and his bungalow in Crosby. I'll do the house. No mobile number yet but I'm working on it.'

'Two telephone intercepts! Okay,' replied Rafferty. 'I'll do a postal intercept too. Ring me tomorrow. Hopefully, I'll have something for you.'

An older man with a walking stick hobbled towards the telephone kiosk and came to a standstill.

Sam nodded at the stranger and said to Rafferty, 'There's a queue for the phone. No problem envisaged but I'm out of here.' Sam closed the call and vacated the kiosk holding the door open for the man who smiled and limped inside.

Walking away, Sam paused, lit a cigarette with his zippo, videoed the man with the walking stick, and then left the area satisfied that the old man wasn't watching him.

'Eyes!' he reminded himself. 'Eyes open! Stay safe!'

In the meeting house at Faversham Mews, Rafferty engaged Messrs Blue and Green from MI5 and MI6 and voiced, 'Thank you for attending at such short notice, gentlemen. Europa has made an advancement that I think you ought to be appraised of.'

'Go on,' from Blue: the MI5 man.

'Our asset has developed contact with a dock supervisor by the name of Malek Osman. He is Turkish and I am advancing technical security upon him at all possible points.'

'Turkish!' exclaimed Green: the MI6 officer. 'Now that is interesting and ties in with the shipment.'

'And if he is from Turkey then he is most definitely in the game.' added Blue. 'Yes! I agree. Authority granted. Full technical surveillance.'

'Ground troops?' enquired Mr Green.

'No! Not yet,' argued Rafferty. 'Let the asset breath.'

'Yes! Yes, of course,' came the reply. 'We rush when we should stroll. Yes, Bernard, the dice are rolling. The game is on.'

~

Chapter Six
~

Monday
Liverpool area,
Merseyside.

Malek's Aston Martin purred like a pussy cat when he tightened his seat belt and set off for Liverpool. Slipping through the gearbox, the dock supervisor turned left out of his driveway and headed along the Serpentine towards the traffic lights in Crosby where he intended to take the A565 to his workplace. The journey would take him about twenty minutes unless the traffic was busy. The distance involved was six miles.

As the Aston Martin cruised towards the traffic lights, the vehicle drove past a junction where a post office van was parked. The van burst into life and the driver turned right along the Serpentine towards Malek Osman's house. Pulling up short of the house, the postman slid from the driver's seat taking his mail bag with him. He locked the van and walked along the footpath delivering junk mail to various houses en route.

A jogger trotted by inspiring the postman to nod before saying, 'Good morning,' to a lady walking her dog.

On reaching Malek's house, the postman was thankful for the short video that Sam had sent Jupiter and turned to walk down the path to the front door.

Dressed in shorts and a Royal Mail high-visibility jacket, Logan felt comfortable and relaxed when he posted a couple of envelopes containing junk mail through Malek's letterbox.

Rummaging in his bag, Logan removed a piece of strong wax the length of his thumb. He gingerly inserted the wax into the front door lock and recognised that he was tampering with a standard UPVC door. Examination revealed that the yale lock was fitted with anti-drill and anti-card measures that enhanced security to a higher degree than one might normally expect.

Logan withdrew the wax impression, opened a small tin in the palm of his hand, and copied the impression into a separate wax substance. He closed the tin and buried it inside his mailbag confident that the impression would help engineer a key for Sam Quest. The key would fit the front door of Malek Osman's house.

Whistling casually, operation complete, Logan strolled back to the post office van and fired the engine. Moments later, the street was bare save for a couple walking their dog and a jogger disappearing towards Crosby beach.

Logan engaged his hands-free mobile, rang Jupiter, and said, 'Operation completed. Impression on its way.'

An hour later, in Bootle, Sam noticed Malek's Aston Martin parked in front of the Regent Road office when he fulfilled his appointment with the dock supervisor. He parked his rundown Ford Fiesta opposite the Aston Martin and made his way to the office. As he strolled purposefully towards the office, Sam buttoned his leather blazer and adjusted the dark blue rollneck sweater he wore. Pausing for a moment, he rubbed his shoes on the back of his jeans near the Achilles tendon and hoped he would pass any critical dress code that might be in force It was a matter he doubted working in the docks, but also an area that he wasn't too sure of.

Knocking limply on the door, he was admitted by an attractive woman in her mid-twenties who introduced herself as Malek's secretary. She invited him to take a seat. It was the woman Sam recognised from the Rope and Anchor as Jenny. His heart missed a beat and he felt himself draw breath. He was sure his pulse was racing such was the excitement that powered the adrenaline in his body.

'Unfortunately, Mr Malek has an important meeting today, Mr…?'

'Quest! Sam Quest!'

'Yes, of course. I do apologise. Your name slipped my mind. Do I know you? You look familiar but I can't think where from.'

'The Rope and Anchor,' replied Sam. 'I'm the general dogsbody that cleans up. I remember you from there. Weeks ago, maybe.'

'Yes!' smiled Jenny. 'Got you! Yes, of course. I remember you now. How are you?'

'Good! Yes, bouncing now. No! I mean good. Yes, good is good,' announced Sam as he fought to control his nervous system in the presence of a woman he had taken to. 'What a fool I am,' he thought.

'Good! I'm pleased,' replied Jenny. 'Look, Mr Quest, don't worry about the absence of Mr Osman. Mr Jackson has been instructed to tend to your needs. He'll be here soon.'

'Mr Jackson?' queried Sam.

'One of our loadmasters,' explained Malek's secretary.

Taking a seat in the reception area, Sam felt immediately dominated by the woman. Possessed of a good figure and long legs emphasized by a short skirt and a less than loose jumper, Jenny was the eye candy on display, and she was beautiful.

Sam's mind went into overdrive trying to recall the last time he enjoyed female company. Nodding, he offered a smile that she returned with such interest that Sam felt he had almost detected a chemical reaction between them.

Idly scanning through a scattering of travel brochures, Sam tried to avert his eyes from Jenny. He concentrated on the office surroundings. They were clean and compared favourably with any of the car showrooms dotted around Liverpool that eagerly showed off their products in modern surroundings. It struck Sam that the immediate environment was far more affluent than he imagined it would be.

The door burst open and a large muscular man with broad shoulders, a square chin, and a broken nose sauntered in. He wore a donkey jacket, gloves, jeans and a yellow safety helmet which he removed and placed on the desk. The man opened with the words, 'Any messages, Jenny?'

'None at all, Mr Jackson.'

Turning to his guest, Jake queried, 'Quest, is it? Sam Quest?'

'That's me,' offered Sam standing up to greet the man.

'I'm Jake, the loadmaster. I've been told to give you a job. Close to Osman, are you?'

'I'd say so, yes,' replied Sam. 'Close enough to be here for a job.'

'Done dock work before have we?'

'No! Not at all.'

'By the look of you, you'll not have enough strength to last a week,' remarked Jake. 'What kind of work are you doing at the moment?'

'Odds and sods at the Rope and Anchor.'

'Ah! So you're an odd sod then?' chuckled Jake.

The remark did not register with Sam.

'Okay! I get it. My mistake,' offered Jake, 'You're close to Malek Osman and all you've done is bar work. No wonder he landed you here. What else have you done?'

'Not a lot recently,' shrugged Sam.

'You'll be a labourer then! Come with me. There's a boat in now at the quayside. It's been emptied but it's berthed where you'll be working.' Jake grabbed his safety helmet, withdrew one from a cabinet in the office, and handed it to Sam saying, 'Here, put this on. Dock rules! No arguments!'

'None at all. Thank you,' replied Sam who donned the helmet and adjusted the chin strap.

Turning on his heels, Jake shouted, 'Jenny! I'll send him back shortly for the paperwork.'

Malek's secretary nodded and struggled to keep her short skirt at a respectable length as the two men left the building.

'You okay carrying, pushing, lifting and shuffling stuff around,' enquired Jake. 'That's all I've got for you. We're not a factory. We're a delivery unit. Stuff arrives to be loaded onto a ship or a ship arrives to be unloaded. Got me so far?'

'I have, yes.'

'Good! Because that's all I have unless you can manage a crane or drive a forklift truck?'

'Sorry, no!'

'Thought not. It's fifteen quid an hour only payable when you're wanted. We load and unload when there's work to do. Some weeks it's eighty hours a week, other times it's maybe only twenty or thirty hours a week. Mr Osman runs the wages department too. You'll pay tax and national insurance when appropriate. It's deducted at the source. I'm the loadmaster. He's the paymaster. That's the job offer, Quest. Take it or leave it. Part-time! Full-time! Your decision!'

'I'll take it,' replied Sam. 'Full-time!'

'Good! Follow me,' ordered Jake in a brusque manner. 'You can meet the team you'll working with if they're around.'

The loadmaster stomped ahead of the undercover detective leading him towards the dock. Jake's black boots thundered on the tarmac and complimented the dark clothing that he wore. He was dressed for work and Sam noticed that his heavy-duty jeans bore knee supports whilst his donkey jacket enjoyed leather elbow patches.

At the quayside, Jake pointed and said, 'You'll see there are quite a few terminals dotted along the Mersey dock system. Every terminal has at least two berths at the quayside. Where we're standing now is one of our terminals. Understood?'

'Yep! That's one hell of a size ship, Jake.'

The vessel towered above the two men but was small in comparison with others berthed further upriver.

'It's a boat, not a ship, and it's slightly bigger than the ferry to the Isle of Man. Never mind, it's the one we'll be filling tomorrow morning. Where are you living at, Quest?'

'A flat in Vauxhall near the Royal Liverpool University Hospital in Everton.'

Jake snarled at the word Everton and said, 'Football! Do you support the reds or the blues?'

'Neither!' replied Sam. 'I have no interest in the game.'

'Good! Because you don't usually get Saturdays off. I want you here tomorrow morning and Tuesday at 5 am. Loading and unloading, can you manage that?'

'I reckon so,' voiced Sam.

'We'll catch the tide for a quick turnaround,' explained Jake. 'It's a three-hour crossing to the Isle of Man and a daily load for a private company involved in delivering stuff for major website retailers. Don't be late!'

'I'll be here,' voiced Sam.

'Good! Get yourself back to the office and sign up with Jenny. She's Osman's secretary. She's a gorgeous gal and she's for Osman's eyes only. It keeps him happy and he's a sad bastard at times. Understood, Quest?'

'Perfectly!'

'Good! I'll see you tomorrow.'

'Will do!'

'By the way,' challenged Jake. 'What relation are you to Mr Osman? Son? Stepson? Cousin? Nephew even?'

'Why do you ask?' queried Sam.

'Because we only employ family and friends on this site. I asked if you were close to him, and you said you were. I presume you are a relative. What's the relationship?'

'I'm not related to Mr Osman,' revealed Sam. 'Not at all! Whatever gave you that idea? I helped him out at the Rope and Anchor a few days ago and he told me he would put a job my way.'

'What?' queried Jake angrily. 'Did I hear you right?'

'Like I said,' replied Sam. 'Not related, just did the man a favour!'

Spinning on his heel, Jake was gone from Sam's presence in a flash leaving the detective to think that Jake didn't want him on site.

'The loadmaster looks a hard man,' thought Sam. 'He seemed to be both bossy and brutish with no time to go into the complexities of where the washroom might be or the location of a canteen or work's hut.'

Sam stood at the edge of the quay and looked out across the Mersey towards the Wirral and the town of New Brighton. Then he scrutinized the boat he was to help load in the morning. Taking a step closer to the edge, he looked down trying to see if there was a hidden platform below that might be used for loading and unloading. He knew that, despite what the loadmaster had told him, there were a couple of deserted docks on the seven-mile stretch of dockland. Bramley Moore, for example, he knew was well over a century old and was derelict. He was also aware that the Bramley Moore dock was scheduled to replace Goodison Park as Everton Football Club's new stadium and work there would begin soon. Sam had done his homework and knew there was a likelihood that parts of the dock system might be locked and secured and out of sight to unwanted eyes.

Dissatisfied, Sam turned around. His mind wandered to an attractive secretary and the thought that he had grown unaccustomed to engaging the female form over the last year.

Three dockers wearing dark blue oily overalls and matching blue and white bobble hats walked towards him.

Head down, Sam ignored them as he stepped away from the quayside. Trying to sidestep the group, the smaller of the trio suddenly nudged him unexpectedly.

Losing his balance, Sam staggered to one side whereupon one of the men let rip with a fierce haymaker that smashed into Sam's face and sent him reeling. Another punch followed accompanied by, 'You're either red or blue. Which are you?'

Landing flat on his backside, Sam struggled to regain his feet saying, 'Neither! I don't follow football.'

'Neither do we,' giggled one of the men who punched Sam on the side of the head and added, 'But we don't like you. You shouldn't be here. You're not wanted.'

Holding his head, Sam replied, 'I don't know who you are. I've done nothing wrong. What are you talking about?'

'You're not one of us,' spoken from the group followed by a kick aimed at the body that Sam managed to avoid by parrying the blow with his arm as the words 'Beat it now. Get lost!' resonated in his ears.

Sam regained his balance and replied, 'Your boss, Mr Osman! I saved him from a beating. He gave me a job.'

'He's not our boss,' replied the smaller assailant who forcefully pushed Sam backwards towards the edge of the quay. 'Jake is the boss around here and you'd best do a runner because you're not a scouser from Liverpool. Beat it, buster. We don't need you.'

Evading the group, Sam gained safer ground and squared up to the trio saying, 'It's a job, that's all. A job! I need a job. I'll not be a problem, I promise.'

'Bet your life on that, buster because you'll not be here tomorrow, will you?' A fist lashed out and caught Sam on the chin. 'Now beat it. We don't want you. You're not local. Move your arse.'

There was a loud shout from afar followed by the sound of rushing footsteps and the appearance of Malek Osman.

'What's going on?' demanded Malek. 'What do you think you're doing.'

'He got in the way,' from the trio.

'He's not from around here,' voiced again.

'I owe him a favour,' explained Malek. 'Now back off and give the man some room. He starts tomorrow morning and that's the end of the story. Understand?'

The atmosphere went silent until Jake appeared behind Osman a moment later.

Ignoring Osman, the assailants cast their eyes on Jake who gestured they should retire.

They stepped away.

'No more trouble, Banshee,' remarked Malek.

'None at all, Mr Osman,' replied Bobby Banshee: the smaller man and group leader. 'None intended. Just our way of welcoming your baby boy to the gang. You're a Turkish guy, Mr Osman, and we're all scousers. You don't understand our ways and neither does your boy. He's not one of us. We just love scousers, and yourself of course, but not foreigners like your son. Sorry and all that!'

'He's not my son,' snapped Malek.

'Just as well,' murmured a voice from the group as they gradually gave ground and walked towards Jake.

The seconds ticked by with Sam rubbing his chin and unsure of what to do next. He held his ground.

Jake stepped forward and said, 'Off you go, guys. That's it for the day. You've said your piece now cool it and get off home. Banshee, you know what to do.'

Banshee nodded, cast an eye at Sam, and walked towards the office block as Jenny appeared trotting at a steady pace. Her long legs reached out and gathered speed as she glided across the tarmac.

'The telephone, Mr Osman. The caller says it's urgent. One of the shipments is running late.'

'I'll be there, Jenny,' replied Malek who turned to Jake and said, 'You didn't have to hit him. Was that necessary?'

'I don't know want you mean,' replied Jake brushing his stubbled chin with his right hand.

'Banshee and his bully boy mates only assaulted the man because you told them to.'

'You should know better, Osman. Banshee is in my tribe. I'll see you in your office later.'

'I'm busy,' snapped Malek.

'Make time!' growled Jake in a threatening manner. 'You need to be reminded of one or two things. Do you understand what I'm saying, Osman?'

Malek visibly shrunk under the verbal attack. The paunch above his trouser belt wobbled nervously. The Turk gestured an admission and then beckoned Sam forward saying, 'Go with Jenny. You've papers to sign. Quickly now.'

Hurriedly, Jenny waved Sam forward and said, 'This way. Sam. Follow me. Come on.'

The quayside cleared and Sam walked back to the office with Jenny. He savoured her beauty but glanced back at the two men still standing on the quay. He wondered who the real boss of the outfit was. Was it the dock supervisor and higher ranking Malek Osman or was it Jake, the loadmaster who everyone was frightened of? One ruled with a pen; the other with fear: pure fear.

Once Jenny and Sam were out of earshot, Jake stuck his face into Malek's and said, 'What the hell are you playing at? Why did you invite an unknown to the team? You bloody fool. You know what we must do now, don't you?'

'He saved me from a beating the other night. The cops were there too. He got me out of the pub. I owe it to him.'

'You owe him nothing, you idiot,' snarled the loadmaster. 'You know nothing about him. He could be anything from a cop to a customs officer for all we know.'

'No, he's not, is he? I mean, I never gave it a thought, Jake. I didn't stop to think. He helped me. I could have lost my briefcase if it hadn't been for him. And you know what that contains. Come on! Look at things my way for a change.'

'You're paid to think, and do as you're told. You're not paid to cause us problems, you bloody clown. I thought he was a close relation of yours and that's why I gave him a job because I trusted your word. You know the score, Osman. Friends and family only on our terminal. All you've done is land us with a problem we don't need. He could be anyone, you bloody idiot. Now get out of my sight before I drop you right in it with the boss.'

'What about Sam Quest?'

'Leave it with me. Banshee knows what to do.'

Sheepishly, Malek turned and made his way back to the office leaving Jake fumbling for his mobile phone.

In the office, Jenny presented Sam with employment papers to sign and then issued him with a security pass explaining that such a document would authorise his entry into other parts of the terminal that he might need to visit.

Accepting coffee from Jenny, Sam sat at a desk and struck up a conversation with her. She replied with equal relish and only moved away from his presence when Malek returned.

'Putting you through now, Mr Osman,' voiced Jenny when Malek approached his office door and she turned to the telephone system.

Pausing for a moment, Malek engaged Sam and said, 'Sorry about all that, Sam. It's these Liverpudlians. They have a welcoming ritual to perform whenever a new employee arrives. I'm trying my best to stop it, but it's not quite sorted out yet.'

'No problem,' replied Sam. 'No harm done and I've got a job. Thank you.'

Malek nodded and entered his office to take that urgent phone call.

'That's not right,' whispered Jenny. 'Those three are bullies and Mr Osman knows it. They've always been like that. They pick and choose who to work with and who not to work with. People are frightened of them.'

'Are you?'

'Me? No! Mr Osman looks after me and I'm as safe as houses in the office. You won't see me down at the terminal. My job is writing letters, answering the phone, running errands and general office work.'

'Good! I'm pleased you feel safe,' ventured Sam with a smile and a softness in his voice that appealed to Jenny.

'They shouldn't have hit you and there's no welcoming ritual that I know of.'

'Oh, I see,' replied Sam listening for more.

'Not right at all,' continued Jenny. 'Everton fans live next to Liverpool fans everywhere in this city. They rarely fall out and fight each other. What they did was wrong. Anyway, it's not for me to say but I think they just didn't take to you, and they are used to having the final word on who works with them. You be careful out there, Sam. Is it alright if I call you Sam? I mean, there are some nasty bully boys out there, I can tell you. Look out for the small guy called Banshee. He's horrible.'

'How do you know that, Jenny?'

'Because I watch, I listen, and I work people out. He's not my kind of fella. He asked me out once, only once. I blocked him right away. No chance.'

'Is it alright if I call you Jenny?' enquired Sam.

'Of course. I've been Mr Osman's secretary for three years now. He's very nice but some of the men… Anyway, I've said too much already. Have you signed those papers?'

Sam set down a pen, pushed the papers across the desk to Jenny, and said, 'You've been very kind, thank you. Between you and me, I didn't hear a word you said about anyone.'

Jenny took the papers and beamed a smile.

'Tonight!' suggested Sam. 'Would you join me for a drink, maybe a meal somewhere? No disrespect intended but I notice you're not wearing a wedding ring, so I assume…'

'Yes! What time?' replied Jenny interrupting Sam's flow.

'Seven! Eight! Which is best?'

'Seven-thirty,' offered Jenny. 'At the Mariner's Hut. It's next to the Premier Inn about half a mile down the road. Yes, I'd love to. I'll see you there. You can tell me all about yourself.'

'And you can tell me all about yourself,' grinned Sam playfully. 'For instance, can I have your mobile number just in case I have to cancel for some reason?'

Jenny scribbled on a scrap of paper and handed it to him saying, 'Can I have yours?'

'Yes! Of course, you can, Jenny, I've just got a brand new one from the shop across the road. I hardly use it. I'm just learning how it works. Did you know it's the first proper time I've been able to afford one?'

'Oh, lucky you.'

'Thinking about it,' ventured Sam. 'As I've started work here, could you give me the numbers for Mr Osman and Jake?'

'I don't see why not,' replied Jenny. 'Jackson! It's Jake Jackson. While I'm on, I'll give you Billy Banshee's number too. Just so you know if he rings you. It's one to avoid at all costs if you can. He's Jake's buddy. Some days they are glued to each other at the hip. Or is it like bookends? Whatever, they are very close mates.'

'Thanks,' smiled Sam. 'Seven tonight then!'

'Seven-thirty,' replied Jenny returning the smile.

'Maybe we can…'

'Go on,' replied Jenny.

'Oh, nothing. I just thought we might make a habit of it. I mean seeing each other… For coffee and such… Tea even, maybe?'

'Maybe,' grinned Jenny. 'Maybe!'

'I mean,' blurted Sam nervously, 'Maybe we can talk about stuff.'

'Stuff?'

'Like Liverpool and where are the best places to go.'

'Okay! Anything else?'

Struggling, Sam gurgled, 'Sport! Yeah! Do you play sports? You know, badminton, tennis, golf, stuff like that.'

'I swim,' replied Jenny with a smile. 'Maybe we could go for a swim one day. There's a pool at the leisure centre in Bootle or there's one at the Aquatic Centre at Everton. Which would you prefer?'

More confident now, Sam replied enthusiastically, 'Either!'

'Okay! We can decide tonight.'

'Yes! Let's do that. Seven thirty!'

'Seven-thirty!' confirmed Jenny.

Exiting the office, Sam strolled to his car and felt an air of relief grip him.

'I've got a date with her,' he thought. 'That wasn't in the plan but she's gorgeous and I like her. Plus, I've got three phone numbers to get stuck into as a result of chasing a woman.'

Sam unlocked his Fiesta and slid into the driver's seat. Arranging his seatbelt, he casually checked his surroundings and spotted Banshee getting into the driver's seat of a silver Audi at the far end of the car park. Sam waited for a while, pretended to scour the glove compartment so he could waste time, and then stole a glance again. The Audi hadn't moved.

Firing the engine, Sam drove out of the car park and onto the main road. Within a minute he checked his rear-view mirror and confirmed that Banshee was following him at a discreet distance.

Sam approached a roundabout, slipped into a lower gear, and maintained a direct route towards his flat in Vauxhall.

'Maybe Banshee lives here too,' thought Sam. 'There's only one way to find out. I'll let him follow me home if that's what he wants. Otherwise, he'll peel off somewhere and my suspicions will be unfounded.'

Banshee clung to his target even when Sam deliberately stopped at a newsagent for a paper and parked outside the shop. Banshee pulled in about fifty yards behind Sam but continued to follow when his quarry returned to the car with a newspaper and a bunch of flowers.

'Yes, he's on me,' thought Sam who drove to Vauxhall and parked in his allotted space. 'I wonder if he's worked out that I bought the flowers for Jenny to give to her tonight. I shouldn't have done that. I dropped my guard. If they know I've bought her flowers then I've given them a weakness, and it's my weakness for a pretty girl and no female company. Idiot! Yes, I'm an idiot. I should have left out buying the flowers. Don't write anything on the label. Not a thing! Don't write her name on the flower label. You bloody idiot. One step forward and potentially one step back. There's only me on my side. Thing it through, you clown.'

Casually, naturally, Sam locked his car and effortlessly strolled to his flat constantly reminding himself to increase his awareness of personal security. He took a quick shower, changed clothing, collected a shoulder bag from the wardrobe, and plucked a hair from his head. Licking the thin wisp, he placed it across the wardrobe doors as a seal and vacated the flat wearing a pair of rear-view sunglasses. The spectacles were popular amongst cyclists since they used semi-transparent mirrors to give a continuous view of the road behind them.

Walking towards a nearby café, Sam checked his sunglasses and saw Banshee following him. On reaching the café, Sam ordered a coffee and took a seat where he could see the front and rear entrances to the premises. He unfolded the newspaper he had bought and pretended to read it whilst simultaneously casting a suspicious eye at his surroundings.

Banshee watched Sam enter the café, used a mobile phone, and then melted into the building line on the other side of the street.

Once satisfied there were no other intrusions, Sam found a phone booth in the café and rang Jupiter adopting the agreed procedure. Drinking his coffee between glances out of the window and updating Jupiter on the day's proceedings, Sam kept his eyes and ears open monitoring everyone in the café and watching for movements that might suggest a new watcher was in place.

'The Audi!' remarked Rafferty. 'Interesting, Quest. It's a hire car on long-term lease to Banshee.'

An hour later, Sam emerged from the café and began his walk home to Vauxhall. Almost immediately, he picked up Banshee following him again. Undeterred, he reached his flat and glanced at the front door. There was no sign of forced entry, but Sam knew the lock was a Yale non-deadlocking night latch. It was possible to force the lock open by exercising pressure on the latch and inserting a thin blade into the holdback mechanism. Mostly used in Victorian and Georgian properties, the lock was still popular despite its replacement by sophisticated systems from the modern era.

Detecting a slight scratch where a blade had penetrated the locking mechanism, Sam entered the apartment and saw that the wisp of hair had fallen from the wardrobe doors. He presumed he was the victim of a burglary. One of the wardrobe doors was ajar and an upended trouser pocket was visible hanging from a clothes hangar. Rummaging in the wardrobe, Sam examined his range of tee shirts and knew they had been scrutinized by the trespasser. A few of his tee shirts carried the logo of a cannabis leaf whilst others carried the word 'skunk' printed on the rear.

Kneeling, Sam studied a small set of drawers situated inside the wardrobe. The drawers had been released but hadn't been closed properly.

'Amateurs?' thought Sam. 'I don't think I disturbed them but it looks as if they didn't tidy up when they left.'

Tugging one drawer fully open, Sam unravelled a pouch and checked his supply of cannabis. It was lying next to a bunch of rizla papers, a box of matches, and a small set of weighing scales. But the dominant factor emanating from the drawer was the pungent smell of cannabis that was rife in the atmosphere. Anyone searching the wardrobe could not have missed the evidence of cannabis.

In addition to the drug paraphernalia, more than a dozen used betting slips lay on the table. Each slip had been stamped by the bookmaker but each one was a loser. Next to one of the betting slips was a letter from a solicitor's firm indicating that Sam Quest owed money on his credit cards as well as the non-payment of a bank loan.

'They've even searched my clothes,' thought Sam as he considered his situation. 'They'll have seen my connections to the drug world and, hopefully, they'll have worked out that I'm a gambler and I owe money. I'm in debt and they can use that knowledge to their advantage if they give it some thought. Will they pay me to do something illegal based on what information I left for them to find? I planted the articles just in case the flat was burgled. My passport and driving licence will have been examined along with letters and bills. Some of those things have a Carlisle address on so that might lead them to contact people in Cumbria. Who knows what else they found out about me during their visit? Nothing was taken so this was all about checking me out and they won't have worked out that I was planning that the flat might be burgled as part of the process leading to whether they could trust me. If they've any suspicions about me, that will confuse them and hopefully lead to an argument between the parties concerned. The loadmaster made a mistake in thinking I was related to Malek. That was the stroke of luck I needed. Confusion will lead to more separation if they argue the point. Upsetting the status quo and dislodging normality have caused problems in the past. Can Sam Quest be trusted or not? He's an outsider. He's a druggie. Where's Carlisle? Get that address checked out. That's what they'll be talking about. I think we were right about one thing we discussed. They might be involved in a massive drug importation operation but they're not as good as we thought they might be. A couple of gang leaders like Osman and Jake fall out, Banshee turns out to be a street soldier, and now I've discovered my flat has been burgled, probably by Banshee's two mates from the quayside. We are slowly uncovering more vulnerabilities in the organisation. The challenge is to prize it wide open, but I think I'm just scratching the surface. Who is running the show? Surely there's someone with brains somewhere.'

Closing the drawers, Sam shut the wardrobe doors properly before climbing into bed. He fluffed the pillows up and checked the time before finishing reading the newspaper.

In a room in central London, some distance from the headquarters of the Security Service in Thames House, a female operative named Becca sat quietly reading a book. She wore earphones and thumbed the pages of a book about the history of Russia and the Soviet Union.

To all intent and purposes, the building was just another call centre the public walked past every day of the week, but the digital platform she was responsible for contained over a score of phone numbers and reference numbers. It was situated in a line of similar platforms where her colleagues sat waiting for a line to activate and their console to burst into life. Each reference number related to a security operation in which she played an integral part.

Becca turned a page and then a light flashed on her console. EUROPA appeared causing her to set aside her book and press the alphabet keys followed by the numeric keys on her keyboard. Activating her earphones, she listened to the conversation between the parties concerned fully aware that she was monitoring an intercepted call on behalf of the Security Service. Becca made sure the language option was set to 'English' and recorded the dialogue. As the conversation continued, she typed onto the screen notes that formed part of the 'preliminary dispatch protocol'. A 'full commentary' version would follow once her supervisor, Janice, had checked the product and verified the same.

'That's the first one from Europa,' revealed Janice. 'Rush that through please, Becca. It's a Priority One.'

'What's the operation about?' ventured Becca.

'Drugs importation!' replied Janice. 'There's no point in telling you otherwise, not when you're the primary listener. Why do you ask?'

'Why not the police or the National Crime Agency?'

'I don't know,' replied Janice thumbing through Becca's book. 'I'll guess it must be a big one. Just produce the reports soonest, please. Who knows, maybe you'll hear enough to work out the mystery yourself.'

Becca smiled, turned to her console, laid her fingers on the QUERTY keyboard, and replied, 'Will do.'

Sam's alarm sounded in his flat in Vauxhall, Liverpool. He swung his feet onto the bedroom floor. Dressing in his usual dark clothing, he hoisted his shoulder bag, donned his roll-down balaclava, and vacated the apartment.

Adopting counter-surveillance techniques, Sam established he was not being followed. Checking over his shoulder was the easiest manoeuvre but also the worst way since it betrayed the fact that he was looking for watchers. Instead, Sam turned sharp corners and stopped, lit a cigarette, waited for a follower, and then repeated the action a short time later. He turned around and retraced his route, stopped, walked through a narrow passageway, used reflections in glass, windows and reflective objects, and donned his sunglasses when he needed to. It took him a while, but he used the skills he had been taught on the streets of Aberdeen and Inverness to ensure he was not being followed by Banshee or anyone else.

Satisfied, Sam reached the multi-level car park and found his new motor. It would be one of the vehicles that Logan would plant in the car park for him whenever a vehicle was needed for covert use or surveillance of some kind. His shabby Ford Fiesta, which was beginning to resemble a rust bucket, was fine for openly driving around Liverpool between his flat and the docks. It was ideal since it reflected his lifestyle and his social standing. The black Mazda 6 Logan had left for him would be used differently.

Sam retrieved the ignition keys from the inside rear wheel. A fresh zippo cigarette lighter was also present and he pocketed it. That made two Zippos in his possession. One is in use and the other is a spare back-up. Unlocking the driver's door, he flipped the sun visor down and seized a Yale key wrapped in a soft velvet bag.

Firing the engine, Sam pocketed the key and drove into the traffic flow heading towards Crosby.

A short time later, Sam pulled into one of the streets that led to the beach. He parked the Mazda and strolled towards Malek Osman's house as he adjusted his balaclava until it covered his forehead, ears, and chin. Apart from keeping the breeze out, his headgear reduced the amount of facial expression on show. He walked cautiously down the driveway towards the front door. Eagle-eyed, he scanned the ground-floor windows and then the bedroom windows assuring himself that there was no one in the house. He knew Malek was a single man and the Aston Martin was in Regent Road.

Sam used the key made by Logan and inserted it into the yale lock. Turning the key, the detective-come-spy felt the pins drop into place. The door opened and he entered Malek's house whereupon he delved into his shoulder bag and removed a pair of clean plastic slip-ons that he placed over his shoes. It was the method by which he knew there would be no soil or grass residue left behind to indicate his visit. He stood for a while and grew accustomed to the light and the sound of the house. All was quiet. Before taking a step, he looked around him searching the building structure for any tell-tale sign of an interior CCTV system. There was none.

Making his way through the downstairs area, Sam entered the double garage via the adjoining kitchen where he found a white Ford Kuga parked in one of the two bays.

'An Aston Martin at the office and a Ford Kuga here,' thought Sam. 'That's a notable difference in car taste. One for work and showing off and the Kuga for, I wonder what?'

Fumbling inside his shoulder bag, Sam recovered his zippo, turned it upside down into a new layout, and began taking photographs of the Kuga. Once finished, he removed a device that sat in the palm of his hand. It was an electronic gadget that he intended to place underneath the car. The device would tag the car electronically and emit a wireless signal that Sam was able to monitor via a separate gadget that was secreted in the glove compartment of his Mazda.

'Remember the training,' thought Sam when he reminded himself to cover the basics first. 'Don't be an idiot again.'

On the walls of the garage, there were cupboards and shelves. The shelves carried the usual tools that you would expect to find in most garages: hammers, pliers, screwdrivers, Stanley knives, trowels, garden shears etc. But when Sam opened one of the cupboards, he was surprised to find an electronic sweeping device. It resembled a short broom and when activated would reveal any electronic interference close by. Sam knew it was the kind of device that spies, and security-conscious criminals, used to make sure they were not being either listened to or followed. The device could be swept across the area like a wand and would betray any electronic device tagged to a car and any listening device secreted in the house.

'Damn it!' mouthed Sam. 'Just what I didn't need, but I remembered the drill. How close was I to crashing the operation?'

Abandoning the idea of tagging the Ford Kuga with an electronic device, Sam began searching the rest of the house. Diligently, he checked the bedrooms, lounge, and office where he found a passport in the name of Malek Osman. The passport carried Malek's photograph and appeared genuine. In the same bundle, he discovered a birth certificate with the same name indicating Malek had been born in Ankara: the capital of Turkey. There was no marriage certificate to be seen. Sam activated his zippo.

There was a knock on the front door shocking Sam to the core and causing him to drop his shoulder bag. He quickly gathered the bag into his hands and ducked low so that he could not be seen.

Another rattle on the door followed. It was louder this time and whistled through Sam's brain.

'Panic!' he thought. 'Sam Quest, you panicked. Get hold of yourself.'

Edging his way into the kitchen, Sam glanced through the windows but couldn't see anything. Sneaking into the front lounge, he concentrated on a mirror on the wall above the fireplace. The mirror reflected the image of a man standing on the driveway outside whilst Sam's position hid him from his view.

The man stepped forward and rattled the doorknob.

A zippo activated and took a photograph of the stranger reflected in the mirror.

Simultaneously, a further man came into view. He was dressed in dark green overalls, and said 'Good morning! How can I help you?' to the man at the doorstep. He then bid him farewell as he moved on down the street.

Having listened to the conversation, Sam picked up that the visitor at the door was a double-glazing salesman canvassing the area. The newcomer in overalls was a neighbour about to cut the grass on his lawn when he reacted to the visitor at Osman's house.

'What to do?' thought Sam. 'Do I go out the back way and climb over the fence or do I sit tight and wait for the neighbour to finish cutting his grass?'

An engine erupted into life outside and Sam noticed that the neighbour was cutting the lawn. Turning, Sam entered an office situated off the lounge and located a laptop on the desk. He switched the computer on, bypassed security by tapping the keypad in a coded format, and then downloaded the hard drive onto a memory stick. Quietly, but methodically, Sam searched the drawers and then made his way through the house exploring the contents and taking photos of documents that proved Malek's lifestyle and disposition in life.

Sam heard the mower die, watched the neighbour disappear around the back of his house, and heard a shed door creak open. Within seconds, Sam was out of the house and down the garden path at a brisk pace.

Locating the Mazda, the detective fired the engine and drove into Liverpool where he returned to the multi-storey car park. He left the memory stick and his old zippo knowing that Logan would collect the gear and analyse the product. Sam checked the car park, made sure no one was watching out for him, and returned to his flat and a hot shower. He had a date that night at the Mariner's Hut and he didn't want to be late.

'Who knows,' thought Sam. 'Jenny might just fill me in on all kinds of little things that are going on in the office. Might be something I need to know.'

The night went well. The two hit it off right away. He with a nervous beginning and her with a warm acceptance of a man she considered to be different from others she had met. They joked. They laughed. They enjoyed each other's company in a way neither expected. There was a special chemistry in play and it was becoming more powerful by the minute. Romance was in the air leaving Sam to forgo asking all the questions about Osman and company that were stacked in his brain. Instead, when his fingers touched Jenny's hand, he felt the sensation of love tingling through his body to his heart. But was it because of his lack of female company over the last year, or was there something else afoot? How close was she to Osman? Just a typist come secretary, or had she been told to find out all she could about the infiltrator?

Whilst holding hands with Jenny in a restaurant, Sam was unaware that a couple of miles away Logan was working late in a surveillance operation organised by Rafferty.

Jupiter's right-hand man had stood in the shadows and waited for his target to vacate the apartment. Once it was confirmed that the target was at his place of work in Walton, Logan used a duplicate key to enter the target's premises. He paused, listened, allowed his eyes to become accustomed to the light, and then cautiously entered the lounge area. Logan switched on a dim light attached to his headgear and approached a television that was fixed to a wall bracket and dominated the room. Reaching up, Logan removed one of the leads and added a thin device to the electronic system before replacing the original lead. He switched on the television and whispered, 'Red Alpha Six! Copy my message.'

'Loud and clear. The audible is good. Vision is good. Proceed!'

Logan moved from the lounge to the bedroom area and removed a lightbulb from the lamp standard before replacing it with another in his possession. Similar visits were made to the kitchen and hall areas. Throughout his visit, Logan whispered his location and his dealings before saying, 'Red Alpha Six! I'm all done here. Sitrep, please!'

'Ten Ten all in place. Audio-visual is now in play. Vacate to the car park for clean pick up. All clear.'

'I have that,' from Logan who secured the apartment and made his way to the pick-up point.

The target address was now covered by technical surveillance of an audio-visual nature.

~

Chapter Seven

~

The Dock Terminal,
Bootle,
Tuesday

Jake Jackson and his team began work that morning before dawn. A score of workers, including Sam, emptied a boat that had arrived from Belfast. It was a normal day that went without mishap and Sam did his bit without saying a word. Polite, and considerate, he blended into the team well and, despite earlier remarks made by Jake, found that he could easily unleash and carry all the packages from the hold to the quayside. A few forklift trucks were also there to assist in the unloading.

Sam watched the crane drivers hoisting the larger containers onto the rear of a heavy goods vehicle and wondered how long an ocean-going vessel would take to unload. He'd heard it might take up to three days depending on the size of the vessel. This boat, however, would take less than a day due to the number of staff involved and its size.

As he studied proceedings, Sam made mental notes of who did what, where and why. His mind was working overtime as he considered how things had changed. Banshee and his mates seemed unsure of him. It was as if he was being watched but there was no one he could tag who might have been the main watcher. Banshee nodded but didn't follow him about the vessel and was content to allow Sam to get on with things.

'Whatever is happening,' thought Sam, 'One day they are all over you; the next they ignore you. The good thing is that no one is bullying me today, but I wonder what is going on.'

'You alright, Quest?'

Sam turned his head slightly and recognised the speaker as one who had attacked him previously. The man was tall, slender, in his late twenties, and wore a blue and white bobble hat as well as his overalls.

'I'm Jason,' continued the man. 'Sorry about the fight the other day. Things got out of hand.'

Sam nodded but didn't engage in conversation.

'I can see you're still upset,' said Jason.

'What do you want?'

'A word!'

'It's over,' replied Sam. 'Unless you intend to repeat history?'

'No, I don't,' revealed Jason in the slightest of scouse accents 'Can we start again?' he added, offering a handshake.

Sam paused for a second or two before accepting Jason's hand.

'I wondered if you had any spare?' asked Jason.

'Any spare what?' queried Sam.

'Dope! You know, hashish, whatever!'

'What makes you think I do drugs?' enquired Sam as he pulled another package from a crate and placed it onto a pallet.

'You look the type,' smiled Jason pushing the package further onto the pallet. 'Where you from?'

'Carlisle,' answered Sam. 'Why do you want to know?'

'Hey! Don't take it personally,' suggested Jason. 'I'm interested.'

'Are you really?'

'I'm interested in why a man from Carlisle should come down to Liverpool docks to work. That's all.'

'I've told you before. I needed the job.'

'And a place to live maybe?' queried Jason with a quizzical look.

'Something like that,' replied Sam. Dropping a package to the ground, Sam squared up to Jason and said, 'Look! What the hell has it got to do with you where I come from or whether or not I do drugs? Why don't you just leave me alone to get on with my job?'

'Because people talk. Word around the docks is that you do drugs: cannabis mainly. Hash! Skunk even?'

'Who told you that?'

'Seen you with a tee shirt on once.'

'Amazing,' laughed Sam. 'I wear them all the time.'

'This one had a cannabis leaf on it.'

Knowing he'd never worn that tee shirt in the docks, Sam realised Jason must have been involved in the burglary at his flat. He might even have been the man who had searched the wardrobe and rifled through his tee shirts and the drug paraphernalia he had deliberately planted for someone to find.

Sam removed his balaclava for a moment to wipe the sweat from his brow. 'So that makes me guilty then, Jason?'

'No! It makes you interesting.'

'And that's all?'

'Unless you tell me more,' suggested Jason. 'You know there's more, Quest.'

Looking over his shoulder, Sam then engaged Jason with, 'I could get you hash, skunk, coke in Carlisle, Newcastle, and some places in the south of Scotland, Jason. What I have at the moment is for me and no one else. Sorry, pal but you're on a loser today.'

'But I was right though. You are a user.'

'Occasionally,' admitted Sam who glanced around again before adding, 'But there's more money in selling than buying.'

'So, you're a dealer then.'

'What makes you say that?'

'Carlisle! Newcastle! The south of Scotland! And where else? Come on, Quest. You just said it. There's more money in selling than buying.'

'What if I did?'

'I can put you into people here,' offered Jason. 'Mal has connections.'

'Mal?'

'Yeah! Banshee's mate. Malcolm! The one with me and Banshee the other day. You remember him, yeah?'

'I remember getting smacked good and hard. I hope everything is sorted now. It's like I said. I didn't come to cause problems, just for a job.'

'Well, you've got a job and who knows,' proposed Jason. 'You might get another one soon.'

'Are you the boss?' challenged Sam. 'Who's who around here?'

'Just feeling you out. Looking to see if you are more than you are. Do you know something, Quest? You're not just a down-and-out begging scrounger looking for a job in the docks. You're more than that. You're into the drugs industry, aren't you? Might even be on the run from the law for all I know.'

'Leave it for now, Jason. I can get you a small supply later this week. But if I deal with you then I don't expect to get kicked around the docks like a football. Is that understood?'

'What you gonna get me, Quest? A couple of smokes or a couple of kilos?'

Sam studied Jason for a while and then pulled another parcel to his chest and heaved it onto the pallet saying, 'Out of my face, Jason. Have you no sense at all? I've got work to do and so have you. Get on with it.'

Sniggering, Jason dropped his package at Sam's feet, turned away, and made his way down the quayside and out of sight.

Loading the last package onto the pallet, Sam stood back when a forklift moved into position and uplifted the load.

'Interesting,' considered Sam. 'That was a deliberate attempt to try and work me out, I'd say. It looks like I've gone from suspect to supplier in less than twenty-four hours. I've tried to present them with arguments about me to try and break them up. I've tried to confuse them. Now I'm confused. Time to ring Jupiter, I think.'

An hour later, it was Sam's turn for a break. He stole away to a nearby café where he phoned Rafferty and updated him on the product of the search at Malek's house, and recent events.

'Thanks for that, Quest,' replied Rafferty. 'One thing at a time. You need to know that recent telephone calls made by the loadmaster, Jake, indicate that he is in contact with Detective Sergeant Brian Doyle of Merseyside police. Doyle is stationed at Walton but he's a supervisor with widespread connections throughout the force area. One of Jake's calls to Doyle was made shortly after the assault upon you on that morning you went to see Osman about a job. Doyle interrogated the Police National Computer and pulled the digital file on you. As you know, it's a false file created by Logan and uploaded to the PNC with a tag that feeds directly to Logan and no one else.'

'You hacked into the Police National Computer.'

'We do have legitimate access to the facility, Quest. As a result, Doyle knows you have a criminal record for drug dealing and are suspected of further drug dealing in the north of England, the northeast, and parts of Scotland. He also knows you were once a detective with five years' service and then you were bombed out for cowardice and the rest.'

'Has it occurred to you that Doyle might be investigating the very same thing that we are? He might be part of a police operation into drugs importation at the docks.'

'He's not,' confirmed Rafferty. 'The phone interceptions reveal that Doyle is the boss, not Osman and not Jake. He's bent, corrupt, and a bad apple. I'm keeping him under wraps.'

'What about informing Merseyside senior command? They'll surely want to know,' insisted Sam.

'I'm sure they will, but all in good time. I'm letting things run. We're aware of his corruption. We'll run alongside him and see where it takes us.'

'You're sure of this?' probed Sam.

'I am. For your information, Quest, technical surveillance is now live at Doyle's home address.'

'I see! You're that sure,'

'Logan has been doing some homework, Quest. Those guys that attacked you the other day, plus Jake and Banshee particularly, have all got previous convictions for assault.'

'That doesn't surprise me,' replied Sam. 'They look hard and act hard whenever it suits them. They're well known in the dock community.'

'What might surprise you is that during the last eighteen months, Jake, Banshee, Malcolm and Jason have all been arrested for various degrees of assault or violent disorder.'

'I see.'

'No, you don't see,' declared Rafferty. 'On each occasion, the charges against them were dropped even though they all had previous convictions and the Crown Prosecutions Service had authorised proceedings from the evidence available.'

'How did that happen?'

'On every occasion, the officer in the case was Detective Sergeant Brian Doyle. What do you make of that?'

Sam paused, thought it through for a moment, and then proposed, 'Are you suggesting that Doyle has used his position to recruit violent criminals to the docks in return for arranging the charges against them to be dropped?'

'It looks that way. You just told me that Osman's secretary, Stacey, mentioned to you that they were well-known bullies. People are frightened of them. Now you know why people are scared of that particular clique. They're hard, violent when they need to be, and live in the shadow of corrupt police protection.'

'Jenny!'

'What?'

'Jenny! She's Osman's secretary, not Stacey.'

'Oh, yes, sorry. Anyway, Quest, Jason's approach to you was arranged over the phone by Doyle via Jake and Osman to test you.'

'Why?'

'They are trying to enlarge the network they are running. They're looking for dealers from outside Liverpool to offload the incoming product. We're on the verge of a breakthrough, Quest. Hopefully, I'll get the full story to you in due course.'

'What do you mean by the full story?'

'Leave it for now, Quest. I haven't time to tell you. Look, finding out that you were once a cop has increased the traffic flow on the phones. You've confused them and got them arguing, discussing, and talking to each other. Every time they talk, we learn a little bit more about them and their lifestyles.'

'I see. Confusion promotes argument and discussion between them. It works then. It looks like they've bitten.'

'I hope it has confused them even more. They will realise you have access to a team of street dealers, hence your conviction and the false intelligence report planted in the digital file in your name. That will be important to them right now if the shipment is inbound and they are building a network of suppliers. Osman may have panicked when he was in danger of losing his briefcase but it looks as if he's normally a cool customer. His phone is quieter than the others. Find out what he's up to. We need more on the Turkish connection.'

'Okay! Will do! Tell me, does Jenny figure in their operation so far?'

'Jenny Higgins! Osman's secretary?'

'Yes, that's the one. What can you tell me about her?'

'She's the same age as you. Jenny is single and originally from Ainsdale midway between Formby and Southport. She lives with her parents at weekends, but she has a flat in Walton throughout the week. Father is a doctor; mother is a housewife and a volunteer patient driver at the local hospital. There's no indication that she is involved criminally but that could change. She's oblivious to everything going on around her. Almost a dumb blonde of a secretary.'

'How can you say she's a dumb blonde when you've never met her?' twisted Sam angrily.

'Oh, no!' gushed Rafferty. 'Don't tell me you are interested in her. It's not in the brief, Quest. Hands off! She might be in on it.'

'I don't think so,' replied Sam. 'I've been out with her a few times now. Socially, I mean.'

'But you don't know for sure whether she's clean or dirty, so back off and leave her alone.'

'What if I fall in love with her?' queried Sam.

'Don't!' snapped Rafferty.

'And she with me?'

'Don't take her out again. See her only at work and only when you're in the office. Keep a safe distance, Quest. As the cops say, you're single-crewed. There's no room for hitchhikers, girlfriends, or secret lovers. Ditch her before she twirls you around her little finger.'

'Mr Rafferty, you are Jupiter to me. You are my Roman God! Jupiter struck down his enemies with bolts of lightning and eagles were his sacred birds. Do you know what Jenny means?'

'I'm not with you, Quest.'

'The name Jenny is short for Jennifer. That's the Cornish form of the name Guinevere. The name is historically attributed to good people who are fair and well-minded. Jenny won't be a problem.'

'But you need to be reminded, Quest, that Guinevere betrayed King Arthur by helping his nephew Mordred usurp her husband's throne. She then ruled by his side until Arthur returned to fight Mordred to the death. Widowed, Guinevere escaped to a nunnery where she lived the rest of her days in shame and seclusion. Hardly a good recommendation for anyone in this game, Quest.'

'No! But one day I hope she will produce the contents of Malek Osman's briefcase from the office safe.'

'I see,' acknowledged Rafferty thoughtfully. 'You decide to challenge the Roman God Jupiter by the use of an irrelevant woman's name. You challenge when you should obey. Have you always challenged authority, Quest?'

'Only when I need to.'

'A word of advice then. She might be harvesting everything there is to know about you and your lifestyle. You are my spy: my asset. Assets do not run assets. I understand what you are trying to do. The briefcase is a long shot, always has been, and I'll not be surprised if it all turns out to be irrelevant paperwork. Expect it to be timesheets, pay scales, the shift rota, the tax handbook, and stuff like that. You told me Osman is an administrator. Remember? You told me he runs the legitimate side of the business. He's the bookkeeper that produces the figures for the accountant. Doyle runs the show we're interested in, not Osman. That briefcase will be full of office stuff.'

'You think so? I told you that as an administrator he could be the man with his hand on everything to do with the money.'

'We'll see. I'll tell you now, Quest, I'm not impressed that you have recruited someone outside the organisation to do a job that we might sanction ourselves should the need arise.'

'The need has arisen in my mind. I trust her. She's not stupid. I can see it in her eyes.'

'Heaven forbid! You've put yourself in more danger, Quest. If they find out you're chasing Jenny or using her, that gang will blackmail her, threaten her, and use her to manipulate you. Back off! Do you hear me?'

There was a brief silence before Sam eventually replied, 'I hear you. I need the postman to action a special delivery.'

'Logan will be playing postman tomorrow morning. Check the mailbox for a small supply of cannabis for the boys.'

'I got that, thanks,' replied Sam. He cradled the phone, shook his head in annoyance at the words spoken of Jenny, and then casually returned to the docks.

Instantaneously, Rafferty pressed a button on the telephone on his desk and said to a colleague, 'Maxwell! Jenny Higgins! I want her flat and home telephone covered as of today. Plus, I want a history of all calls from her home address over the last three years. When you've done that, I want a background report on her education, political views, and social views. I want to know all about any criminal activity she's been involved with in the past. What are her likes, dislikes, and hobbies? What books does she read? What films does she watch? What perfume does she use, everything, the works? Spin the drum. Understand?'

'Sir! I'm on it,' replied Maxwell. 'The drum is spinning.'

'Thank you! Class the intercepted phone calls as secondary primaries. Let let me know if anything contentious drops out.'

Rafferty waited for a moment, heard his colleague Maxwell reply, 'Will do!' and then put the phone down.

'Quest!' thought Rafferty. 'I hope you're right about that girl because if you're not, Jupiter will strike you down with his bolts of lightning and my eagles will fly down and destroy you. Assets recruiting assets. Not on this watch, Quest.'

In an office in central London, Becca adjusted her headphones, intercepted more phone calls, recorded the main details of the conversations, and presented reports for Janice: her first-line supervisor.

There was a quiet, almost inaudible, tapping on the black and whites as Becca's fingers glided over the keyboard at phenomenal speed.

Janice sidled up to her, waited for a time to speak freely, and said, 'More phone numbers, Becca. They should be appearing on your workstation shortly. They are classified as secondary primaries.'

Another call came in when the 'Europa' console burst into life.

Becca shook her head, exhaled, and gestured to Janice saying, 'I need help here. I've got office phones, home phones and mobiles, and it's only a question of time before they all start talking to each other at the same time. It's all going down and I'm close to being swamped.'

'Can you stay on a little longer until I sort things?'

'It won't be the first time. Yes!'

'I'll divert staff,' revealed Janice. 'I'll check with the operational officer. Keep on it, Becca. We need you on the button.'

'The button,' chuckled Becca. 'I need an off button.'

Another light activation; another conversation. Fingers and thumbs chasing the keyboard.

~

Chapter Eight

~

Wednesday
Carlisle
Cumbria

The sun had barely opened its eyes over the Mersey before Sam Quest had finished for the day. A storm out in the Atlantic delayed a landing from Bilbao in Spain and the crew had to be content with unloading another small vessel inbound from Belfast. Half the team, including Sam, were laid off.

Walking towards the office Sam bumped into Bobby Banshee and Jason who gestured an enquiring face.

Sam nodded positively, shook hands, and simultaneously handed Jason a small wrap containing cannabis.

'On the house,' said Sam softly.

Pocketing the wrap, Jason replied, 'That was quick.'

'I told you I'd get you some.'

'No, I meant the handshake. Cool, man! Cool!'

'Well practised,' suggested Banshee with a suspicious tongue and an unsavoury look on his face.

'Only a fool makes such things public,' replied Sam quietly. 'Now button it before the whole world hears you. I'll catch you later. That's all I have for now.'

Sam entered the office, winked at Jenny, and noticed that Jake was busy with paperwork. Signing off in the logbook, Sam divulged, 'I'll be back shortly. I've left my hat down on the dock. I'm not the same without it.'

Jenny laughed, gestured to the presence of Banshee and Jason who joined Jake in the office, and replied, 'You can't go anywhere without that balaclava, can you?'

Sam waved and walked back to the quayside as Banshee and Jason watched him from the office window.

Jenny took some files into an adjoining room.

'Cop, drug dealer, a coward or just a sad bastard?' quizzed Banshee as Sam trotted towards the quayside.

'The boss says all four,' chuckled Jason. 'Did you see that switch with his hands? One wrap straight out of his pocket like lightning curled into his palm and passed in a handshake. Less than a second, Banshee. They don't teach cops how to do that. Not even bent ones. He's got balls if he does that in public regularly and I'd say he's done that before many times. It's not the kind of thing you pick up in a classroom. Practice makes perfect and that switch was a prime example. I reckon he's good to go. What about you, Banshee?'

'Still not sure. I've told Jake to give him a wide berth.'

'What about the boss? Doyle told us he wants dealers like him. Swift, sure and confident, isn't that what he said when all this began? I get Doyle's drift. We'll make more money quicker if we can push it out faster.'

Jenny approached the office door, held it ajar, and listened to the conversation between Jason, Bobby Banshee, and Jake.

'Quest was a coward apparently,' revealed Jake. 'They didn't get rid of him; he did a runner because he couldn't hack it. If he's a cop we don't want him here, even if he's a former cop or a bent cop. If he can be corrupt in the police, then he can be untrustworthy anywhere. We'll get rid of him quietly if need be. He just might have an accident on the dockside and topple into the Mersey. Who wants to push him in? Hey, it's a fast-flowing river and on an outbound tide - Well, it's a deep sea out there.'

'He's not bent,' argued Jason. 'That's not why the police got rid of him. If he's not an undercover cop, then he has a key to a network where we can sell the product on. Even if he was a bent cop, and I don't think he was, he looks as if he's now as bent as the rest of us. We should take him on. We've no network in the northeast or Scotland. He's the man with the contacts up there according to Doyle. And Doyle will know. He's not stupid. We know Quest. Better the devil you know than a stranger who racks up to the docks and wants in.'

'Put it this way,' added Banshee. 'If Quest is an undercover cop, then why worry? He's got nothing on us. We're as clean as a whistle. Or are the cops going to raid us and lock Jason up because he's got a wrap in his pocket? I don't think so.'

'Why not test him properly with a delivery?' proposed Jason. 'Doyle can get him arrested. Let's find out what he says to the cops when he's lifted.'

'You mean he'll tell them he's on an undercover assignment and walk out the door without being charged?' replied Jake.

'You got it in one,' nodded Jason.

'It's been discussed recently,' replied Jake. 'I think we should settle it once and for all otherwise we'll argue all day and all night, and that's not doing any of us any good. I'll arrange it with Doyle. Meanwhile, Jason, get hold of Malcolm and stick with Quest this afternoon. I want to know what he does with his afternoon off.'

Jenny had heard enough. She gently closed the door and contained herself in the filing room until Jake, Banshee and Jason had left.

Fifteen minutes elapsed before Sam returned with his balaclava and signed off in the logbook.

'I overheard Banshee, Jake and Jason talking,' revealed Jenny hesitantly. 'Sam! They think you are a cop. Is that right?'

Suddenly, it dawned on Sam that Rafferty might have been right all along. Had Jenny overheard a conversation? Was she in the enemy camp; the girl he was falling in love with? Had she been briefed to woo him and twirl him around her little finger? Did the plot involve the demure Jenny Higgins? He'd come so far since that night on Botchergate. He still remembered the sound of gunfire pounding in his skull when the barrel of a weapon lowered towards his eyes and shell casings ejected from the weapon of a crazed gunman intent on murdering him in cold blood. Now, and only now, a lifetime later, did Sam query his very existence, the decision he had made, and the life he was leading at that precise moment.

'Sam!' repeated Jenny. 'Are you a cop or not? They think you are and if you are then they're going to kill you.'

'I am no longer that Sam Quest,' thought Sam to himself. 'Who am I? Where am I? What am I? What's it all for? Is it worth it? Have I been a fool, taken for granted, or used by others to better their agenda? Or something else? Do Jupiter and his bosses look upon me only as an asset? Assets running assets was the term Jupiter spoke of. I may be his spy, but I'm just an asset. I bet I have no name when he talks of me to others in his command line. So, I do all this to be called an asset and nothing else? Am I done? Can I go the distance? It's all rather tiring.'

'Sam!' pleaded Jenny. 'Are you listening to me?'

Looking into Jenny's eyes, Sam couldn't find a hint of falsehood. Just an emotion that seemed to join rather than divide. Had she already wooed him into her stockade with the help of a short skirt, tight jumper, attractive looks, and a chemistry called love that he'd not experienced in the passage of his life? For a moment, Sam was unsure of how to respond until he decided that from the outset, he'd never seen Jenny close up and personal with any of the gang he was investigating. Was that because she was much cleverer than he had judged? Or had she become an ornament that others around her ignored because she was merely an office secretary who kept the logbook, worked out the shift rotas, answered the phone, and was Malek Osman's private eye candy? He didn't know but it was time to make his mind up and either obey Rafferty's words of wisdom or deny them. And that was Sam's weak spot, he had a reputation for challenging authority.

'Jenny, I was a cop once,' admitted Sam. 'The force got rid of me because I got involved in investigating too many robberies. I had to leave because I wasn't brave enough to stand the pressure.'

'Well, they are planning to get you to deliver some drugs and you'll be arrested if you do. They're even talking about killing you and throwing you in the river.'

'Who said that and when?'

'I was in the filing room. The door was ajar. I heard the three of them talking about it just after you went to look for your balaclava. They didn't see me and if they did then they just look upon me as the dumb blonde with the short skirt.'

'Way too short,' smiled Sam. 'Thank you.'

'Are you free tonight, Sam? I enjoyed the Mariner's Hut the other night.'

'Sorry!' twisted Sam painfully. 'I would love to take you out, but I have an appointment at the 24/7 dentist in Norris Green.'

'I didn't know you had a toothache.'

'I haven't. I'm being treated for gum disease, and I'll be there a few hours.'

'Oh! Maybe another time,' said Jenny with an air of disappointment.

'Definitely,' replied Sam. 'I don't want to lose you now that I've found you. I enjoy your company and…'

'And the short skirt?'

'Too short,' advised Sam with a smile. 'Way too short. Wear trousers next time out.'

'Cheeky!' laughed Jenny. 'You're too cheeky. I'll wear what I want when I want.'

'I know you will. I can see an independent streak in you. It's partially hidden because you choose it to be. But I see it.'

'Do you really?' whispered Jenny.

'Yes, and I think… One day, I'll tell you what I think,' replied Sam: a man whose uncertain mind wrestled with the sanctity of the life he was leading.

'Tell me now,' replied Jenny.

'I can't. I've things to do, but…'

'Go on.'

'Malek Osman's briefcase!' replied Sam. 'Has he lost it? It's just that after all the fuss he made about it, I've not seen it around the office.'

'That's because he keeps it in the safe until he goes off with it to wherever,' revealed Jenny. 'Why are you bothered about his briefcase?'

'Jenny! Do you have the combination to Mr Osman's safe?'

'No! Oh no! You are, aren't you? Oh, dear God, why do you want to know?' queried Jenny her voice rising as she spoke. 'No! Don't tell me! The bully boys are right, aren't they? You're an undercover cop!'

'Listen to me, Jenny. Do you have the combination to his safe?'

'Yes! I use the safe every day. It's his briefcase that you want, isn't it? Oh no, Sam. You really are, aren't you?'

'Jenny! Listen to me. I need you. I need you like I've never needed anyone before. I want you to do something for me. Something special!'

Midday moved closer. Sam left the office and within minutes of leaving knew Jason and Malcolm were following him in Jason's motor.

Pressing the digits on his mobile, Sam called Rafferty and worked his way through the agreed security protocol.

'The system shows you are using a mobile, Quest. If the opposition takes you and scrolls through your calls, they'll be more suspicious than ever. You're finished! Get a grip, Quest. You're losing it.'

'It's urgent. I'm being followed by Jason and his mate. I reckon they're with me for the day. I want you to get Logan to stage a road closure as soon as possible. I need a clean break so that I can pick up on Osman and find out where he goes on his day off. Don't worry about the mobile, I'll ditch it when I need to.'

'See that you do,' replied Rafferty. 'Or I'll send Jupiter's eagles to strike you down.'

'Logan!' snapped Sam. 'Yes or no! Your shout.'

'Where are you now?'

'Bankhall Street, Kirkdale! Where are you?'

'Too far away but Logan is close.'

'I'm stopping at the café at Brasenose for half an hour. Then I'm into Stanley Road where I want the stop. I'm after Osman but can't do it with these two on my tail.'

'Give me an hour,' voiced Rafferty. 'Take a left at the crossroads and you'll hit it.'

'Thirty minutes, and not a second more,' snarled Sam as he slammed the phone down and turned into the café's car park.

Time flew by swiftly thanks to black coffee, toast, a borrowed newspaper and no sign of Jason and Malcolm in the café. Just the front of Jason's car poking out from a row of parked cars in the café's car park.

Sam's mobile sounded a notification which he glanced at and realised Logan was ready.

Paying for his snack, Sam strode purposefully to his car, fired the engine, and drove from the café to the nearby crossroads where he was held at the traffic lights. A glance in his mirror revealed Jason's car three vehicles behind.

The lights changed to green. Sam was through the lights and into Stanley Road with no one behind him and a clear road ahead.

Seconds later, the lights changed to red. Jason pulled up baulked by the traffic immediately in front of him, and a set of faulty traffic lights.

Logan appeared from a parked British Telecom van, waved an acknowledgement to the waiting drivers, and opened the power supply cabinet situated on the footpath close to the lights.

Moments later, the adjoining lights changed to green. Traffic advanced across the junction. Jason was held at the lights.

There was an almighty jump to safety by Logan when Jason mounted the pavement, bounced across the footpath, and landed on Stanley Road intent on chasing Sam Quest to wherever he was going.

It was too late.

A short time later, Sam pulled into the multi-level car park and switched into the Mazda 6. He popped the boot and removed a bag which he opened, checked, and then took to the nearby toilets. Five minutes later, an old man wearing a grey wig, spectacles, a thin moustache, and a walking stick, hobbled with a limp out of the toilet.

It was Sam Quest disguised and ready to go.

Pausing, Sam used a reflection in the lift stairwell, confirmed his appearance, and fired the Mazda driving back towards the docks.

Back in Liverpool, Jason drove into the multi-level car park searching for Sam. He saw the old Ford and said to Malcolm, 'He's on foot. Probably at his flat. He's going nowhere. We'll give it an hour or two just to make sure then we'll call it a day and go for a pint. No point in trying to follow a man who is banged up in his flat all day. He's okay. I can't see a problem with him.'

'Couldn't agree more,' offered the thin-faced Malcolm. 'But I'm not sure, Jake would agree.'

'Don't you start,' scolded Jason. 'The last thing I want today is another argument. Give it a rest.'

Sam located Malek Osman leaving the Regent Road office. He followed him discreetly to his home in Crosby where Malek parked the Aston Martin and took his white Ford Kuga towards the motorway.

'Why the Kuga and not the Aston Martin?' puzzled Sam. 'Presumably, wherever he's going, whoever he's meeting, he doesn't want to reveal his Aston Martin and the wealth that one might associate with such a car. He's taken one of the most popular household cars in the country to.... Where's he going? That car switch alone is telling me he deliberately drove home from the office, changed cars, and is back on the road again. Malek Osman has moved on. He's up to something, and I'll guess he needs to be quieter, less noticeable, and more refined. Is he in the process of changing his lifestyle for someone, or himself?'

Sam changed gears when the car in front turned off and he moved up in the queue behind Malek. He had ten car cover on Osman. That was the distance between Malek and Sam. Ten cars separated them as they headed towards the M58 motorway.

'The sticks!' thought Sam. 'He's heading for the sticks.'

Sam fumbled for his mobile, rang Rafferty, and said, 'Got him! I'm Maghull towards Skelmersdale. I'll put my money on the M58 and then north or south on the M6. What you got that I don't know about?'

'Nothing,' replied Rafferty. 'Nothing at all.'

'You got a Red Alpha Six surveillance team on the M6 by any chance?' probed Sam.

'No, they are tied up elsewhere, but I can get you an eye in the sky in fifteen minutes. Yankee Zulu One is ours. I'll brief a follow only on a vehicle of interest. Get back to me when you know where he's headed.'

'Yankee Zero One in the sky! Got that!' voiced Sam. 'We're approaching Pemberton junction on the M6. Just one thing while I have you on the phone.'

'Go on,' replied Rafferty.

'If you can do technical surveillance on Doyle's flat why can't we do the same on the office block at Regent Road? Osman, Jake and the boys seem to talk amongst themselves. Surely there's a wealth of information to collect.'

'I agree but we need access to the building at the right time, plus no CCTV. Did you know they have a system of twenty-four-seven security guards on duty and they are all tied to Doyle's recruitment? We might get lucky if we mounted a technical attack but right now I don't want to jeopardise the operation by such a gamble. Understood?'

'Okay! I'll get back to you.'

The traffic was busy but on closing with Pemberton, on the outskirts of Wigan, Malek took the M6 north towards Lancashire. Sam followed suit, realised he had only one car cover and was grateful for the presence of a helicopter that emerged as a distant dot in the sky above.

'Yankee Zero One has the eyeball. Drop back,' appeared in a text notification on Sam's phone. He reduced speed, located the helicopter in the sky to his offside, and relaxed as Malek headed north at seventy miles an hour in the third lane.

They were through Skevington, Bamber Bridge, Garstang, Scorton, Farleton, Killington, Tebay, and Shap with Malek at a steady 70, Sam in tow half a mile to his rear, and Yankee Zulu One reporting from eight thousand feet.

All hell broke loose when Sam hit the Thrimby Straight in Cumbria and realised the police were chasing a maroon Jaguar that was hurtling down the motorway at a phenomenal speed.

In the third lane, the stolen Jaguar reached Hackthorpe travelling at over one hundred and twenty miles an hour as it overtook Sam and then Malek. The Jaguar headed north towards Skirsgill Interchange at Penrith with a posse of police cars on its tail. Headlights flashing, blue lights rotating, and sirens blaring on a ferocious and dangerous afternoon.

'Yankee Zero One breaking off and returning to base. Fuel is now a crucial point. We are breaking off… breaking off… Broken. We're Out of here. Message ends,' appeared on Sam's mobile screen.

'Not now,' murmured Sam. 'Damn it not now.'

The detective thumped his foot to the pedal and felt the speed of his Mazda accelerate as he tried to close the gap between himself and Malek's Ford Kuga.

Ahead, two police patrol cars adopted the middle and third lane trying to slow the Jaguar down. As the Jaguar was baulked it swung to the nearside to overtake but found that the patrol cars had repositioned and were denying free passage.

The following police cars closed with the Jaguar and dominated the highway causing both Malek and Sam to significantly reduce speed.

Weaving from the nearside to the offside, the driver of the stolen Jaguar tried to overtake the police, hit the brakes, swung to the nearside again, and tried to squeeze down the inside of one of the patrol cars. The Jaguar remained contained on the motorway with two police cars in front of it and two immediately behind it. Gradually, the Jaguar cut its speed as the driver weaved from left to right trying to find a way through. The following traffic was held back. Drivers were baulked by the police with a chase developing right in front of their eyes.

Malek selected a lower gear. Sam followed suit and they both slid into the slower nearside lane.

Suddenly, the Jaguar nudged one of the police cars and broke through the gap onto the grass verge next to the hard shoulder. With lights flashing and sirens sounding, the chase continued with the Jaguar breaking away from the police. Grass and mud spat from the Jaguar's rear tyres as they bounced from the grass verge back onto the main carriageway. There was an explosion of noise and noxious gas when the Jaguar's exhaust growled, and the vehicle made the middle lane home free.

A fifth patrol car roared into view from Sam's rear, tore down the third lane, and then sideswiped the Jaguar to the nearside

The Jaguar spun out of control and pirouetted in a madcap frenzy with the driver's hands working overtime on the steering wheel. The rear of the Jaguar collided with the front of a police car as it spun around. The police car ricocheted into another police car, and the Jaguar pulled onto the hard shoulder facing the wrong way.

Downhill, the Jaguar slid backwards towards Mayburgh Bridge with the posse of police cars now surrounding the stolen vehicle.

Opening the car door, the driver of the Jaguar was out of the vehicle, across its front, and running towards the central reservation with only the flashing blue lights and piercing sirens blaring in his ear.

There was a scream when the car thief ran into the front of a moving police car and hit the bonnet. The body catapulted into the sky and landed some fifteen yards away bent over the barrier of the central reservation with complete mayhem surrounding the crash site.

Seizing the opportunity, Malek saw the gap widen. The carriageway ahead was free when he dropped a gear and accelerated away from the crash site as he followed a line of traffic that was also heading north.

Sam steered to the nearside intent on following through.

One of the police drivers swung his vehicle into the gap, slowed the traffic, and watched the steam escape from his engine as the chase came to an end.

The Mazda came to a standstill. Snatching a powerful handheld telescope from the glove compartment, Sam zoomed in on Malek's Ford Kuga and watched it disappear northwards.

Holding the telescope to his eye, Sam located the Kuga and watched it travel beneath the Skirsgill interchange on the motorway. There was no deviation. Malek continued to travel north on the M6.

'Pull into the side, please,' directed a uniformed policeman tapping on Sam's side window. 'My colleague says you are a witness. We'll need a statement from you.'

Glancing at the policeman, noticing the police car reversing into the middle of the carriageway, Sam replied, 'Sorry! I didn't see a thing. What happened?'

Before the policeman replied, Sam seized the moment, saw the gap, snatched a gear, and drove through the space with a cheery wave to the officer and a foot on the accelerator.

The policeman stood up, scratched his head as the Mazda took off, and then turned his attention to the next car in line.

Sam's eyes transfixed on the rear-view mirror as the Mazda gained speed, hit seventy miles an hour, and then cruised towards one hundred miles an hour. Malek was nowhere in sight. Sam continued the pursuit as the needle on the speedometer moved further up the scale.

The Mazda was through Catterlen interchange and close to Southwaite when Sam finally caught sight of the Ford Kuga. He checked his speed. It was one hundred and forty miles an hour. He checked his rearview mirror. There wasn't a police car in sight.

Easing off, Sam tapered the speed right down and moved to the nearside lane as Malek's Ford Kuga signalled it was turning off at interchange 42: the first turn-off for Carlisle.

Cruising into the city centre at a law-abiding speed, Malek remained unaware of the Mazda following half a dozen cars behind.

Sam breathed out, wiped the sweat from his brow, and tailed Malek to the Crown and Mitre Hotel on Blackfriars Street. Malek stopped close to the locked gate at the rear entrance of the hotel. He got out of his vehicle and spoke into the intercom system fixed to the wall next to the gate. He waited for an answer intending to gain access to the hotel and arrange security of his Kuga.

Parking in a delivery lay by on the same street, Sam left the Mazda and immediately reckoned that this was not Malek's first visit to the hotel. Only a regular visitor would know that the hotel car park was situated in its rear yard surrounded by a gated complex and walls on three sides.

Sam sprinted down Barwise Court into English Street, turned left, and then walked casually to the hotel which he entered through the front door.

Composing himself, hobbling slightly, Sam felt emboldened by the disguise he had worn since leaving the multi-level car park. He made his way warily into the lobby. Wearing a grey wig, spectacles, a thin moustache, and leaning on a walking stick, he paused, studied a tariff fixed to the wall next to the reception, and then observed Malek entering a lounge bar halfway down a corridor from the rear entrance.

Sam strolled down the corridor noting the entrance to his right and a mirror on the wall to his left. He stopped at the mirror, straightened his tie and brushed his moustache whilst using the mirror to scan the lounge bar. Taking his time, Sam observed Malek approach a man he recognised as Caleb Cartwright. The two shook hands and the man gestured for Malek to join him at his table.

Malek sat down opposite the man unaware that Sam confirmed that Malek was with Caleb Cartwright: a notorious professional crook from the city.

Using reflections in the mirror, Sam scanned the rest of the lounge bar and then revisited Malek and Caleb.

'I remember the photograph of Caleb Cartwright from my younger days as a detective,' thought Sam. 'Never met the guy or had any dealings with him but I do recall other detectives telling me that Caleb had a minor conviction for supplying drugs at the local level. Problem was, in those days, Caleb Cartwright was known to be a prime mover in the city's underworld and was often suspected of involvement in the more serious crimes that took place. A good criminal that was seldom caught because of lack of strong evidence against him.'

Osman ordered a brandy and began talking to Caleb.

Sam entered the bar and took a seat with his back to the pair. He focused on a blank television screen and used dark reflections to study the body language of both men.

'Just don't turn the telly on,' thought Sam. 'Otherwise, I'll lose sight of these two.'

A brandy arrived and was gulped down in one by Malek who shook his head and returned the glass to the table.

Adjusting a mini hearing aid, the size of a stud, Sam inserted the device into his ear cavity to amplify the sound. Situated half a dozen tables away from the two men, who sat in a corner some distance from any other customers, Sam heard Malek apologise for being late. Caleb gestured the unimportance of such a problem and then listened to Malek recount the harrowing details of the chase on the motorway and the death of a car thief trying to escape the clutches of the police. Caleb responded by blaming the motorway police for the entire incident even though he wasn't there.

'Your voice is too low,' thought Sam who casually raised his right hand to his ear and adjusted the hearing aid. The device was more than a normal hearing aid. Its complex scientific design allowed Sam to increase the volume, target the direction of the conversation, and amplify the sound.

A waitress arrived and Sam ordered a coffee, a scone and jam as he listened to the small talk of his two targets.

A short time later, the coffee arrived followed by a tour guide escorting a group of American tourists around the hotel.

'The Crown and Mitre Hotel was built in 1905 on the site of the original Crown and Mitre coffee house,' declared the middle-aged brunette attired in a dark blue two-piece suit aided by the presence of a clipboard.

'Just what I need,' thought Sam. 'Verbal interference.' He turned his head slightly to better target the Caleb-Malek conversation.

'This site has a history dating back to before the Jacobite Rebellion,' continued the tour guide. 'The landlord in those days supported Bonnie Prince Charlie and gave shelter to the rebels once they entered the city following the 1745 siege. By the end of the 18th century, the Coffee House was the main coaching inn in Carlisle. It was a stopping place for both mail and stagecoaches on their way to London, Glasgow and Edinburgh.'

Head down, Sam avoided the tourists as they glanced around the lounge bar and appreciated the pictures of the city covering the walls. Sam ignored them and watched Malek and Caleb. The two men glanced up, realised there had been an American invasion in the lounge bar, and stopped talking until they moved away. Sam then heard Osman explaining to Caleb Cartwright how the next shipment of coffee would take place.

'It will be delivered to the coffee warehouse in Kingmoor Industrial estate, Carlisle, where you will process and package the consignment into coffee bags for sale at various retail outlets throughout Carlisle,' voiced Malek. 'The coffee will be delivered locally immediately and some of it will be transported onwards into Dumfries and Galloway. Happy with that?'

'Not enough,' thought Sam. 'Tell him the coffee is cocaine because that's what I want to hear.'

Listening to Malek, Caleb nodded his understanding.

The talkative tourist guide, conscious of her intrusion on the customers, escorted her group to the other side of the room and continued, 'The Crown and Mitre Inn boasts a romantic episode in which a Miss Margaret Carpenter and Sir Walter Scott, the novelist, stayed here the night before they were married in the city's Cathedral. It was on a Christmas Eve. The original Inn was demolished in 1902 to make way for the existing hotel which took three years to build. When the hotel first opened it was said to be one of the finest hotels in the north of England. Many other famous people have visited this hotel. They include Woodrow Wilson: the President of the United States who visited the hotel in 1918. His mother was born in Carlisle.'

'I wish she hadn't been,' thought Sam. 'Get out of my ears, woman. You're spoiling the job.'

Sam turned his head slightly to hear, 'The consignment of coffee is packed in thick sacks,' voiced Malek. 'In the middle of each sack is another sack of refined cocaine. We call it pearls. Some people call it coke.'

Caleb nodded his understanding whilst, at the other end of the room, Sam breathed a sigh of relief and took a slurp of coffee.

'At last,' thought Sam. 'Pearls: a Liverpool name for cocaine.'

The scone and jam arrived as the brunette guided the tourists out of the lounge bar towards the ballroom.

'Each sack has four kilos of refined cocaine worth £60,000.'

'The weight of four bags of sugar,' thought Sam.

'You will receive twenty sacks of coffee, ten of which will be coffee only, and ten of which will contain pearls. This amounts to forty kilos and a payment of £600,000 in cash is expected.'

Caleb drew in a sharp breath.

'Half within forty-eight hours and half on delivery,' disclosed Malek.

'How much did you say?'

'Half within forty-eight hours and half on delivery.'

'It's not cheap this time around.'

'Caleb! This is a one-time-only deal for a proven and trusted customer. You have earned a fifty per cent discount which I am happy to offer you. The price today is £300,000.'

'That makes cocaine as cheap as chips,' smiled Caleb. 'We'll make a fortune at that price.'

'Potentially,' argued Malek. 'That theory is entirely possible, but I want you to join my special club, Caleb.'

'Club?' queried Caleb as Sam spread margarine and jam across his scone and listened to the conversation.

'You've been specially selected to join the club because you have an extensive street market across the county and beyond,' declared Malek. 'Am I right in thinking you are Cumbria's number one supplier, Caleb?'

'Probably! Hard to say but I'd reckon so. I don't make a habit of looking up the league table. I rely on an army of lieutenants to line up the street dealers for me. You'll not find my hands on the pearls or whatever you choose to call them in scouse land.'

'Take a tip from me, my friend. You're currently talking to the UK's number-one supplier. Don't worry about how much you can make but concentrate on how much you can sell.'

'What do you mean by that? I don't understand you. I buy to sell and make money because of it.'

'I'll have another consignment coming in next month,' disclosed Malek. 'Sell the delivery we are talking about now, as quickly as you can, at the lowest price possible. If you can do that, the same half-price deal will apply. We can all get rich quicker if we sell at lower prices, increase the love of pearls, and encourage street dealers to widen their activity. The next shipment is guaranteed, Caleb. We're going big. I mean really big, Caleb.'

'How do you work that out? I'm not on your wavelength.'

'It's all about economics, my friend. If we lower the price, we'll create more demand. More people will become reliant on drugs. When demand increases to a higher-than-ever-before level, we can then increase our prices. The club you are invited to join is dedicated to increasing the number of people reliant on cocaine. Making more users equates to making more money. All the time, we know we are in charge. The supply is under our control and will meet any demands that are put upon it. Do you understand that?'

Gradually a smile crossed Caleb's face. He nodded and queried, 'Electronic transfer?'

'Never!' replied Malek. 'Too risky these days. We don't want to leave a digital trail for the cops or the customs boys to follow. It's cash only.'

'Three hundred grand?'

'Can you manage it?' probed Malek.

'At a push, yes, of course. Electronic would have been better but I can raise the cash. I just need a day or so.'

'Good! I suggest you hire a mule to deliver the cash.'

'To you in Liverpool?' queried Caleb.'

'No! Skelmersdale! Like you, my hands never touch the pearls or the banknotes. Keep your fingerprints and your DNA out of the picture. I want you to deliver the money to Tawd Side Close, Skelmersdale. It's as simple and as safe as that.'

Caleb scrolled the internet on his mobile phone and realised it was not a street. Google maps showed it as the name of a house in Skelmersdale close to the River Tawd.'

'It's an accommodation address, Caleb. One of my lieutenants will be there to receive the money from you between 1 pm and 3 pm every day. Have you got it all worked out?'

'Will twenty-pound notes do?'

'Mixed with tens, and the odd fifty, yes. I don't see why not. It's all cash. No counterfeit, Caleb. My lieutenants have orders to dispose of the mule and the sender of the mule if there is any hint of impropriety.'

'The cash will be straight. It has been in the past and it will be in the future. Yes, it's more than usual, Malek, but your new club sounds like it is a band of well-chosen elite customers. Count me in, and count on me to deliver.'

Both men shook hands and left the lounge bar leaving Sam to finish his coffee and ignore the pair when they parted and went their separate ways. Caleb took the front door; Malek made for the rear car park.

Once they had gone, Sam was out of his chair and out of the revolving front door watching Caleb walk towards the market. Turning into St Cuthbert's Lane, Sam immediately bumped into a uniformed police officer whom he recognised as Bill Barnes. There was a brief feeling of panic in Sam's brain before he thanked himself for a well-worn disguise, dodged around Bill Barnes, and headed towards the delivery layby and his Mazda.

As Sam neared the end of the lane, Osman's Ford Kuga crossed his path and headed towards the city centre.

Moments later, Sam was on the trail again with the Kuga clearly in sight and the Mazda safely located in a discreet position in the traffic flow.

The two vehicles meandered south through the city, hit the motorway, and began the long journey back to Merseyside.

Once south of the city, on the M6, Sam's fingers rattled his mobile and he connected with Rafferty from the phone holder on the dashboard.

'Quest!'

'Jupiter!'

'What a day,' began Sam. 'Thanks to Logan I followed Malek to Carlisle, would you believe it? All safe, no problems.'

'Fruitful?' queried Rafferty.

'Yes, from the beginning,' replied Sam. 'It goes like this.'

As Sam followed Malek south on the M6, he gradually recounted his meeting with Jenny, took another warning from Rafferty who did not approve of the relationship, and stuck to his guns arguing, 'All I'm doing is telling you what she told me. Do me a favour, I need to trust someone and right now, I trust her. I can see her, touch her, talk to her, and understand her. You! Jupiter! You're a bloody planet somewhere in the solar system to which I have no access. You're a voice on the end of the phone and I'm a rat caught in a trap. Give me a break!'

'You're losing it again, Quest.'

'You want me to penetrate the gang, but you don't want me to use Jenny as a route. Why not?'

'I don't want you to penetrate Jenny and that's an order,' thundered Rafferty. 'Understand?'

'You're not my boss,' argued Sam. 'Right at the beginning, you told me you would never be my boss.'

'Times change,' howled Rafferty growing in rage.

'Only because you're holding the timepiece and want your own way. Well, tough, Rafferty. I'm doing things my way.'

'Now slow down and don't get agitated, Quest. Once we're done, we'll whisk you away to anywhere you want to go and rest. But right now, I want you to forget the woman for a while. She's clouding your mind and will get you into trouble. Now tell me, Quest! Tell me what happened when you arrived in Carlisle?'

'A moment!' replied Sam who tried to ignore the phone before taking a deep breath and replying, 'Give me a moment. I didn't ring up to argue with you.'

'Take your time, Quest. 'It's all we've got at the moment. Time!'

The seconds ticked by before Sam disclosed the conversation overheard between Malek and Osman and ended with the comment, 'We've got something concrete at last. They are into drug smuggling in a big way. Osman imports and Caleb Cartwright is one of many being recruited to sell the drugs once they arrive. It's a club alright. A dangerous club but we've got a foot in the door.'

'Keep it there,' ordered Rafferty. 'I'll arrange for technical surveillance on Caleb Cartwright. He sounds like we should know more about him. I'll brief a Red Alpha surveillance team to cover him. Low level to begin with, and only relevant to the local supply of drugs, but let's see where he runs and what he does with his life.'

'Sounds good!' replied Sam.

'Now I've got news for you, Quest. Do you recall giving me a list of telephone numbers relevant to people working at the dockside: Osman, Jake, Banshee and the team?'

'Yes, I do,' confirmed Sam. 'They were given to me by Jenny, but they wouldn't be any good as you don't trust her.'

'Then maybe I am wrong,' admitted Rafferty. 'We've used the information to intercept calls and learn more about the gang. Jake Jackson is identified as Lionel Martin Jackson. He has a long list of convictions mainly for assault. He's travelling to Manchester by train on Thursday and I want you on his tail.'

'Why not use Red Alpha Six: one of your surveillance teams?'

'This operation needs to remain as tight as a drum, Quest. It's down to you and no one else. In Carlisle, I can deploy a surveillance capability in the knowledge that any connection to the target in Liverpool will not be easily discovered by the local police. It's an intelligence-gathering operation on Caleb Cartwright. In Liverpool, I've got one corrupt cop on the board. He might be the only one. There could be others with him. We don't know but we're watching and listening. I don't want to overplay my hand in Merseyside. You're the main player, Quest. You were recruited for a one-man operation with minimal support and one day you'll know the full extent of everything that's going on. Don't follow Jake on the train to Manchester. Meet him at the railway station.'

'What's going on?' probed Sam.

'I think the shipment from Colombia is organised although I've nothing from our sister service to confirm that. I suggest our targets in Liverpool are just firming up the buyers and extending the sales ground. Person-to-person marketing, Quest. We believe Jake is going to a meeting in Manchester to expand the street network. I want to know who he meets, why, when, where, and all that is said. Understand?'

'Carlisle repeated?'

'Except it's Manchester. Be there, Quest. We need you firing on all cylinders. But there's more you should be thinking about, and his name is Doyle.'

'The bent cop,' replied Sam. 'Oh, I hadn't forgotten about him. Part of my mind tells me he's not the boss because Osman was clearly in command when he met Caleb Cartwright in Carlisle. Then I'm telling myself that he's only doing what Doyle told him to do at the outset. It's complicated, don't you think?'

'It's also why the brief has always been to keep in touch with yours truly so that I can give you a different slant on things and make sure you stay on the right path.'

'Here's a slant, as you call it, going through my mind. If you accept that what Jenny told me about the conversation she overheard is true then they will ask me to do a drug delivery for them. It might be part of the consignment or just a dummy run and the man behind it all will be, as you say, Detective Sergeant Brian Doyle. What do you think?'

'I think they'll test you to see if you're up to it, Quest.'

'Do we tell the local police?'

'What do you think?'

'Of course not,' replied Sam. 'For me, Doyle is running things on the docks on his own. The local cops don't know. We do.'

'And we've no plans to tell them,' said Rafferty.

'What if he turns out to be the man who tests me?'

'Then you'll get locked up with an amount of whatever on you and we'll take it from there,' proposed Rafferty.

'You'll take it from there,' sighed Sam. 'It'll be me in the cells, not you.'

'Logan has your back. Go with the flow and see what happens. Look if they've got the money, they'll need to get a good load for you to carry.'

'Logan might have my back,' replied Sam. 'But he won't be sitting in the cells with me.'

'You're overthinking the future, Quest.'

'I need to because I'm on my own and your brief was to confuse the opposition. Let me tell you, Jupiter, that sometimes the loneliness of my position confuses me as much as them.'

'Manchester, Quest!' replied Rafferty. 'Keep in touch. We're with you and will be all the way.'

'Words!' replied Sam ending the call. 'Just words.'

~

Chapter Nine

~

That Night
Faversham Mews
London.

'**An** interesting update, Mr Black,' voiced the Director General of the Security Service.

'Very,' added the Chief of the Secret Intelligence Service. 'Most useful, Mr Black.'

'I'm obliged, Mr Blue and Mr Green,' replied Rafferty. 'To recap, before we discuss the matter further, the loadmaster has been identified as Lionel Martin Jackson a.k.a Jake. He has previous convictions for assault in the Merseyside area and according to our analysis of telephone interceptions, he works with Malek Osman and the others mentioned in my update. The boss of the gang is Detective Sergeant Brian Doyle who is stationed at Walton Lane police station.'

'Yes, we have that,' replied Mr Blue. 'What's new that is not in your current update?'

'Earlier today, Malek Osman travelled to Carlisle and met Caleb Cartwright in a hotel. Osman asked Cartwright to join his club and Cartwright accepted. The man has one minor conviction for supplying drugs and is suspected of being involved in serious crime in Cumbria. Osman offered a deal to Caleb that reduced a drug's buy from £600,00 to £300,000. I'm pretty sure the drugs being discussed are part of the inbound shipment from Colombia.'

The two leaders exchanged knowing looks before the Director General insisted, 'Go on!'

'Osman's idea is to increase the flow of cocaine without raking the money in. Odd, don't you think, perhaps confusing?'

'In what way?'

'Part of the intelligence we have gained indicates Doyle is the gang's leader. Yet here we have Osman making significant progress and striking a partnership with Cartwright.'

'Technical surveillance clearly shows Doyle to be the leader.'

'And the police still don't know of Doyle's involvement?' queried Rafferty.

'No, not all. I think Doyle has recruited a good team of people to do his bidding. Osman is a good example of the choices he has made. Doyle likely identified Caleb Cartwright as suspected of supplying drugs via the Police National Computer system. If not that, then probably by the normal meetings and exchange of intelligence that you would expect detectives from surrounding forces to share.'

'That would correspond with how Doyle and his friends cottoned on to our asset and are now wondering if he's an undercover cop or one whose knowledge and contacts they can use in supplying drugs to another part of the country.'

'Agreed!'

'You know more than I,' proposed Rafferty. 'Do you think Doyle is Misha or linked closely to Misha?'

'We think Misha is a Russian spy working out of London. That would rule Doyle out, but the truth is we don't know.'

'You are less than forthcoming about Misha, gentlemen,' argued Rafferty taking centre stage as he stood and poured each of his colleagues a coffee from a steaming hot jug. 'That may be because I do not match the status in the organisations that you represent. You are both chiefs. I am merely a foot soldier employed to do your bidding. However, I'd like to remind you that I enjoy a significantly high-security clearance due to my continued handling of black operations: the kind of operations that the majority of members in both organisations, and the entire population of the country, are not aware of. I need a break, gentlemen.'

'A break!'

'Not a rest,' continued Rafferty. 'I need a break in your silence. I know that Operation Europa is about drug smuggling and that the operation is part of Operation Misha: the search for a top-grade Russian spy working in the United Kingdom. But that's all I do know. You have kept the secret under wraps.'

'That is correct.'

'I like to think you picked me to handle our asset and Operation Misha because of the service I have given and my proven capabilities. You are not obliged to comment on that, but I ask you again, how did Misha come to light?'

Mr Blue leaned over to Mr Green, cupped his hand over his mouth and whispered something.

Green considered the comment, nodded in agreement, and addressed Rafferty as follows:

'Mr Black, it is time to enlighten you somewhat. You will know that the FSB controls the Russian military intelligence service and maintains its own special forces units. It is the main directorate of the general staff of the armed forces of the Russian Federation.'

'Yes, I am fully aware of that,' responded Rafferty.

'Five years ago,' continued the MI6 chief, 'A member of the FSB working in the Aquarium mounted surveillance on a man working in the British Embassy in Moscow. The FSB officer convinced himself that he had identified an MI6 officer and duly offered his services.'

'Whoa! Wait a minute,' voiced Rafferty. 'What the hell is the Aquarium?'

The MI6 Chief chuckled and replied, 'It's the current nickname for the headquarters of the FSB. We've got Legoland at Vauxhall; they've got the Aquarium in Moscow. Their headquarters are located on the outskirts of Moscow at the Khodinka Airfield.'

'An airfield?' queried Rafferty. 'Why an airfield?'

'You asked for more. I'm giving you more. Pay attention!

'My apologies,' offered Rafferty. 'Pray continue.'

'The FSB headquarters can be accessed either through an entrance located on the Khodinka airfield or through a narrow lane behind the Institute for Cosmic Biology.'

'Cosmic biology and aquariums somehow don't go together,' suggested Rafferty.

'I can't help you there, Mr Black. It's the way it is.'

'The FSB man! What services did he offer?'

'He wanted safe passage to the west for himself and his family in return for information he volunteered to provide us.'

'And you believed him?'

'Such a process isn't that simple,' replied the MI6 chief. 'We met him covertly at various times over the next 18 months in Moscow and became interested in what he had to offer.'

'For example, if you don't mind,' interjected Rafferty. 'Everything! It's time to come clean about Operation Misha.'

A further exchange of looks took place between the leaders of MI5 and MI6 before a reply sounded and a coffee cup broke the silence with a chink on the saucer.

'The Aquarium is surrounded on three sides by a variety of restricted-access facilities. These included the main headquarters of Aeroflot, the design bureaus for Ilyushin, the MIG fighter plane, and various aircraft production organisations. The National Aviation and Space Museum, the Rocket Enterprise, the Military Aviation Academy and the Moscow Aviation Institute are all situated in the area. The Institute for Cosmic Biology is located on the fourth side of Khodinka. Cosmic biology is a scientific discipline concerned with the possible correlation between the universe and organic life and the effects of cosmic rhythms and stellar motion on man.'

'You mean the search for life in the universe?' suggested Rafferty.

'And a whole lot more. From military capability to outer space via the aircraft industry.'

'I can see why our intelligence services would want an insider working there for them. What else can you tell me about the fishbowl?'

'The main FSB office is somewhat neglected in its appearance. That said, it's a glass-encased nine-story tower surrounded on at least three sides by a two-story structure. An adjacent fifteen-story structure outside this area is also an FSB facility. It includes offices and residential accommodations for current and former FSB staff and their families.'

'I take it your man once lived in the residential accommodation there and is now working for us?'

'He's with us, that's all you need to know,' revealed the MI5 man.

'And he knows Misha?' probed Rafferty.

'No,' replied the MI5 director. 'But he tells us that a source named Misha is tasked with organising the large-scale importation of Class A drugs into this country. We presume that means heroin or cocaine as they are the most common rather than others with a lower addictive process. The object is not one large importation but multiple large importations that will flood the country with drugs. Misha is at the centre of the operation.'

Rafferty nodded and listened.

'The gist, however, is that Russia is providing the money for the drug buys from the Colombian cartels. We believe now, thanks to you and our FSB source, that the bulk of the money is being paid by the Russians to people like Doyle. Such a person then arranges the buy from the Colombians via his network of drug dealers. He keeps his share, passes over the buy money to the dealers, and waits for the delivery. When it arrives, the dealers attend the docks, collect the drugs, and circulate into the UK selling the product and preparing for the next buy. Millions of pounds are involved! Our asset tells us that the target is to wipe out our society not by nuclear attack or economic downfall but to turn both the upper echelons of life in the UK and the lower echelons, into a state where Class A drugs are cheaper than a bag of crisps. A kilo of heroin may soon be the same price as a kilo of sugar, and that price may well drop in the coming weeks if we don't terminate the attack. It's the biggest assault on this country since the end of the Cold War.'

'You jest? That seems to replicate Osman's deal with Cartwright.'

'Precisely! Cheap to the point that they are available for all. That way, they can ruin our society via drug abuse, addiction, and... well, need I go on?'

'There has to be a connection in Colombia.'

The MI6 chief edged into a more comfortable position in his seat and replied, 'Don't we know it? We're aware of the problem, but the fact is the illegal drug trade in Colombia has been controlled, historically, by four major drug trafficking cartels: The Medellín, Cali, Norte del Valle, and the North Coast cartel. They've been the most prolific since the 1970s, but the situation is now made worse by several right-wing paramilitary groups acting in opposition to revolutionary Marxist–Leninist guerrilla forces and their allies among the civilian population. These right-wing paramilitary groups control a large majority of the illegal trafficking of cocaine and heroin. Paramilitary violence in Colombia is targeted against left-wing insurgents and their supporters.'

'Left-wing?' queried Rafferty. 'That hardly seems commensurate with Russian politics.'

'Which is why the Kremlin is financing organised crime syndicates in the United Kingdom to do their dirty work for them. The Russians supply the money. British organised crime is doing the buying and arranging the deliveries. The Russian strategy is to destroy the UK as we know it today. One of their tactics is to fund organised crime to achieve that political goal.'

'If we were to inform the cartels of this, do you think they would halt supplies of cocaine and heroin?'

'No! There's too much money at stake and money is power.'

'What about the Colombian government?' quizzed Rafferty.

'Efforts to reduce the influence of drug-related criminal organizations is one of the aims of the Colombian government,' replied the MI6 chief. 'There is an ongoing war among rival narco-paramilitary groups, guerrillas and drug cartels fighting each other to increase their influence. The Colombian government struggles to stop them because of the violence they exert and the platform of power from which the cartels operate.'

'One day a drug cartel could run a country,' suggested Rafferty.

'And if successful, the country would then be a cartel,' added the MI6 chief. 'Cocaine production in Colombia reached an all-time high in 2017. Colombia is the main global producer of raw coca, as well as refined cocaine, and one of the major exporters of heroin. The cocaine trade is assessed at ten billion dollars a year. Drug addiction affects everything from environmental damage to education, health, and the economy.'

'I get the picture,' nodded Rafferty. 'Colombia has a problem, and the rest of the world is either standing by idly watching or helping the Colombian government to defeat the cartels. It all depends on their political views and aspirations. Tell me, how come the defector is aware of all that but doesn't have a clue who Misha is?'

'That remains the mystery,' intervened the boss from MI5. 'Who is Misha? We can tell you that our informant has told us about a travel agency in Central London. He tells us that the agency is used by the FSB as a safe business from which to launch covert operations. We believe that it is the access point where the money from Russia finds its way to a legitimate business in the UK. A technical surveillance operation on the travel agency was mounted some time ago, probably when you were recruiting Europa. Everyone who enters the premises is covertly photographed and we have identified three Russian trade delegates and a Russian diplomat who are regular visitors and seem to be central to the activities of the agency. We're photo-scanning everyone who visits the premises and trawling through every phone call made either into or from that shop. It's in Piccadilly. We've harnessed historic CCTV records from our operation.'

'Tell me you have a result,' ventured Rafferty.

'Yes! You put up Brian Doyle as the leader of the gang. Their photographs were added to the system. We ran a comparative analysis with those already recorded as having visited the travel agency. We got a hit, only one but Doyle has been a regular visitor over the last twelve months. Interesting! He's seen entering regularly with a holdall. I wonder why!'

'Thank you, Sam Quest,' muttered Rafferty quietly.

'Indeed,' continued the MI5 Director. 'I believe we are closer than we ever have been, but we are not close enough and need to prove beyond a shadow of a doubt that the travel agency is operating under a false flag. If that proves to be the case, we will action the removal of every suspected FSB officer working out of those premises, and possibly more whom we suspect may be housed in the Russian Embassy. Evidentially, we need to be able to prove our actions in a court of international law so that, politically, our action against the FSB officers working in London is supported by the global community. Our government does not want to be seen as pointing the finger. It wants to be seen as politically correct and backed up by strong evidence rather than unproven accusations. If we are successful, it will be the biggest event in the world of espionage since the Cold War. That's why it's been under wraps and Operation Misha is never discussed outside these walls. When we go chasing spies, Bernard, not everyone in the organisation knows what we are up to. Everything is locked down just in case we have a leak that we don't know about. Historically, we know that works.'

'Trust!' voiced Rafferty. 'Trust! The whole thing, gentlemen, is about our asset, me, you, and … It's all about trust and how we get on with each other, isn't it?'

'To some degree, but we are a team. The relevance of your comments needs explanation."

'If you were our asset then you're on your own,' replied Rafferty. 'It's worrying. Our asset, Europa, is in tremendous danger from various sources. Do I pull him out?'

'No! More than one drug tsar in the UK and elsewhere has been recruited by Doyle and his gang, on behalf of the FSB in London, to import hard drugs from the South American cartels. We may be able to police some of the naval routes to stop them, but we have little chance of stopping multiple import routes by land, sea or air. The country could be awash with drugs within a year or two. We must locate and destroy Misha and the network he has built up.'

'Or she,' proposed Rafferty.

'Yes! It may be a woman. We don't know.'

'Europa is on his own. He might go to prison since he is taking steps to improve his status in the gang. To penetrate the target, and gain more trust, he has placed himself in a position that neither of you would wish to emulate. The danger to him grows by the hour. If he is imprisoned, what do we do to keep him safe and the operation on track?'

'We'll cross that bridge when we come to it,' replied the MI5 man. The MI6 chief agreed and sat back when the Director General added, 'Just get him deeper into the organisation and closer to Brian Doyle and the rest of them. The asset has opened the door for us. We have a foot in the gap. By finding a weak point and causing them to argue and become a little confused, he's got himself inside. Now we need to twist him further. If we're inside, we can break them. If we are outside, we will be onlookers.'

'I think it's time I told Europa about Misha,' proposed Rafferty. 'He needs to be alert to the fact that we are looking for someone called Misha. It must become a top priority for him. He needs to know that Misha is at the centre of our operation.'

'What is he doing at the moment?'

'Getting ready for his next trip.'

'Good! You know what to do. Use him to the best of your ability.'

'Use him, but don't protect him, is that why you mean?' argued Rafferty.

'I note the challenge in the tone of your voice, Rafferty. Your job is to obey, not challenge. The welfare of the United Kingdom is at stake. There is no time for pleasantries. We're not interested in recovering the drugs. It's a one-off operation even if it's the biggest ever. We can kill this attack off, and future attacks, by nipping it in the bud. We want the Russian diplomats and FSB officers involved in this and if that means letting the drugs run when they've arrived, then so be it.'

'And Europa?' contested Rafferty.

'May be expendable,' voiced the MI5 leader authoritatively.

Rafferty poured more coffee from a steaming pot and said, 'Pleasantries? Let the drugs run? Europa is expendable! I'm beginning to understand how he must feel, gentlemen. Perhaps I have misunderstood his position in life. But that's the problem with jobs such as ours, isn't it? To deny the evil that threatens us we sometimes must be evil to win.'

'Precisely!'

'More milk? Sugar?'

A saucer rattled and a spoon unloaded a hundred grains of sugar into a hot brown liquid that was the only witness to the decisions of the night.

~

Chapter Ten
~

Thursday Morning
Manchester

Sam drove to Manchester railway station, disguised himself in similar attire to what he wore when he visited Carlisle, and then parked the Mazda in a long-stay car park. He walked back to the railway station on foot.

Jake arrived, stepped down from the train, and strolled purposefully along the platform. He wore a bright blue puffa jacket and blue coloured cap when he passed Sam who was disguised as a man in his sixties. Jake ignored his adversary.

Commencing the follow, Sam noted how Jake stood out on the street with bright clothing and a hat that signposted his position. He soon felt happy that Jake had no idea he was being watched.

On reaching a café about half a mile from the railway station, Jake entered and took a seat in the front window next to a middle-aged man smartly dressed in a suit and full-length black woollen overcoat.

Sam held back, crossed the road, and lit a cigarette using his zippo from a safe distance. With photographs taken, Sam sauntered into the café and occupied a seat a few tables away from Jake and the man he had met. The café was busy and there were few empty tables left.

'Too noisy,' thought Sam. 'I can't use the hearing aid here. It's too enclosed and won't work properly.'

Ordering coffee, Sam seized the moment, turned to the waitress, and ordered, 'Sorry! I've changed my mind. A couple of slices of toast as well, please.'

'No problem,' came the reply and at that precise moment Sam lit another cigarette with his zippo. This time he got a good picture of the two men in deep conversation.

'I wish I could lip read,' he thought. 'Something to remind Logan and Jupiter about.'

The watch continued for half an hour and Sam decided their conversation had been quite specific. Leaning back in his chair, he occasionally heard the words, 'Pearls, coffee bags, and club.' The talk reminded him of Osman and Cartwright's meeting in Carlisle. It sounded similar but he couldn't elaborate on the content.

Swallowing the last of his toast, he washed it down with the remnants of cold coffee and realised that Jake and his colleague were making ready to leave. Taking the initiative, Sam dropped a ten-pound note on the table for the waitress and left the café before Jake and his friend.

Secreting himself in a doorway close by, Sam watched Jake and the other man step across the road and head deeper into the city centre.

Ten minutes later, the two men entered a casino, paid an entrance fee, and made for the gambling tables. Sam followed suit, made for the bar, and used the reflections in the mirror to monitor the pair who were playing on the roulette wheel.

The day wore on. Both men took turns buying Krug champagne at £500 a bottle. Again, it was too noisy for Sam to deploy the hearing aid device, but he took up a closer position at a blackjack table nearby and tried to hear what was said.

To no avail, Sam decided that all he could hear was the talk of gambling, what to select, and what to bet. But he did notice how popular Jake's friend was. As the two men played the table, close to a dozen people approached, spoke to the mystery man in the suit, and paid him their respects. Although Sam had picked up little of the conversation, it had registered that the mystery man was rich, popular, and well-known in the casino.

Activating his mobile, Sam phoned Jupiter. He knew he might be overheard so immediately used the agreed proceed and put a bet on a horse running that afternoon.

'Are you safe, Quest?' probed Rafferty.

'In a casino in Manchester. Have you got me?'

Rafferty moved to another console in his office, checked Sam's mobile signal, and replied, 'Manchester city centre! We have you covered, Quest. What do you need, a loaded dice?'

'Not a bad idea,' chuckled the detective turned spy. 'No! I want you to hack into the casino's CCTV and then the outside systems in the immediate locality of the casino.'

'Why?' enquired Rafferty gesturing to his colleague Maxwell to listen in to the conversation and progress Quest's need.

'I have a...' Sam paused when a customer came to close and changed tables. Once out of earshot, Sam continued, 'Our man has met a very rich Mr Big in a café down the road. They're in the casino now and he now spending money like it's going out of fashion.'

'Money? In what way?'

'Krug at £500 a bottle and money on some bets being pushed around the roulette like there was no tomorrow. Single number bets, red or black bets, group numbers, you name it Mr Rich Man is game for it. Wins every time but loses at the same time because he's multi-betting hoping for the odds to deliver him a big win.'

'Do you see that as part of his personality, Quest? Whatever he does in life there's a backstop where he'll always walk away with something.'

'That sounds about right,' replied Sam. 'Who is he?'

'We're on it, Quest.' Rafferty watched Maxwell hacking into the local CCTV system and continued, 'Might take a while. Ditch Jake. Follow Mr Big. I'd like to know all about him.

Phone the office with an address once you house him. I'll arrange full surveillance once he's identified.'

'A done deal,' from Sam as he closed the call and realised Jake and Mr Big were heading for the exit.

Casino staff fluttered around Mr Big like butterflies nosing the latest bud in the garden. The word, 'Taxi' exuded from the group and Sam responded by second-guessing what was going to happen next. Once again, he was out of the building before his two targets. He raised his hand. A taxi approached and drew up. Sam slid into the back seat and watched the casino entrance.

A cloakroom attendant helped Mr Big adjust his overcoat whilst another emerged from the casino and signalled a taxi to attend. The driver stopped directly outside the entrance and waited.

A twenty-pound note changed hands to the delight of the cloakroom attendant who escorted Mr Big to the waiting taxi. There was a handshake with Jake who set off walking towards the railway station. Mr Big spoke to the taxi driver and moments later the taxi drove off in the opposite direction.

'Do you want to go somewhere, pal?' enquired Sam's taxi driver. 'Or are you happy just to sit in the back and watch the crowds?'

Kickstarted into life, Sam leaned forward and replied, 'Follow that taxi.'

'Really! And where is he going to, pal? Liverpool, Birmingham, Cardiff, London, which?'

'I don't know but I want to find out where he lives.'

The taxi driver fired the engine and said, 'You a cop? Run out of petrol, have we?'

'No! Don't be stupid! The bastard is having an affair with my wife. I want to know who he is and where he lives.' Sam thrust a wad of money into the taxi driver's hand and finished with, 'Get on him. Nice and easy but follow that black cab.'

Mr Big's taxi was halfway down the road before Sam's taxi driver snaffled the cash into his pocket, set off after his quarry, and replied,' Never fancied marriage myself. Expensive! Not worth it! Too much trouble they are... Women! Still, let's go. I don't like dirty tricks men myself. Hang on tight.'

The taxi took off at speed with Sam rolling into the back seat shouting, 'Easy does it. Not too close.'

The two taxis meandered through Manchester city centre, were held at traffic lights, baulked by other vehicles, forced to stop by pedestrians crossing the road, and generally annoyed others before they made the M62 and increased speed.

They were through Westwood Park and Risley before turning off onto the M6 north. Close to Pemberton, Mr Big's taxi took a left onto the M58 and then turned off into Skelmersdale.

'Skem!' ventured Sam's driver. "Lover boy lives in Skem by the look of it. You got fifty miles on the clock, pal. Double it to take you back to Manchester. You all in?'

'Follow him home,' ordered Sam. 'The wife's car will be close by I reckon.'

'Look, pal,' said the driver. 'I'm gonna drop you soon. It's a hundred-mile round trip at least and I don't want to give evidence in any divorce court. Not me. I was never here. Never saw you. Never been to Skem before. You got my gist?'

'Oh, yes, loud and clear! I've never seen you before and will never see you again,' replied Sam. 'The house, pal. Follow him home. I'm paying you good money so do as I ask.'

The driver felt the wad of cash bulging in his pocket, patted it, and did as he was bid.

Mr Big's taxi drove through a housing estate, found the countryside, and pulled in at Tawd Side Close. The house was a detached bungalow standing on an acre of land. The garden was huge, encircled the house, and needed the grass cut.

'Here we are,' voiced Sam's taxi driver. 'Home sweet home.'

'I don't think so,' proposed Sam. 'The wife's car isn't here, and he's not sent his taxi on its way. He's either collecting something or dropping something off.'

'Solicitor's letters?' suggested the driver.

'Could be. Wait.'

Less than five minutes later, Mr Big emerged from the bungalow carrying a bundle of envelopes. He emptied them into a briefcase and then re-joined the taxi.'

'Off again?' queried Sam's driver.

'Yes, back off a little,' advised Sam. 'You're too close.'

The surveillance continued before Sam eventually housed Mr Big in a detached house in Skelmersdale. It was one of the more salubrious estates in the Lancashire town. The building bore no signs of individual design or architecture. The entire street was festooned with similar-looking houses.

A woman opened the front door, kissed Mr Big tenderly on the lips, and then stepped back as he entered the house.

'She yours?' enquired the taxi driver.

Sam made a mental note of the address and replied, 'Yes! I'm afraid so. Liverpool, driver! Take me to Liverpool, please.'

'Will do,' replied the driver. 'Sorry, you've had such a bad day, pal. I really am. That can't have been good for you.'

'Not to worry.'

'Not my business but I can see one big difference, pal.'

'Which is?' replied Sam.

'He's younger, suited, booted and housed on a posh estate in Skem. You're what, say ten years older, maybe fifteen?'

'Something like that.'

'Age! That's it. No disrespect intended, pal but you look like an old man. She's taken a younger version. Sorry! Whereabouts in Liverpool?'

'Lime Street.'

'On our way,' revealed the taxi driver as he swung the taxi around at a convenient turning point and headed towards Liverpool.

'Tawd Side Close,' thought Sam as he tried to relax in the rear of the taxi. 'That's where Malek Osman told Caleb Cartwright to deliver the money for the drugs buy. It's all coming together now. The network is weaving itself into a band of proven country-wide drug dealers who run scores of local street dealers. Another 'man in the middle' who is well off, seems to be rich, very popular and well-known, and won't be a mystery man much longer if Jupiter's team can work their magic.'

Sam's mobile sounded. It was Jupiter.

'Quest,' revealed Sam. 'Good to go. What you got?'

'I want to see you at the Victorian bus shelter on the promenade at New Brighton, on the North Wirral coast, tonight. Eight o'clock! Be there.'

'Understood!' Sam closed the call and wondered what was so important that he had been summoned to a face with face Jupiter. Were the eagles about to fly?

That night, Sam joined Rafferty at the bus shelter and the pair set off along the promenade. The awkward drizzle rained down on their faces as a sea breeze wafted into them and made conversation difficult. They returned to the shelter and took a seat.

'I love the rain,' chuckled Sam. 'How about you?'

'I can do without it,' replied Rafferty.

'Strange old world,' remarked Sam. 'The two of us are embarked on an investigation into a multi-million-pound drugs racket and we can't even find a dry place to meet and chat. What chance have we got?'

'The rain always wins,' replied Rafferty. 'But I have something for you, and I thought the sooner the better for everyone involved.'

'Let me guess,' voiced Sam. 'You've won the lottery and you're packing all this in. Gonna retire, aren't you? Tell me that's the truth.'

'I wish,' chuckled Rafferty. 'No! I'm here to tell you about Operation Misha.'

'Never heard of it.'

'No, but you're part of it.'

'Misha! I'm part of Operation Misha?'

'Central to it,' replied Rafferty shuffling in his seat.

'What does Misha mean?'

'In Russian,' explained Rafferty. 'Misha is short for the Russian male name Mikhail, or Michael as we would say in England. It's also Russian slang for a bear.'

'A big brown one?'

'You got it,' admitted Rafferty.

'What has a bear got to do with drugs importation?'

'It's everything to do with drugs. The problem is that the Russians are in the process of weaponizing Class A drugs that are being imported into the UK. Can you get your head around that one for a moment, Quest? Weaponizing drugs that addict the population!'

Looking out to sea thoughtfully, Sam shook his head and watched the raindrops fall from his balaclava and trickle onto his forehead and then his nose. He wiped his face dry and ventured, 'Well, that's one way of ruling the world. I take it they've discovered a new drug that they want people to use?'

'No! You're so deep inside that you've missed the bigger picture, Quest.'

'What do you mean? It's not what I think it is, is it?'

'British Intelligence has a source inside the Russian military. They plan to flood the British market with a constant supply of Class A drugs. The first one due will be the largest you could ever imagine, and it won't be the last. To do that, they've recruited the top crooks in the UK's drug world. They are paying them well above the odds.'

'What about the Mr Big who Jake met in Manchester?'

'We followed your suggestion, Quest. Took images from the casino CCTV as you proposed and ran checks. We came up with trumps. Your Mr Big goes by the name of John George Turnbull of Skelmersdale. The property at Tawd Side Close you told us about is an accommodation address. It was last lived in three years ago by a family now deceased. The premises are for sale under the tenancy of a solicitor with links to both Osman and Turnbull.'

'Well, well, well! He's known?'

'No previous convictions but the National Crime Agency have a two-inch thick intelligence file on your Mr Turnbull. Never gets his hands dirty. Just collects the money, launders it, hides it, arranges his street dealers, and their street dealers, and their street dealers, and the next layer of street dealers, and so on, to collect the drugs and sell it to Joe Public and every addict this side of Preston. That's why he's rich and that's where his weakness lies. I've put a surveillance team on him, and telephone interception is up and running as we speak. The NCA is following the money and some of it is digital. They're gradually bending the dealers, but it takes time.'

'Good, but too long if what you say is true.'

'He's getting away with it because he's clever. He'll fall one day. If the NCA doesn't take him, we will.'

'John George Turnbull! Not much in a name?'

'Just a name!'

'Tell me more,' pleaded Sam.

'The drugs are imported from the Colombian cartels at the usual top dollar. The Russian plan is simple. When the drugs reach the shores of mainland Britain they will be sold at the cheapest possible price.'

'Of course,' mulled Sam. 'I was wondering if that might be the case, but I couldn't quite get my head around the size of it all. Just what Osman and Jake have been doing, recruiting the top dealers.'

'You got it,' nodded Rafferty. 'I'd say you're so up to your neck in it that you've not had time to sit down and work it all out. Well, Quest, you've got it now.'

'But there's no Russian connection on the docks. The closest is Osman and he's Turkish. Not the same.'

'We have a trace on the bent cop called Doyle. Since you raised him to our attention, we've discovered that he has connections to the Novikov travel agents in Piccadilly, London. We believe the travel agents lie at the centre of the Russian plot.'

'I see. What does Novikov mean?'

'It's Russian for 'newcomer'. We're working on how the money gets from Moscow to London and we think Novikov is an open door for the operation.'

'How is that?'

'The money arrives from Russia in the diplomatic pouch which, as you know, can be whatever size they want it to be as long as it is properly identified as a diplomatic pouch and then sealed.'

'In a circus with a bear called Misha?' chuckled Sam.

'I'm open to all suggestions,' replied Rafferty. 'I want to know who Misha is. Who else is in the supply network and which Russian in the UK is recruiting the runners, providing the money, and running the show? Doyle is the main connection. When he was spotted entering the Novikov travel agents there were three members of the Russian Embassy already inside. We need to know which one was dealing with Doyle. Or was it two of them, or all three? You'll have to get deeper inside the network, Quest.'

'I thought you might have bugged the place,' remarked Sam.

'There's a secure room inside the building that rejects our technical expertise,' replied Rafferty.

'Why would a travel agency need a secure room that afforded protection from the eavesdropping capabilities of British Intelligence?' ventured Sam. 'We know why. It proves your theory.'

'Not enough,' replied Rafferty.

'Were any of the three Russians in the agency called Mikhail?'

- 143 -

'No! There's no one in the frame called Misha or Mikhail. We're running all kinds of concoctions into our records and the only thing we've come up with is the Ankara Queen. Our historic records show that the last known captain of the vessel was Michael Alvarez who was born in Colombia. We don't know if he is still the captain or changes have been made.'

'Mikhail! Michael! Bit of a long shot that one then, I'd say,' voiced Sam.

'Agreed! So far, we have no line on Misha. It's down to you, Quest. Keep those ears open.'

'You might have to bail me out if Doyle, Osman and Jake agree that they want me to deliver by way of a test. You wonder why I don't have time to theorise like you guys. The truth is, I have a lot on my mind and can't remember the last time I had a good night's sleep. Think of it my way, Doyle will have me arrested and put out of the game.'

'If that happens, admit the charge, ask for bail, and tell the arresting officers that you are an ex-cop. Don't hide anything. Doyle thinks he can win but we have brought the National Crime Agency into the fold for Operation Europa and there will be a huge police presence when the Ankara Queen arrives. I want you on that boat unloading. It will take three days to unload the ship at least and I need to be sure that when we hit it, we go straight to the drugs. Give me a signal when you are sure the drugs are on board.'

'Where will you and Logan be?'

'We'll be using a drone or on a rooftop. I'll be watching you. Wherefrom is unimportant.'

'Balaclava off and a wipe of the brow,' declared Sam.

'Once we see your signal, we'll lock down the docks and raid the Ankara Queen. Simultaneously, we'll carry out raids and arrests across the country from Dumfries in Scotland to London via Cumbria, the North-East, Skelmersdale and every other suspect dealer on the books between here and

Timbuctoo. There's now double the number of officers working on this operation than there was in the beginning. We will be able to prove a huge nationwide conspiracy if it continues the way it is going.'

'That's not helping me beat Doyle and it doesn't take a genius to work out he's going to get me locked up.'

'There is a way to beat him,' explained Rafferty.

'Such as?'

'He's a leader of men despite his low-level rank in the police.'

'I'll go with that,' replied Sam. 'The DS is often the backbone of the force, but what the hell has that got to do with it?'

'Leaders don't like to be seen to have made a mistake. The boss is always right. If we can disrupt his thought pattern and prove him wrong, it might work for us. I plan to cause him to have to come to terms with a mistake of his creation no one else's. The problem is that you are the only one capable of making it happen.'

'What do you want me to do?'

'Go a step further for us.'

'More danger?'

'Probably!'

'Explain!'

'The rain is easing off,' remarked Rafferty. 'There's a coffee kiosk a few hundred yards along the way. Walk with me and I'll tell you what I'm thinking. Then I'll tell you how the raids will go down. We'll be using over a thousand officers if it all goes to plan. All you need to do is find Misha.'

'All I need to do is stay alive,' replied Sam. 'Then I'll find Misha.'

Half an hour later, Sam was on his way back to Liverpool. His mobile rang. It was Jenny.

'Sam! I did it.'

'Did what?'

'The briefcase! You wanted the contents of Malek's briefcase.'

'No! I wanted you to find out what was in the briefcase, Jenny. Not to steal the contents. Was it in his safe? Please tell me no one saw you.'

'Mr Osman had his annual monthly meeting at the harbour master's office.'

'Why?' asked Sam.

'The harbour master directs and oversees the daily harbour operations. Mr Osman sorts out all the times of arrival at the dock with the harbour master's office. He's been away most of the day and the boys have been on the docks. I was on my own, so I got into his briefcase.'

'I thought you didn't know the combination to the briefcase.'

'Not officially, Sam. I just remembered it.'

'What do you mean, you just remembered it?'

'I've always believed that Mr Osman hired me a few years ago because he's on his own. He's single. I think he thought he would employ someone like me in the hope that they might be friendly to him if you know what I mean. A lovey-dovey type who wants a girlfriend but doesn't know how to go about it properly.'

'You mean he was looking for female company?'

'Well, that's men for you, particularly bosses like Mr Osman. I heard them all saying I was Osman's eye candy and that's all I would ever be because I was a bit snooty and hard to chat up.'

'Was that when Bobby Banshee and the boys were asking you out too?'

'Yes! I told you about Banshee earlier. Horrible man thinks we should fall over him because he's a big name on the docks. They might all think I'm attractive or whatever, but I don't like any of them. I was nice to them, for the sake of my job, but kept them all at bay including Mr Osman.'

'Good for you. You're a tough cookie when you need to be.'

'Over the years, they gradually lost interest in me. I went from the secretary everyone wanted to take out to the dumb blonde with the short skirt and no brains.'

'Because they are used to getting their way,' suggested Sam. 'When someone like you comes along, and you say no, they don't know how to respond, do they?'

'That's it. Anyway, I remember watching Mr Osman locking his briefcase in the safe. It's either in the safe or on his desk. I learnt about his habits so much that I got to know the combination of his briefcase without him telling me.'

'How did you do that?'

'His favourite number is 3. I know that because I get him a lottery ticket every week from the Spa shop across the road. He always picks 3, 13, 23, 33, 43, and 53. I played about with the combination lock on his briefcase. It's a three-dial combination lock.'

'Three again!' remarked Sam.

'Exactly! I entered all the 3's into both locks and guess what?'

'The briefcase opened?'

'Yes! Hilarious, Sam! It was so easy.'

'Brilliant! Funny how everyone thinks you're a bit of a dumb blonde when you're not. You're a bit of an observer of life and people, aren't you? Much cleverer than people think.'

'Thank you, Sam. Do you know what that number 3 means?'

'I'm not with you, Jenny.'

'To me, it means that if it was so easy to get into his briefcase then the contents can't be valuable. I did it but it's just rubbish.'

'Rubbish! You did what? What rubbish?'

'I got my mobile out and took photos of the contents. There's nothing important in there, probably just irrelevant notes that he hasn't thrown away yet. I thought there might have been some handwritten notes for me to type once he'd decided to pass them to me, but no. Nothing!'

'What was in the briefcase?'

'I found a list of names and addresses with telephone numbers beside them and things like one K, three K, ten K. I don't know what that means but it's all on my mobile.'

'K for kilo,' suggested Sam. 'Kilo is a weight.'

'Yes! I know. I'm not stupid!'

'Ten K next to a name and an address might mean someone has ordered ten kilos of something.'

'Could be, Sam. Hey, whatever it means, it's yours. I know it's getting late, but I can meet you in the car park of the Mariner's if you have time. I want to get rid of it all from my phone before I go to work tomorrow. If Mr Osman or one of the boys borrows my phone or starts tinkering with it, I don't want them to find those photos.'

'You're right there, Jenny.'

'I thought that if I sat next to you in the car park at the Mariners, I'd send you the photos from my phone to yours. Once you've got them, I'll delete mine and I'll be safe. Is that okay?'

'Yes! I'll be there. Brilliant idea!'

'How long before you can make the Mariners?'

'About an hour!'

'Good! See you then. Don't be late.'

'I won't be,' said Sam as he closed the call and thought, 'She's done it. That just might be the delivery list for all the contacts Osman has made. It sounds like a list of dealers and what they've bought. The Mariners! Oh yes, I'll make the Mariners alright. I do believe I'm falling in love with the reincarnation of Mata Hari. Love! Oh dear, how will I know if I'm in love? '

Buzzing, his mind working overtime, Sam put his foot down. How could he say no to Jenny Higgins? She was about to reveal the entire network of the Doyle-Osman drug dealers to Sam Quest.

'Bernard Rafferty,' thought Sam. 'You were wrong, so very wrong. She's a smooth operator, is that one. Yes! Jenny Higgins is on the right side of the law. Now I want her on the right side of me. She's the one for me. I just feel it in my bones.'

~

Chapter Eleven

~

Friday
The docks,
Bootle.

Malek Osman gestured for Sam to take a seat at the other side of the desk and said, 'You got my message then?'

'Sure did,' replied Sam who had been relieved from the dock terminal so that he could attend a meeting with Osman. 'What's the problem?' His eyes took in Jake and Banshee who, grim-faced, sat close by. Banshee had his feet on the table when Sam replied, 'Why three of you? Did you hear what I said? What's the problem?'

'There is no problem, Sam. I just wanted to go over a few things with you before an important shipment comes our way, that's all,' replied Osman.

'In that case, fire away!'

'We met in the Rope and Anchor. You got me out of a tricky situation for which I extended my gratitude by arranging a job for you. Perhaps I was wrong. I don't know but I intend to find out.'

'The briefcase, Mr Osman. You had a briefcase with you that night and I assumed the contents were important since you clung to it as a man possessed. I knew you were influential because not many people walk the docks carrying a briefcase.'

'Was it convenient or contrived?' probed Osman quizzically.

'I don't understand.'

'Yes, you do. You're a cop, aren't you, Quest?'

Sam shifted slightly in his seat, tried to muster more courage, and replied, 'I used to be a cop. That was years ago.'

'But not now?' queried Osman.

Feeling the hairs on the back of his neck bristling, Sam replied, 'No! Not now! They wiped me from their books. They didn't want me, so I jacked it in. Is that the problem?'

'You resigned because if you hadn't, they'd have sacked you. Correct?'

Sam shrugged his shoulders and said, 'I can't answer for what someone else might have done.'

'Where did you go when they sacked you?'

'Around!'

'Define around,' growled Jake from the corner of the office.

'Scotland mainly,' revealed Sam. 'Then I came down here to get a proper job.'

'You came down here because you're wanted by the cops,' said Banshee. 'You're up to your neck in warrants, Quest.'

'Not me! I'm clean.'

'Or undercover?' suggested Jake.

'Undercover!' exclaimed Sam before continuing, 'Oh yeah! I forgot to tell you, Mr Osman, that when we were lying on the floor behind the bar in the Rope and Anchor, I should have told you that I was an undercover cop. I mean, it was so obvious, wasn't it? And I knew there were either a dozen gold bars in your briefcase or the wages for the entire dock work force. Do me a favour, guys. I didn't want them. I'm not that kind of thief, It was the job I was after.'

'Not that kind of thief!' remarked Osman curiously.

Banshee suddenly stood up and approached Sam with a fierce scowl saying, 'Don't get smart with us, Quest. You've no idea who you're dealing with. Get too smart and we'll feed you to the fish in the Mersey.'

'Sorry,' replied Sam trying to hold his nerve. 'But you said there was no problem. So why the questions about the Rope and Anchor and all this rubbish about being an undercover cop?'

'We know all about you, Sam Quest,' declared Osman as he gestured to Banshee to sit down. 'Detective Constable Sam Quest was born in Carlisle on…'

Initially surprised, Sam leaned back in his chair and listened to Malek Osman read out his life story. It was all true except for the ending which had been engineered by Logan and added to the Intelligence Section of the Police National Computer. Sam knew for sure that they were reading a copy of Logan's file, and he presumed the file had been given to Osman by the corrupt Detective Sergeant Brian Doyle of Merseyside Police.

'They sacked you because you're a coward,' stated Osman. 'And let's be honest, you've hardly shown yourself to be a hero on the docks, have you?'

'He can't fight and can't take a punch,' growled Banshee. 'He's a weakling. Maybe that's his cover, being a weakling.'

Sam forced a chuckle and replied, 'If I wanted a cover story it wouldn't be as a weakling. I wouldn't even be using my right name. I'd have a false one. Don't you ever watch crime shows on telly?'

Banshee threw a glance at Osman and Jake before continuing, 'You're suspected of running a drugs racket in Dumfries, the Newcastle area down towards Grimsby, and Carlisle. Is that right?'

'You're well informed,' suggested Sam.

Osman smiled and replied, 'We need to be.'

'But you are wrong,' voiced Sam.

'Wrong?' argued a surprised Jake.

'Yes! I don't run Carlisle. Someone else does. As for the other places, well, that's my business, not yours.'

'Today, Sam,' intervened Osman. 'We're making it our business.'

Sam replied with an understanding nod.

'But you admit you're into drugs?' insisted Jake.

'Was,' replied Sam. 'I've never used drugs but we all know the financial advantages that we can gain from them.

Look, I had to take a break. Get away for a while. Melt into the background.'

'Escape the police you mean,' suggested Jake. 'They're onto you in Newcastle, Grimsby, Dumfries, places like that. Quest, I think the saying goes that they would like you to help them with their enquiries. They're in the process of getting arrest warrants out for you. Did you know that?'

Sam didn't reply.

'Who runs Carlisle?' enquired Osman.

'Why do you want to know?'

'Because you're from Carlisle so why didn't you say you were running the drugs into Carlisle?'

'Because I'm not and I wasn't. When the police got rid of me, I went to Scotland. I got involved, made money, and spread the net. You know how it works. I can see you've done your homework.'

'Who is the main source in Carlisle? Who runs the city?'

'I'm not grassing anyone up,' stated Sam with a defiant surge in his voice. 'Banshee! You can get your boys together and throw me in the Mersey if you want. You nearly did it once before, but I'm not grassing up a fellow operator.'

Osman, Jake and Banshee exchanged glances and nods before Osman squared his tie and ventured, 'We have a supply of pearls coming in soon. Valuable things, pearls.'

'They can be,' nodded Sam. 'If the price is right.'

'So many pearls that we need to get rid of quickly. You interested in pearls?'

'I could be. What's in it for me?'

'More pearls!'

'Really! They don't last long. I'd be careful what you do with your pearls.'

'Interested in helping us?'

'You mean you've no orders?' argued Sam. 'Are you telling me you're expecting a delivery of pearls and you've no one to sell them to? You chose not to believe me, but you expect me to believe you when you sit there and say you have to get rid of the pearls quickly. Really?'

'We have outlets, but we need more,' replied Osman.

Sam nodded thoughtfully, offered a slight grin, and replied, 'Like mine?'

'It may be up for discussion,' suggested Osman.'

'Now ain't that the word of a good operator?' offered Sam.

'A friend in Carlisle, is it?' probed Osman. 'The main dealer there. It could become another outlet. A friend, is it?'

'No!'

'But you have a list of dealers you can tap into,' suggested Osman. 'Where's the list?'

Sam tapped his head with his index finger and said, 'Here! Where it's nice and safe.'

'Carlisle?' argued Osman. 'In the head, is it? I want the list, Sam. The Carlisle list!

Jake leaned forward and added, 'Now!'

Nodding, Sam replied, 'Caleb Cartwright runs the city and some of the county. I've never met the guy, never had any dealings with him, and because I was once a cop there, I never did any dealing in Carlisle, or Cumbria for that matter.'

Osman said, 'Describe him?'

Sam's brain rolled back to that day in the Crown and Mitre Hotel. He described Caleb and then added his clothing saying it was often the usual attire he wore.

Malek Osman's eyes brightened. He glanced at Jake who engaged Sam with, 'Give me a Lancashire contact.'

'Quite a few. I'd start with Turnbull from Skelmersdale. Not well known. A clever man who never lays his hands on the pearls. A bit like me really, but then you'll know that.'

Jake threw a sideways glance at Osman and said, 'Turnbull, is that what you said?'

'That's him. I'm told he ought to stop throwing his money around. He draws attention to himself by spending too much. Turnbull needs to stop being a big shot. If he continues like he is he'll eventually come to the notice of the police and they'll have him. That said, my people tell me he's got the Skelmersdale area in his pocket.'

'Your people?' queried Osman.

'Business associates,' replied Sam with a forced grin.

Jake said, 'I want you to make a delivery for us.'

'Pearls?' queried Sam aware that his pulse was racing.

'Just a delivery,' replied Jake taking the lead in the office.

'When?'

'Now!'

'What about work?'

'This is work,' declared Jake. 'Your choice. Yes or no?'

'Yes!'

Bending over, Jake lifted the office phone, hit the digits, and waited for a reply before eventually saying, 'It's on. Now!'

Sam's breathing drew less shallow when he remembered that Jupiter's office would be listening to Osman's phone as well as Doyle's phone. Within a short time, he hoped, those people working in the Jupiter office would tell Rafferty and he would be aware of what was about to happen.

'You'll take your car,' insisted Jake who produced a briefcase from under his chair. Jake donned a pair of leather gloves as he studied Sam's eyes. Flicking the catches open, he removed a brown manilla envelope and handed it to Sam saying, 'You'll take this directly to an address that I give you and you'll hand it over to the occupant. No conversation. Just a handover. Once that's done, you'll come straight back here and wait for one of us to meet you. You won't stop anywhere on the way there and you won't stop anywhere on the way back. Understand?'

Sam nodded and listened to the address upon which he replied, 'Bolton?'

'You got satnav in the motor?'

'Yes!'

'Then follow the A58 route,' ordered Jake. 'The A58 route. Got that?'

'When?'

'Like I said, now!'

'I thought you were joking.'

'We weren't joking when we asked you yes or no.'

'No! You weren't,' admitted Sam weighing the envelope in both hands. 'I'd say a kilo in here, wouldn't you?'

'Just deliver it,' growled Jake.

Sam was up on his feet and out of the door with the envelope under his arm making for his motor when Jenny appeared in the car park walking towards the office.

Shaking his head, Sam whispered, 'Not now!' and walked straight past her. She stood still, turned, and watched him go with a look of annoyance on her face at the way she had been ignored. Sam was into his Ford and driving off without a further look at Osman's secretary.

Jake stood at the office window, watched Sam take a right turn out of the car park, and said to Osman, 'He's taken the bait. Ring the boss and confirm the delivery is taking place.'

As Osman made the call, Banshee said, 'I take it you don't want him followed to Bolton?'

'Bolton?' queried Jake. 'He'll not get out of Merseyside, Banshee. There's a bottle in the bottom drawer. Pour three glasses, pal. We'll have a drink to pass the time of day.'

Sam was through Old Swan and Knotty Ash when he hit the A58 and checked his mirror. There wasn't a police car in sight, just a couple of taxis and a handful of saloon cars on the roads out towards the motorway routes and Manchester.

Reflecting as he drove his ageing Ford Fiesta, it occurred to Sam that Jake and the boys knew nothing of the Mazda 6 he had been driving on his long journeys. That vehicle was still parked in the multi-level car park. For now, his battered old Fiesta would do.

A crossroads came into view and Sam caught sight of a police patrol car parked close to the junction. Through the crossroads, Sam glanced in his rear-view mirror and watched the police car pull out to join the traffic queue behind him.

'Game on,' thought Sam as he accelerated to fifty miles an hour and the A58 opened before him. Adopting a casual attitude, Sam drove at a leisurely pace

The police car pulled out, overtook the line of traffic, and then slid in behind Sam's Ford. Sam held his speed with one eye on the road ahead and the other in the rear-view mirror. He saw the officer in the passenger seat pick up the radio handset and talk into the mouthpiece.

Another police car came into view. It was parked on a layby on the nearside of the road and pulled out as soon as Sam's Fiesta approached leaving the undercover detective nicely wedged in the middle. There was one police car in front and another behind, and Sam was the meat in the sandwich.

'Two cops in both cars,' thought Sam. 'It's four to one in their favour, but when?'

Sam held his speed. What were they waiting for? They had him. There was no way his old Fiesta could outrun either of the three-litre patrol cars, and a glance at the satnav confirmed he was still in Merseyside.

The blue lights went on. The siren of the following patrol car sounded causing Sam to glance in the mirror and see the officer in the front passenger seat gesturing to him to pull into the nearside.

There was a layby ahead and a police dog van had activated its blue light and slewed broadside across the road effectively closing the road.

'The odds are mounting,' thought Sam. 'Two cars and a dog van make at least five cops and one dog against me. There's no point in running away. Barking mad? Well, here goes.'

Sam held his left hand high for the following police car occupants to see his acknowledgement. Then he covered the brakes and gradually reduced speed as he flicked a switch. His nearside indicator began to flash.

The police car ahead slowed with him. The police car behind drew nearer to the Fiesta's bumper. The blue light on the police dog van rotated on the roof and the driver's door opened. The police were forcing him to stop in a gentle and controlled manner with the driver of the dog van opening the driver's door and stepping onto the tarmac.

Sam moved to the nearside, entered the layby, and slowed almost to a standstill. He glanced in the rear-view mirror. The driver of the police car was smiling. It had all been so easy.

Old Ford Fiesta or not, Sam snatched second gear, swung the steering wheel to the offside, and slammed the accelerator pedal to the floor.

The dog handler jumped out of the way. Sam mounted the grass verge on the offside, bumped the Fiesta back down onto the highway, and heard the engine screaming as he swung back to the nearside narrowly missing an oncoming brewery wagon.

Increasing speed, Sam watched the needle on the speedometer climb towards seventy and then touch eighty as he stole a mile on his pursuers and left them flummoxed. Within seconds, a simple quiet stop-check had become a fail-to-stop followed by a high-speed chase and the suspect was ahead of the game in a rattling old Ford Fiesta that had seen better days.

Racetrack!

The A58 became a racetrack with all three police vehicles chasing Sam and an embarrassment of radio signals emanating from the police reporting the pursuit.

In an office in Walton Lane police station, Detective Sergeant Brian Doyle listened to the radio commentary, slammed his fist on the desk, and snatched the phone from its cradle.

'I want a roadblock before he gets out of Merseyside,' snarled Doyle. 'I want that car stopped and the driver locked up within the next fifteen minutes and before he reaches Haydock. Understood?'

'We've responded to your recent intelligence-led briefing by bringing the suspect vehicle to a standstill on the edge of the city, Sergeant Doyle,' replied the voice of a quietly spoken duty control room officer. 'Unfortunately, the suspect has failed to conform to stop signals and has absconded. We are in pursuit and arrangements are in hand to stop the vehicle again.'

'Again!' blared Doyle. 'Cut the crap, you clown! Sheer bloody incompetence the first time. Move it! Don't let that car out of our sight or I'll have your balls hanging from the top branch of the Christmas tree, you bloody clown. Get it stopped!'

The phone went dead. Doyle slammed his phone on the cradle. He turned the volume up as he listened to a string of instructions on the wireless network. Somewhere inside his head, a normally composed brain pattern faltered and raised a notch. Doyle hated it when things weren't going his way.

Tilting around a corner, Sam was sure he was on two wheels for a moment before he felt all four wheels regain the tarmac. The suspension system groaned and reeled from the relentless pressure of high-speed cornering.

A glance in the mirror confirmed the chasers were catching him. Sam slammed on the brakes as he met a sharp curve, grabbed a lower gear, and then accelerated around the bend with the suspension audibly creaking and the Fiesta rolling from one side to the other.

Then they had closed on him, caught him, and were shining their headlights menacingly into Sam's rear-view mirror with the town of St Helens ahead and the likelihood of a dozen natural traffic holdups that would only assist the chasing pack.

Ignoring the sirens and flashing blue lights, Sam checked his satnav. He slowed, allowed the first of the wolves to overtake him, and then swung violently to the nearside down a single-track road.

The second patrol car following braked late, swung into the same junction, and collided with the offside hedge. Only the police dog van negotiated the corner correctly and was able to continue the pursuit.

A glance in the mirror led Sam to realise he was ahead of the game. His nimble brain and those crazy driving techniques taught by Logan had ensured he was still holding that 'get out of jail card'.

Holding his course, Sam recalculated the satellite navigation system and plotted a route that bypassed St Helens and led to the A580 East Lancs Road. The first purpose-built intercity highway was his target, his passage to freedom, and the way ahead. He flicked the headlights onto full beam and gunned the Fiesta along the single-track route as fast as it would take him. Gasping for what semed an eternity, Sam eventually took a deep breath and prayed that he was the only vehicle on the single-track road. If he wasn't, a head-on collision was on the cards.

Minutes later, another fleeting glimpse in the mirror revealed no following traffic. Sam had outdriven and outwitted the dog handler and the best Merseyside had to offer. Reducing speed drastically, he felt the manilla envelope, rolled the driver's window down, and opened the envelope. As the Fiesta cruised gently along the lane, Sam emptied the contents of the envelope and watched the constituents fall towards the grass verge, saw the grey-white substance scatter to the winds, and then scrunched the envelope into his clenched fist. Continuing his journey at normal speed, Sam threw the envelope into the countryside and rolled the window back up.

Making the East Lancs Road, Sam swung towards Haydock and hurried down the carriageway at seventy miles an hour.

Ahead lay a trap. The police closed the junction where the A58 met the A580. Above him, a police helicopter circled. Sam eased back and checked the mirror. A speck or two in the distance revealed a police dog van, a police transit van, and two patrol cars growing larger in the mirror. The chasing pack had reformed and were still in pursuit albeit some distance behind.

An articulated wagon had been highjacked by the police, swung across the road blocking the carriageway, and was surrounded by half a dozen patrol cars with their headlights flashing and blue lights rotating.

All Sam could see on the side of the wagon was a huge advert for Country Life butter. He was sure he didn't want it to be spread all over the tarmac by colliding with it.

'Only one thing left to do,' thought Sam as he repositioned the Fiesta in the offside of the lane and accelerated towards the roadblock. 'All or nothing.'

At the roadblock an Inspector held his mobile phone, 'Here he is, Sergeant Doyle. We've got him. The rat is about to jump into the trap. He's all ours. Would you like him gift-wrapped?'

'On my way,' snapped Doyle happily. 'Hold him! Search him! Turn the vehicle upside down if you must but, be assured, my informant tells me there's a kilo of cocaine in that car and he's going down. Get him locked up.'

'Understood! Everything is under control. Leave it with us,' from the Inspector in charge of the roadblock. 'Safe journey!'

Sam hurtled down the carriageway towards the articulated vehicle, a welcoming committee of police cars, and a pompous police Inspector who thought he knew all there was to know about how to catch a fly in a trap. Except Sam Quest was no fly and with his headlights on full beam, he banged the horn with his fist and kept the pressure on as the distance between the Fiesta and the roadblock closed.

'He's not slowing down,' from the roadblock.

'Recording on video,' from the helicopter.

'He's going to kill himself,' from a police driver.

'The man's mad,' from the Inspector loosening his collar.

A horn blaring. A Fiesta at top speed; its suspension light and easy cruising to a roadblock that might potentially kill. A police helicopter circling, watching, recording, and an Inspector easing his shirt collar close to panic.

The police scattered, jumped out of the way, ran for cover, and waited for Sam to smash into the articulated wagon.

Sam hit the brakes at the last second and swung the car to its nearside and up the embankment. Swathes of turf spat from the rear wheels of the Fiesta as its tyres fought for traction in the damp grass. Sam urged the car towards a wooden fence at the top of the embankment.

The police helicopter zoomed low, banked to the offside, and was gone from Sam's sight as the Fiesta dislodged the wooden fence and began its slippery voyage down the embankment.

Sam swayed from left to right in the driver's seat, accidentally activated the windscreen wipers, and felt the car pitch over onto its side and roll down the bank.

The Fiesta rolled over, dented its roof when it became upside down, and then allowed the severity of the embankment's incline to take over and deposit it on the carriageway with a loud thump. The rear window popped out and exploded into dozens of glass fragments on the tarmac.

Another police officer jumped out of the way.

The Fiesta had regained all four wheels and was stationary on the tarmac in an upright position.

Steam escaped from the radiator. The wipers flew across the windscreen at top speed. The horn blared continually now broken beyond repair and stuck in the on position.

The Inspector's bottom lip dropped. His mouth opened but his tongue froze. He was lost for words.

Sam shook his head, burst out laughing, and pressed the clutch. He snatched a gear; he knew not which and thumped the accelerator pedal to the floor.

The Fiesta took off towards Manchester with steam escaping from the radiator, a broken exhaust dragging along the tarmac, no rear window, and an engine close to seizure.

'Move the wagon!' screamed the Inspector. 'Clear the road!'

'What? Turn this around?' queried the overweight ageing wagon driver. 'It took me ten minutes to line it up for you. Now you want me to turn it around. Do me a favour.'

'Driver,' screamed the Inspector angrily. 'Move it!'

'Take me five minutes, boss. I'll sort it,' replied the wagon driver as he climbed into the cab.

'You lot!' shouted the Inspector. 'Get after him. Get those cars turned around and get after him.'

Pandemonium broke out at the roadblock when mayhem descended and there was an uncontrolled rush to turn all the police vehicles around and give chase.

The Inspector hit the digits on his mobile, waited for an answer, and then said, 'Greater Manchester Police! Force Control Room, please. This is Merseyside in pursuit of a dangerous drug courier. Immediate assistance is required at Ashton-in-Makerfield. Yes! He's through Haydock and headed your way.'

Closing the mobile, the Inspector felt it vibrate, answered the call, and said, 'Ahh! Detective Sergeant Doyle.'

Sam was through Haydock and approaching Ashton-in-Makerfield when he saw a road sign revealing he was now in the

Greater Manchester area. A hundred yards further on two police vehicles were located at the side of the road.

As Sam drew closer, the two cars pulled out blocking the carriageway. Sam activated his indicator to pull into the nearside, but everything was broken except for four wheels and a steering wheel.

The Fiesta drew to a standstill. The exhaust fell off, and a windscreen wiper began to scratch the glass surface.

Winding down the driver's window, Sam put both hands through the window into the open air. He spread his fingers and shouted, 'I give up! I'm unarmed! I am your prisoner!'

Cautiously, two police officers closed with him, opened the driver's door, and pulled him out of the car. They took him to the ground, handcuffed him, and said, 'You're under arrest.'

'What have I done?'

'You are in illegal possession of drugs.'

'Is that why they were chasing me? Look, I'm sorry about doing forty-odd in the thirty-limit way back in Liverpool but drugs! No way! I don't use drugs and I haven't got any drugs in my possession.'

The two officers exchanged puzzled glances.

'I said I'm sorry. Can I go now?' queried Sam. 'My car needs fixing, probably scrapped. I need a tow to the nearest garage. Do you want my driving licence?'

'You are being detained for a drugs search at the local police station. Your vehicle will also be searched.'

'The car too?' queried Sam. 'It's a wreck now. Still, that's what you get for not stopping for the police. Will I get an endorsement for speeding?'

Dragging Sam to his feet, one of the officers said, 'Are you taking the piss, son? Where are the drugs? The boot or the glove compartment? Maybe under your seat! Or did you hide them somewhere else?'

'I don't know what you mean. I haven't got any drugs.'

'Get in that police car. We'll turn you and your car upside down if we have to.'

'Just been upside down,' remarked Sam. 'Didn't like it!'

'He's taking the piss out of us,' shouted again. 'Sort him!'

The arresting officers bustled Sam to the ground. Struggling to free himself from their grip, a fist rammed into his face followed by a knee smashing into his groin. Sam groaned, exhaled loudly, and collapsed into a lifeless pose when he twisted onto his stomach and handcuffs were applied behind his back.

Unceremoniously, moments later, Sam was bundled into the back of a patrol car. Half an hour later, he was in the cell block at the police station listening to the custody sergeant explaining his rights.

Sam nodded, protested his innocence of the drugs, and admitted his speeding offence in Liverpool asking to see his solicitor as soon as possible.

The cell door closed behind Sam and he dropped onto the wooden bunk provided. He glanced at the door flap. It was down. The custody officer was gone from view. Breaking into a cold sweat, the adrenaline that had pulsated through Sam's body for the last few hours vanished leaving him cold and sweating. Ice cold!

In a state of extreme shock, Sam lurched from the bunk and clung to the enamel toilet in the corner of his cell. His stomach heaved and he emptied the contents into the bowl. He watched his hands shaking as if they were warning him of the dangers ahead. Sam tried to steady himself, but the tremors continued and he listened to his heart beating like a bass drum. Then it missed a beat or was it two when a knifing pain attacked his chest and shoulders? Every muscle in his body seemed to collapse as his mind switched off and fatigue invaded his brain. Eventually, his stomach empty, cold, in shock, and overcome by despair and the rush of it all, he curled up into a foetal position. Lying on one side, Sam gradually fell asleep. He was exhausted, with his knees bent towards his chest, a faulty heartbeat racing, and a cold dampness that had overcome him and reduced him to a spent man.

Forty minutes later, at the scene of the roadblock, the uniform Inspector was holding Brian Doyle at bay using a dozen excuses as to why the suspect had evaded arrest. From the versatility of the Ford Fiesta, and the inexplicable actions of its driver, to a wrongly parked wagon. From the steepness of the incline to the lack of preparation, every excuse he could think of was offered to the detective.

To no avail, Doyle was not amused. 'Give me your phone. Call yourself an Inspector! You're overpaid and over-promoted.'

The Inspector handed his phone over but did not reply.

Doyle searched the phone, pressed the screen, and immediately found himself talking to Greater Manchester Police. He asked to be put through to the holding police station and waited.

'Ashton-in-Makerfield! How can I help you?'

'Merseyside Police! Detective Sergeant Doyle speaking! Put me through to the detective dealing with the prisoner Sam Quest. Pronto!'

Moments went by before the custody sergeant engaged Doyle and said, 'What's your problem, Sergeant Doyle?'

'Quest? What do you intend to charge Quest with? Possession of cocaine, I presume! I'm coming through to interview him. Hold your local man off until I get there. It's my case and he's my prisoner. I want him in court tomorrow morning. I'll be with you very shortly.'

'That's not possible,' replied the custody sergeant. 'Quest is being released.'

'Released?' exploded Doyle. 'What the hell is going on? Am I surrounded by idiots today? Cocaine! He's got cocaine with him. He's in possession of Class A drugs.'

'No! He wasn't,' came the reply. 'There were no drugs found. He was searched by a detention officer and his vehicle was searched by a trained sniffer dog. We even used the portable X-ray machine to examine the bodywork of his car. What a wreck! Nothing incriminating was found. I suggest your information may have been well sourced, Sergeant Doyle, but the fact remains he has not committed any criminal offences in this police area.'

'What about dangerous driving?'

'Not in this police area,' voiced the custody sergeant. 'He was requested to stop and did so. The car he was driving was a write-off. A dozen traffic offences have been committed by Quest but they are not criminal. They are summary offences which may lead to his appearance in a magistrate's court. However, given the fact that he was arrested on what has turned out to be false information, that is highly unlikely. Indeed, very unlikely. He admits to exceeding the thirty-mile-an-hour speed limit in Liverpool. You and I both know that is not an arrestable offence and the only evidence against him is his admission. It would not stand up in court if he pleaded not guilty. I'm sorry, Sergeant Doyle but you need to put this matter behind you and move on.'

'But the intelligence on him is colossal,' argued Doyle.

'But not evidence! Sorry! I'm releasing the prisoner. There are no grounds to keep him in custody.'

'Keep him locked up,' bellowed Doyle. 'He could have dumped the drugs before he was stopped by the police.'

'Or never had any drugs with him to start with,' argued the custody officer. 'Either way, there's no evidence against him.

'I'll get a warrant out for him. He's suspected of being a drugs courier. We need to search the roads between Liverpool and Haydock.'

'Then you can arrest him when he returns to Liverpool.'

'No! I want him now.'

'So does his solicitor.'

'To hell with his solicitor,' argued Doyle. 'He's wanted here.'

'Sergeant Doyle,' explained the custody sergeant politely. 'I'll remind you that as far as I am concerned you have no jurisdiction in the Greater Manchester Police area. It's our patch, not yours.'

'I'm a Merseyside officer. I have authority throughout England and Wales. I'm coming to arrest him. He's mine. Hold him for me! I'm on my way!'

'What are you going to arrest him for?'

'Just hold him. I'll sort it out when I get there.'

'I'm aware of your powers of arrest, Sergeant Doyle. Yet again, I remind you that Quest hasn't committed any criminal offences here. Intelligence is not evidence and you have no warrant or information that would cause me to keep the man in custody for either you or any other force. I'm releasing Mr Quest into the care of his solicitor. End of story! Good afternoon!'

The phone went silent leaving Doyle dead in the water with no hope of turning the tide.

The custody sergeant gave Sam a pen and asked him to sign the release forms relative to his property being returned to him and the administrative side of an arrest and release. Then he looked up and said, 'Your client is free to go, Mr Logan once he has his property and has signed all the papers. Is there anything else we can help you with today?'

'Nothing, at all,' replied Logan. 'I note that you did not tell Sergeant Doyle that my client was assaulted by your officers during his arrest.'

Smiling, the custody sergeant replied, 'But then you will have heard that I explained to Doyle that Manchester is my patch, not his. My decision is final, Mr Logan.'

'Of course,' replied Logan.

'Can you confirm that your client will not be pursuing the complaint against the police that he made to me regarding an alleged assault upon him by the arresting officers?'

'Absolutely!' replied Logan. 'It would be quite wrong of me to suggest we have made a deal, Sergeant. I think it is better defined as a meeting of the minds. I consider it a recognition of the adrenaline and excitement that Sergeant Doyle wrongly caused both you and my client. I suggest it is best left that way with no further action in any way, shape, or form. As far as I am concerned, you are releasing my client into my care and the matter between us is closed.'

'Excellent!' replied the custody officer. 'Can I ask which practice you are with?'

'Logan! Logan and Logan!' smiled Logan. 'Three brothers! We are based in Aberdeen, London and Birmingham, hence my slightly Scottish accent. Here's my card.' Logan handed his business card over adding, 'Please don't hesitate to phone our main office in London should you need any further information.'

The custody sergeant accepted the card, read it, and placed it on the desk whereupon Sam glanced at the business card and recognized the telephone number as the same number he used to ring Jupiter's office.

'I knew they were close to me,' thought Sam.

With the procedures complete, Sam Quest walked free from the building with Logan.

Doyle looked at the grassy embankment where Quest had made his daring escape, studied the vehicle tracks embedded in the grass, looked at the Inspector, and handed the phone back to him. He took a step, got into his car, and sat looking at the steering wheel before glancing at his colleague and offering him a withered reluctant nod.

'I'm always right,' thought Doyle as he fired the engine. 'Always right! Where did the cocaine go? Did Quest ditch the pearls or did the cops nick them? No! I know those guys in Ashton. They're not like that. They're straight whilst I'm.... More self-indulgent is a good term. Better than corrupt or bent. As it is, today, right now, I'm just looking for a scapegoat, someone to blame. It's Quest! He's dumped the bloody pearls to avoid arrest.'

Doyle selected first gear.

'Well, I'll be damned! I'm always right,' thought Doyle. 'He should have been locked up at Haydock, remanded in custody here in the Merseyside police area where I have control, and then filtered out of the system until the Colombian delivery was done and dusted.'

With a forced grin to the Inspector, Doyle worked the clutch, squeezed the accelerator, and drove off thinking to himself, 'That's what happens when you have to decide if the man is an undercover cop or a drug dealer. The best way, if not sure, is to lock him in the cell the first time around and see what happens. Put him on ice. It's his network we want, but I want it clean with him begging for freedom and me completely sure he's not undercover. To hell with you, Quest! I've no option now!'

The Inspector shook his head, placed his hands on his hips, and watched the detective drive off thinking, 'Bastard! First-class bastard of the highest order. Never wrong, always right. Well! That's chopped him down to size. Big style!'

'What the hell do I do now?' thought Doyle as he returned to Liverpool. 'I never thought for one minute that he would dump the pearls. But he did, and Jake and the gang will find out when he returns because he'll tell them. Potentially, he's made me look a fool in front of them all. I expected him to make the delivery. Not for one minute did I think that he would dump the pearls, but he did, and it was never discussed with Jake, Osman, and the team when I told them to set Quest up for a test run. I didn't think it through. The team I've put together will think I'm a fool. They'll detect a weakness in me and have less confidence in me. We'll see about that. Oh, yes. We'll see about that. For this operation with Yurov to work, the dockers need to have total confidence in me. I'll find a way around Quest and his bravado. I knew he'd do that. Just knew it, that's what I expected him to do. Yes! I'll tell them that. Yes, that's my way out. I knew all along he would dump those drugs. We all expected Quest to make the delivery. I made a mistake so what now? Yes, that's the answer for the boys. He's passed the test. I'll tell the gang that I expected him to dump the drugs if he was in danger of being arrested. No one makes a fool out of me. No one! And Quest! He beat me! The bastard beat me because he outthought me. I'll use him. Not the first time around, but I'll use him in the future because I want his network. Yurov will pay me handsomely for details of Quest's network.'

That night, Sam returned to the office in Regent Road, Bootle, Liverpool, where he met Jake, Osman and the crew. He recounted the events of the day and then took a seat at the table and waited for a response. Now composed and with a settled mind, Sam wondered how they would respond, wondered if things would go to plan, and just sat patiently as his eyes gradually scanned the audience before him.

Jake uncorked a bottle of whisky, poured Sam a tot, and slid the glass towards him. It was obvious that Jake and the boys had been drinking for a while. Perhaps it was the calm before the storm.

'Well done! Dumping the pearls was a masterpiece of thinking,' suggested Osman. 'You saved yourself and the team. By the way, it was never discussed but we thought that's what you would do if you were comprised. The boss is well pleased. You've acquitted yourself well, Quest. You could have sold us all down the river. Now, all we want is details of your network.'

'Okay! It'll take me a while to unload my head into a list but I'll oblige you and the phantom boss. And I've told you before,' remarked Sam. 'I'll never grass on a fellow operator, and if that means you guys, then that's the way I am. Take it or leave it, your decision?'

'Good one!' returned Jake. 'Shows you thought it through. The boss wants you on the team. Cheers!'

Jake raised a glass and waited for the rest to join him. They did and Sam stared at them for a while before raising his glass and returning, 'Cheers!'

The whisky went down in one and Sam probed, 'Boss! Boss! Boss! I thought you two were the bosses. Anything I should know about who the boss is?'

'Nothing,' intervened Malek Osman quickly. 'The boss was on the phone just before you returned. There's no problem, and nothing you need to know other than you'll be unloading the Ankara Queen when the vessel arrives later this week from Colombia. That's all you need to know and it's a recognition of the sharing of your network that has partly earned you this. No network, no interest, no test, and goodbye. As it is, we want you on the team and you'll be well paid.'

'Thank you,' replied Sam chinking glasses with his new teammates and taking a deep slug of whisky.

Jake reached forward and topped up Sam's glass.

'Jake will issue the orders regarding times and offloading,' explained Osman. 'Each of us here has a different job in the team. We are all bosses of something. You'll get to know about that as we move through the next few months. As of tomorrow, you'll be told what to lift and where to take it. Comply with Jake's orders at all times.'

'Yes! Yes, I see.'

'Do you normally carry?' probed Banshee.

'Carry?' replied Sam. 'Carry what?'

'A shooter!'

'Never found it necessary,' replied Sam.

'No problem!' smiled Banshee. 'You'll manage the Ankara Queen. Just keep your mouth buttoned and don't be late. Work like a trojan when it's time to unload and make sure those around you don't slack. The quicker the unloading is done the better for all of us. The gear arrives, it sits, and it goes in a flash. I want you on top-notch that day and with your eyes on the others around you. No slacking.'

'The others around me,' queried Sam.

'He means our shield,' explained Jake. 'Nothing more. Another glass?'

Jake offered the bottle and Sam accepted before Jake then topped up the other glasses and set the almost empty bottle on the table.

'When is the Ankara Queen in?' asked Sam gesturing to a panel on the office wall. 'I don't see it on the planning board.'

'Soon,' declared Osman. 'Not long to go. Just keep your eye on your mobile. You'll get a text when it's in and you'll be expected at the terminal within the hour. Understood?'

'Yes, definitely,' replied Sam who raised his glass again and said, 'Cheers! Thanks for the pearls of wisdom.'

There was laughter in the office when Sam's words hit the minds of those who raised their glasses, chinked the glassware yet again, and drank the bottle dry.

'Gonna be a long night,' quipped Banshee as he reached across and took another bottle from a cabinet. 'One for the road?'

The glasses chinked once more to a chorus of voices all repeating, 'Cheers!'

~

Chapter Twelve
~

Later,
The Bunker,
The Defence Intelligence Section
Portsmouth

Digital sea charts dominated the enormous screen fastened to one wall of the underground bunker that was manned by the men and women of Naval Intelligence. Part of the nation's Defence Intelligence Section, the unit acted on behalf of various British intelligence concerns. Primarily, their main customer was MI6: the Secret Intelligence Service.

Dedicated operators sat at their computer stations wearing radio earphones. They were tuned in to multiple sources of naval intelligence. These included ships at sea, submarines, aeroplanes, helicopters, drone activities and, in one specific secure area, data transfer from low earth satellites in orbit.

Each operator enjoyed touch screen capability that instantly transferred the product from their computer to the enormous screen that filled one of the walls in the command area. It was here that the officer in charge, and his deputies and assistants, oversaw the operations and communicated with those agencies that were part of the British Defence Intelligence Section.

One of the lieutenants stepped forward, touched the screen, and watched as the latest observation reached the unit and was transferred to the command module.

'Sighted in Saint George's Channel midway between Wexford and Pembrokeshire,' declared the lieutenant. 'Course indicates movement north into the Irish Sea. Radar and aerial coverage are active.'

'Identity confirmed?' enquired the Commander.

'Awaited, sir,' from the lieutenant. 'An aerial reconnaissance patrol callsign, Jackdaw Three Three, is deployed to the area.'

A keyboard rattled quietly in the background and a computer operator sat back for a moment. She readjusted her seating facility before pressing 'Enter' and from the corner of her eye was aware that the data transfer had hit the command screen.

'Jackdaw Three Three reports a confirmed sighting of a target of interest to M16, sir,' remarked the lieutenant.

The Commander stepped closer to the screen, touched the image of a ship in the middle of Saint George's Channel, and replied, 'The Ankara Queen! Make a signal to Jupiter. The Ankara Queen is midway between Wexford and Fishguard. Current course and speed indicate the vessel will arrive at Liverpool docks in approximately eight hours.'

The lieutenant repeated the message and said, 'All received, sir. Priority One?'

'Yes! Priority One! Inform Jackdaw patrols to tag the Ankara Queen. Likewise, all assigned desk operatives. Report immediately any change in course and speed, as well as wireless traffic emanating from the tagged vessel. Execute the instruction!'

'Will do, sir.'

The Commander studied the computerised image of the Irish Sea whilst the lieutenant sat at a nearby console and transferred the latest information regarding the Ankara Queen to Jupiter and other parties to the operation in question.

In the Jupiter office, Rafferty nodded his thanks to Maxwell who passed him a flimsy received from the Bunker relative to the sighting of the Ankara Queen entering the Irish Sea.

Rafferty moved to his desk and took a seat. Dialling a number, he waited for the Director General of the National Crime Agency to respond. He covered the telephone mouthpiece and said, 'Maxwell! Priority One message to DG 5 and Chief 6.... Reads Europa advancing rapidly. Operation Denial is now in the organisational stage. Ends.'

Maxwell repeated the message. Rafferty confirmed the content with an acknowledgement and the operator moved to transfer the message electronically.

The Director General of the National Crime Agency answered the phone and allowed Rafferty to update him as to the location of the Ankara Queen. He replied, 'After all this time and you give me eight hours to deploy a nationwide task force to counter the threat from a ship from Colombia that you've known about for several weeks?'

'I'm afraid so,' confessed Rafferty. 'The matter is complicated further by the requirement not to utilise Merseyside Constabulary in the operation that is being planned.'

'Yes! I am aware of that. I have recently had conversations with your Director-General. I understand the problem, but do you understand mine?'

'Staffing levels?'

'Correct! I am curtailing some of our operations at the request of your service and on the order of the Home Secretary. I presume I have only been told part of the story and not the whole of the story?'

'That is correct,' admitted Rafferty. 'I can assure you that all will become clear when we activate Operation Denial.'

'Denial?'

'The strike operation,' revealed Rafferty. 'We are relying on you to take the ground when the strike is called. Once we have ground control and arrested the primary subjects then, and only then, will we be able to involve Merseyside Constabulary. It follows that the Home Secretary may well instruct surrounding forces to assist if necessary. Until that time comes, Operation Denial is not a police matter.'

'A matter of national security, it would seem.'

'Closer to the truth.'

'A matter involving local police officers, I suggest. Perhaps the word 'corruption' is closer to the truth?'

'Director! Can I be assured of your tactical and strategical assistance on the ground when Operation Denial takes place?'

'Mr Rafferty, of course. You can rely on us. Just pray that I can move the resources into position in good time.'

'A successful raid on the Ankara Queen will be a good result and will be the foundation of, and kickstart to, a nationwide sweep of dealers whom we are aware are also involved and are part of the nationwide network that is in place and needs to be dismantled.'

'I will make the necessary arrangements.'

'Thank you!' Rafferty ended the conversation and shouted, 'Maxwell! Message Logan and all Red Alpha teams to activate their response to Operation Denial. They have all been briefed as to the requirement. Tell them that Operation Denial will involve the NCA and is the strike operation. We are gearing up to deny organised crime at the very least.'

'Logan and three Red Alpha teams are on site,' replied Maxwell. 'The DG phoned whilst you were talking to the NCA. He wants a regular update commencing in seven hours.'

'When the Ankara Queen is expected to dock!'

'Precisely,' replied Maxwell. 'I'll put the kettle on. It's going to be a long day?'

'And night,' remarked Rafferty. 'Yes! Good idea! Thank you, Maxwell! We have work to do to try and get the best result all around.'

Later, in the bunker in Portsmouth, one of the operators was gliding her fingers over the keyboard like a woman possessed.

'Intercepted wireless conversation,' she remarked to the lieutenant. 'The captain of the Ankara Queen is talking to the skipper of another vessel about landing procedures and Customs and Excise. Not yet confirmed, am recording, stand by for the preliminary report.

I'm also doing an internet search on the names being discussed. Sending you a document trail very shortly.'

The lieutenant stood behind her, watched the words appear on her computer screen, and then moved to the command module where he informed the Commander.

Suddenly, the radio went quiet. The conversation had ended. A button was pressed, and the content of the operator's report appeared on the commander's screen next to the image of the Ankara Queen.

Reading the report, the Commander ordered, 'Lieutenant! Priority One! Make to Jupiter a copy of this report!'

'Aye! Aye! Sir,' replied the lieutenant.

The electronic transfer was made and would appear in Jupiter's office in the time it took to say 'Jackdaw!'

In the docks surrounding Bootle, three Red Alpha surveillance teams from MI5 casually, but swiftly, moved into pre-determined positions where they could watch, and report upon, the comings and goings at the terminal where the Ankara Queen was expected. As the teams arrived, they gradually thinned out along the ribbon of land that ran from the Liverpool Dock in the north to the Stanley Dock in the south. By such location planning, the team had positioned themselves to cover the main roads into and out of the target area.

Here and there, a van appeared and parked conveniently close to an area of interest; its unseen occupants used the technology inside the van to activate the watch. Elsewhere, a small fleet of saloon cars found car parks and parking places from which to perform similar duties. And on one or two tall buildings, an empty office was occupied and became a surveillance observation point when high-powered binoculars swept the area and became accustomed to life in the Docklands.

The net was beginning to close but the National Crime Agency were still absent from the plot, and there were still problems to encounter.

Rafferty wiped the sleep from his eyes, brought a mug of coffee to his lips, realised the content was cold and slid it across the table out of reach.

The night had been long. The planning had been done and the resources were gradually moving into place. But still, the questions haunted Rafferty. When and where would the Ankara Queen dock? Where were the drugs hidden in the vessel? Was the illegal consignment below deck in the hold, in the bodywork of the ship, being towed underwater from the stern, or in possession of a crew member, or multiple crew members? Historically, that's where such illegal drugs were often hidden. It was all to play for and there were no clues available to help the watchers and those who might have to board the ship and carry out a search.

As the surveillance teams took up their places, Logan and Sam Quest parked on the beach at Crosby and dragged two kayaks from the rear of a dark-coloured Transit van. Logan dressed in a wet suit and handed Sam an encrypted radio. Quest had prepared himself for the cold water and wore his balaclava, a black neoprene wetsuit, and skin-tight gloves.

Logan's brief from Rafferty was simple. He would supervise a shore patrol watching for an off-harbour criminal team that might deploy a small vessel to visit the Ankara Queen and receive the consignment of drugs before it docked in the port. Logan had telephone links to Naval Intelligence if that turned out to be the case. There was always the possibility that a movement might cause another surveillance team somewhere to be activated.

Quest's brief from Rafferty was to paddle down the Mersey and look for any new speed boats or vessels of interest that were newcomers to the docks; newcomers that might be connected to the shipment of drugs away from the Ankara Queen and back out to sea to places like Ireland and seaports in the north of England. Not all dealers were land-based miscreants from England's big cities. Some preferred to transport illegal cargo by sea. Once again, Naval Intelligence was on standby.

To win the drugs war, and make Operation Europa successful, Rafferty's team needed to have enough staff to be able to cope with every planned delivery or collection involving the drug dealers who were signed up for the illegal operation. Rafferty's plan was such that known drug couriers would be allowed to collect their drugs, be followed to wherever they had arranged to deliver them, and then arrested along with the main recipients of the drugs.

The Operation Europa plans looked good on paper, but they all enjoyed one major flaw, namely the undisputed fact that the people under surveillance always enjoyed the upper hand. They were the only ones who knew what they were doing, where they were going, and how long it would take to achieve their objective. What was heard on an eavesdropping operation involving intercepted telephone calls didn't always turn out to be kosha. Only the courier: the collector of the packages, knew the when, where, and how. Such people had a streak of independence that was often above the understanding of others in their various networks. None of them wanted to get caught. They all had their backup plans.

Rafferty's brief was simple. Trace and arrest Misha, identify the Russian connections, and, if necessary, allow the drugs in Operation Europa to run. Misha and the Russian attack were more important than the drug operation. Operation Europa was secondary to Operation Misha.

Logan and Sam launched their kayaks. Logan checked the radios, confirmed they were working, and waved. The two men split up and began paddling their chosen paths.

Rafferty poured more coffee. He was grateful to the stimulant for the kick start and mulled over his plans looking for weak spots. There were so many, and he knew it.

The Mersey was choppy from the number of different-sized vessels that were plying the waters. The wake of several vessels caused the kayaks to float up and down on the surface. Sam made the New Brighton area, recorded a negative search, and then turned towards the docklands of Liverpool.

Sam's radio was activated. It was Rafferty.

'Quest!'

'Speaking!'

'Great news!' bellowed Rafferty. 'Naval Intelligence has just informed me that they have uncovered a document trail relevant to the Ankara Queen.'

'And?' queried Sam as he hugged the coastline and negotiated the river.

'The captain of the Ankara Queen is called Mikhail Jamilla. Enquiries reveal he is Colombian born with a Turkish mother and a Russian father.'

'Really? Are they sure? That's something of a concoction.'

'A search of the internet reveals that before enlisting in the commercial navy in Colombia, Mikhail Jamilla worked in a circus. He trained bears for a living before giving it all up for a life on the ocean wave. Quest! It all fits. The name of the captain, the Russian bear, it's obvious. The captain of the Ankara Queen must be Misha.'

'Russian for bear! Fantastic!' replied Sam. 'Are you sure it fits? Misha may just be coincidental. As I said, that's something of a crazy concoction of a relationship.'

'Not these days, Quest. People travel whether they are in the circus, the navy or whatever. Yes! It fits. We've found Misha. All resources will now be channelled to the Ankara Queen where the strike will take place. I've tightened the surveillance teams and armed NCA officers are en route to bolster the front line. Surveillance teams have noted a build-up of vans and saloon cars in the general area of Bootle Dock.'

'Dealers here to collect and distribute?' queried Sam.

'Quite a few known to us on the police national computer,' confirmed Rafferty. 'When the Ankara Queen docks, make sure you never let the captain out of your sight. He's the link we've been looking for.'

'Understood!' replied Sam.

'Good luck!' from Rafferty.

Sam closed the radio and headed towards a line of vessels that were mustered on the Liverpool side of the river near Canada Dock.

'Moving into the mouth of the Mersey,' radioed Logan as he adjusted his binoculars. 'I need a long view. I need to think like one of them.'

'Understood,' acknowledged Sam.

Half an hour passed and neither man had found anything unusual or out of place.

Sam relaxed, eased his paddle out of the water, and let his kayak drift aimlessly towards the Bootle Dock. He allowed himself the luxury of a short rest before reminding himself not to get too close to his place of work.

Backpaddling, Sam turned his kayak away and headed for the beach at Crosby.

The radio gurgled and Logan shouted, 'Got it! The Ankara Queen is approaching the New Brighton Lighthouse. The estimated time of arrival at Bootle Dock is thirty to forty minutes. Speed is very slow as the vessel begins to negotiate the passage into the docks. What a size. It's massive and preceded by two pilot vessels. That's a three-day search at least.'

Sam's mobile sounded. It was a text from Jake telling him to attend the terminal in forty-five minutes. Acknowledging the text, Sam then replied to Logan with, 'Got that! I'm heading back to the beach. I've just been called to the docks. It's going down.'

Rafferty engaged the radio with, 'Excellent work, gents. I have received confirmation from the Bunker. The Ankara Queen has been spotted inbound from the lighthouse. They are relinquishing surveillance control to us. You are ahead of them. I'm placing all units on full alert. Resume! You know what to do.'

Sam smiled and began to paddle hard towards Crosby.

Two minutes later, there she was. Sam took a deep breath, shook himself, and looked again. There was no mistake. Sam Quest had found a yacht called Misha.

Sam slowed, checked the name on the bow, and studied the forty-feet long yacht. It was named Misha alright. The name was written in gold paint on the bow and stood proud below the sails that dominated the deck.

'It's only recently docked,' decided Sam. 'The crew are only now stowing the sails properly.'

The yacht was a sight to behold with her classic lines. It was an ocean-going cutter, relatively smaller than other yachts, but a speedy sailing vessel like a sloop. Misha enjoyed a single mast rigged fore and aft and carried a mainsail and at least two headsails. The hull was deep and narrow and caught the eye.

'Four men in the crew,' thought Sam as he resumed paddling with one eye on the river and the other on Misha's deck.

'Get back to the docks,' radioed Logan. 'You need to be at the terminal pronto.'

'I'm en route,' replied Sam. 'Got a surveillance taxi handy?'

'Yes! One of our black taxis will attend the shoreline where you launched the kayak from. Move it! We'll need a signal when you spot the drugs.'

'As previously discussed,' voiced Sam. 'But we have a problem?'

'Such as?' ventured Rafferty intervening in the radio. 'What's wrong?'

'A yacht called Misha! It's not long arrived, and it's moored at the same terminal that the Ankara Queen is expected.'

'There's no time for jokes,' growled a tired Rafferty. 'Get back on land, Quest. You need to be on the docks. Now!'

'I am on my way, but it's not a joke. There's a forty-foot ocean-going yacht named Misha that's just moored at Bootle Dock. That's the problem. An hour ago, there wasn't a Misha in sight. Now we have two to play with.'

The radio went quiet as Rafferty and Logan considered the ramifications of what Sam had just told them.

Sat in the rear of a forward control van, Rafferty engaged a secure linked computer facility which enabled him to speak directly to the Chief of the Secret Intelligence Service and the Director General of the Security Service. Rafferty opened the conversation with, 'Sorry for the alert call, gentlemen, but Misha has been identified and I'm sure you will wish to be appraised of that knowledge.'

'Excellent!'

'Bravo! Who is it?'

'That's the problem,' explained Rafferty. 'The captain of the Ankara Queen is called Mikhail which can be translated into Russian as Misha. Misha is also Russian for bear. Mikhail once trained bears in a circus. He's a Colombian with a Turkish mother and a Russian father. Mikhail has all the hallmarks of being Misha.'

'So, what's the problem?'

'Our asset has identified an ocean-going yacht at the same terminal. It's called Misha. Which one, gentlemen? Which one do we take out?'

'Both!' barked the MI5 man. 'Simultaneously!'

'Easier said than done,' argued Rafferty. 'Whichever is the innocent party will be onto the press within minutes. We could upset the plan by backing the wrong horse.'

'I favour the Ankara Queen,' ventured the MI6 chief. 'It's been the Ankara Queen since the beginning. That's what

Naval Intelligence was briefed to look out for. That's the target vessel. Carry out the strike there.'

'I favour my colleague's comments,' remarked the M15 chief with a change of heart. 'How on earth will we ever know?'

'Leave it to Europa,' proposed Rafferty. 'The clock is ticking and he's the only one with a foot in both camps.'

'Misha,' muttered the two intelligence chiefs together. 'Just what we didn't need. Another puzzle!'

~

Chapter Thirteen

~

A short time later
The Shipping Terminal
Bootle Docks

Mikhail Jamilla mastered the bridge of the Ankara Queen when the ship moved gradually into the dock and berthed in its allotted place. It was the dock where the largest vessels ever to visit Liverpool were catered for. The dock was used exclusively for post-Panamax container ships: those ships that were too big to negotiate the Panama Canal. The ship was 950 feet in length and 165 feet in width, carried 75,000 tons of cargo and rose 150 feet above the waterline. The Ankara Queen was a beast of a vessel: a floating dinosaur!

The anchor dropped and the crew busied themselves with mooring the vessel using three hawser points to the front and three to the aft. The pilot vessel let go of the lines when it was joined by the chief pilot who waved farewell to Captain Jamilla.

Jason and Malcolm appeared on the quay, signalled the crew, and immediately began helping them to secure the hawsers. The huge ropes were so heavy it took three men to manipulate them effectively.

Dressed in his normal working clothes, Sam jumped out of a taxi, trotted into the office, briefly acknowledged Jenny, and nodded at Jake and Banshee.

'Just in time,' said Jake. 'Come on! We're off! It's going to be a busy day. You fit for this?'

'Absolutely,' chuckled Sam joining the duo as they walked from the office. 'I've been in the gym all night getting fit. I'm as strong as an ox. I take it the ship's in?'

'You mean you've been in the pub all night and just got here in time,' returned Jake with a sly dig.

'Well, something like that,' grinned Sam.

'The ship has docked! You're on the Ankara Queen with Jason and Malcolm. They're just hooking her up. Give them a hand with the boarding ladders and platforms. We need them to be tight in place. Make sure they are solid before the unloading begins.'

'Understood! Access for forklift truck drivers?'

'They'll be granted access when we're ready. Until then, they'll form the usual casual barricade at the immediate entrance to the dock. They know what to do.'

'A barricade?'

'Yes! A barricade! Just a loose parking arrangement that closes part of the entrance down whilst providing access for specific vehicles of choice. We can get on with the job in hand without any unwelcome visitors deciding to take a stroll around the quayside.'

'Sounds like a good idea,' replied Sam.

'It's been like that since you joined us, Quest. You've just never noticed the common security practices we exercise when a ship with a valuable load is in the dock.'

'Felt a few security practices though,' remarked Sam with a chuckle as he stroked his chin. 'Which reminds me, where's Malek?'

'His job is to sort out the paperwork with the captain and the port authorities. He'll be around later. Now keep the job in your mind. Do it quickly and then we're done.'

'How long?' probed Sam.

'A day or two, maybe three. Who knows? You just need to concentrate on unloading. Now crack on, pal. No more time wasting.'

'I'm on it,' voiced Sam striding towards the Ankara Queen.

As the three men climbed aboard the ship, members of the National Crime Agency moved into covert positions around the target area. Armed plainclothes officers gathered in the area whilst uniform officers from the NCA assembled at a golf course near Mossock Hall, on the edge of Bickerstaffe, in Lancashire. They were a fifteen minutes drive from Bootle Dock, not in the Merseyside police area, and not conversing with any of the surrounding police forces on the radio network. The only figure of authority in the immediate area who knew of their presence was Bernard Rafferty, callsign Jupiter, who sat at the command desk in the rear of a control vehicle and checked the screen coverage of events taking place outside.

Sam reached the Ankara Queen and helped prepare the gangways, platforms and fittings that preceded the unloading of the vessel.

Meanwhile, Logan's team closed on the home address of Malek Osman, confirmed his presence, and watched the house as the operation moved into another phase.

At various addresses in Skelmersdale, from Tawd Close to the urban sprawl, eyes watched, researched a surplus of vehicles visiting the target known as John George Turnbull, and prepared a response the like of which might shock Skelmersdale to the core. It was said that Turnbull was so blasé about his role in the drugs world that his security was poor, found wanting, and a blessing in disguise for the team designated to watch over him and enquire into him. He'd even banked the cash received from multiple transactions into his account. His run of luck was surely coming to an end.

In Carlisle, the watch on Caleb Cartwright and his associates continued. One team monitored his home address whilst another recorded the movements of those visiting a nearby trading estate where Caleb was understood to horde coffee bags for distribution. The watchers noted that a supply of new coffee bags had been delivered to the distribution centre. The bags were smaller than usual. Caleb's organisation was gearing up for a large consignment that it would split into much smaller deliveries. There wasn't a coffee grinder in sight. Just a line of local dealers calling to pay for their share of the coming load.

In places like Leicester, Blackburn, Chester, Leeds and Sheffield, the watchers grew in number. Years of intelligence gathering had all come together in recent hours. Now the snare was being set to catch all those who had figured on the wrong side of the fence over the past few weeks. Hours of watching, recording, researching who was who, and building profiles on the suspects, were about to pay off. The telephone links had been proven. The couriers had been identified as driving and delivering from one address to another. In some places, the money had been banked. The networks were now close to penetration thanks to the smooth and quiet passage of intelligence via the National Crime Intelligence cell and the Security Service.

At the golf course near Mossock Hall, the street maps were spread out on the vehicle bonnets as supervisors indicated how the docks at Bootle would be locked down.

Simultaneously, half a dozen more vehicles linked to organised crime and drug peddling mimicked the law enforcement officers and waited for the Ankara Queen to be unloaded.

But the barrier remained in place. A haphazard line of forklift trucks straddled the entrance to Bootle dock. They were often parked there. It was their usual position when a ship of that size was being unloaded. The usual straight line of driving had been replaced by the need to zig-zag down the same road at a much slower speed, and between the forklift trucks. The forklift trucks prevented the docks from being overwhelmed by visitors, unwanted traffic, and those who had no legitimate business in the docks. You could be sure that anyone parked inside the ring of forklift trucks was welcome, known to the likes of Osman, Jake and company, and had called only to collect a product delivered by a ship for delivery elsewhere. Many of them were well-known and highly respected traders dutifully collecting legal products that had been imported from South

America. Not everyone on the block was a drug dealer, but the drug dealers were the main interest to the watchers.

The unloading continued at a feverish pace.

~

Chapter Fourteen

~

Dawn, the next day
Operation Denial,
Bootle and The North of England

High in the sky, a drone flew across the docks spying on the Ankara Queen below. It paused, hovered, and then moved on recording the vehicles and occupants parked on the streets leading to the docks at Bootle. It paused again, held its attitude, but tilted slightly as the technology inside recorded the line of forklift trucks that held firm at the terminal entrance.

Nimble fingers teased the binoculars, challenged the optics, and allowed the watcher to zoom in on the Ankara Queen. A heavy degree of surveillance from the National Crime Agency and the Security Service was taking place.

Captain Jamilla remained on the quarterdeck. He checked his watch, nodded to the Chief Mate, and relaxed slightly when half a dozen dockers under the command of Jake and Bobby Banshee climbed aboard and split up. Some headed for the hold, others made for the containers and began to call forward a handful of wagons waiting in the wings for legitimate loads.

'Day two! Unloading has begun,' whistled across the radio network as Jake's twenty-strong team of labourers separated into specific groups and began work.

Sam checked his wristwatch, considered the events taking place, and realised a well-rehearsed unloading operation was now underway.

'This way!' waved Malcolm. 'We're on this part of the deck. No containers! Just boxes for the forklift trucks. Lend a hand!'

'On my way,' replied Sam when he walked along the deck of the Ankara Queen watching every movement that took place. 'Were the drugs hidden in the boxes?' he wondered. 'Or the containers?

How will I know? Will it be obvious when Jake and Banshee take centre stage and call the first line of drug couriers to the collection point? How many of them will they need?'

'Here we go,' remarked Jason heaving the first of many boxes from the deck onto the quayside. 'Stand in line, Quest. We use a human chain to get things from the hold onto the deck and into the waiting wagons.'

'Got that,' nodded Sam taking his place.

A crane moved along the dockside. The driver worked the mechanism of the lifting and lowering power unit. Jason stepped forward and used the hook to snare a large net containing dozens of packages from the hold.

The crane lifted and delivered the net onto the dockside where eager hands helped empty the net and load the contents onto a waiting wagon. There was a short break during which the crane driver repeated the operation and Malcolm and Jason rummaged in the hold bringing loose packages onto the deck. The unloading progressed. The hold was being emptied and another forklift truck attended the party as the dockers swarmed over the ship and Captain Jamilla looked on without a care in the world.

A mop of ginger hair and a broken nose betrayed the presence in the human chain of Sean O'Leary.

Sam glanced, saw the heavily built Irishman who he had last encountered at the battle in the Rope and Anchor, and pulled tight his balaclava as he consciously decided to keep his back turned to Sean O'Leary. The problem was Sam had nowhere to hide.

O'Leary dominated the middle of the human chain, yelled at the others to work harder, and had no idea that his enemy Sam Quest was on the same ship.

'Nowhere,' thought Sam. 'Nowhere to be seen! Maybe it's me but I would have expected a quiet controlled rush to where the drugs are hidden followed by a quick removal of the same accomplished by Malcolm and Jason. Nothing yesterday! Nothing today! What's going on? Is the information false or am I so impatient that anxiety is now my biggest enemy?'

Rafferty watched the input from the drone on his screen in the control vehicle and began tapping his fingers on the desk. The drone coverage concentrated on the activities of those on the deck of the Ankara Queen. Occasionally, a slide on the controls broadened the view and images of the dockside, the waiting vehicles, and the line of forklift trucks that stood available. Another flick of the switch repositioned the drone above a line of cars and vans that Rafferty and the team knew were dealers waiting to be called forward. But despite studying the images and talking on the radio to those watchers equipped with high-powered binoculars, there was still no sign that the drugs were being moved. There was no indication that anyone had boarded the ship and moved directly to an area where the drugs were hidden. No one seemed to be worried about the drugs. Surely someone would have checked to see if the drugs had arrived safely before arranging for them to be unloaded. Concerned, and unsure, Rafferty contacted his top-line managers in Faversham Mews via a secure satellite link.

'It's possible the current people on board don't know where the drugs are,' from Mr Green.

'Malek Osman has arranged all the paperwork. He'll know exactly where the drugs are located. When he leaves the house, Logan's team will follow him to Bootle where he'll board the Ankara Queen to oversee the seizure of the drugs,' suggested Mr Blue from M15. 'I recommend that is the best time to strike because you will have most of Doyle's team in situ at the time of the arrest. There is no history of Doyle attending the docks. He seems to communicate with them only by phone.'

'That's correct,' nodded Rafferty.

'You need to think like the enemy, Bernard. Has it occurred to you that Jake and company deliberately haven't been anywhere near the drugs?'

'Why not?'

'They're waiting to see if the police or Customs will pounce. They're checking to see if all is good, making sure they haven't been betrayed. They'll move when they're ready and not before.'

'That makes sense,' replied Rafferty.

'We can tell you're tired, Bernard. It's been a long operation. You're no longer thinking straight. You've got yourself too involved with the planning and procedures. Are you alright to continue? We'll appoint a substitute if we need to.'

'You will do no such thing,' argued Rafferty. 'I may be slightly tired, but I am more than capable of finishing the job.'

'Now you're sounding like a man called Brian Doyle,' chuckled the MI5 Director-General. 'He doesn't like being beaten either. Relax, Bernard! Have a coffee. Maybe even a slug of vodka or a beer. Take time out for a moment. Don't get so wound up inside.'

'Thank you. I don't drink alcohol. Coffee will do.'

'I take it there have been no sightings of any of our Russian friends in the Bootle area?' queried the MI6 Chief. 'We shouldn't forget that they are the masters of the drug importation scenario, not Malek Osman and company. One might have expected the moneymen to have paid a casual visit to see Misha. Captain Jamilla must be of great importance to them.'

'No trace so far,' replied Rafferty.

'Let's see what day two brings. That said, Rafferty, we do expect the Russians to show somewhere.'

'Are you sure?'

'The CCTV footage from the travel agency in Piccadilly reveals Brian Doyle's involvement with the Russians. An examination of his bank account reveals he has become a very rich man in the last twelve to eighteen months. So much so that he must think that his countless thousands will sustain life in clover far above his current lifestyle. He lives in a flat in the middle of Liverpool. If he wants, he has the resources to be able to live in a palace in Dubai or a castle in South America. Doyle is rolling in it due to his involvement in the illegal drug trade. That's why the Russians recruited him. However, he obviously can't be seen to be spending money on these shores. I suspect he may have plans to vacate the UK soon so that he can enjoy life elsewhere. It's all thanks to the Russians and this nationwide operation that he has masterminded. If we are successful, he'll make a break for it with his newfound friends. If he stays, he'll be imprisoned. If he runs with the Russians, we'll never see him again.'

'We do have a surveillance team on his flat in Hope Quarter,' stated Rafferty.

'Yes! We are aware of the status. Developments in that area may be interesting. Any other problems that need airing, Bernard?'

'To strike or not to strike?' queried Rafferty.

'Bernard!' from the MI5 Director. 'You've been in control all night. You're tired and restless. The ship has not long arrived. It's a three-day unloading schedule. We're not even halfway yet. As I mentioned earlier, be patient and let matters mature. They'll get to the drugs in due course.'

'Have any of the known drug dealers attended the ship with their vehicles yet?' probed the MI6 chief.

'No!' replied Rafferty. 'We have a line of such vehicles parked in the waiting area of the terminal. They are being watched by a Red Alpha team who have checked the intelligence database. We've got the main dealers under surveillance. Quite a few of them are close to the terminal or on the road immediately inside the terminal where there are a few waiting zones. I suspect they will be called forward to collect when it's their turn but there's no movement at the moment.'

'Then there's your answer, Bernard,' from Green, the MI6 chief. 'They're not moving because they've not been called forward. When they are, our team in the intercept department will record the conversations and let us know the who, where and when. You're a party to that security protocol and can use the intercept intelligence to respond accordingly. For the moment, those drugs are still in the hold of the Ankara Queen. I'm sure our asset is switched on enough to find out.'

Rafferty nodded and signed off with, 'Very good!'

The day wore on. The early morning moved towards noon. Unloading the ship continued and the situation remained static.

'Are we done yet?' asked Sam as he paused for breath.

'No way,' replied Jason. 'Not even half empty yet. Just bash on, Quest. Stop lagging.'

'I need a break, that's all,' voiced Sam. 'It's hard work. I take it the pearls are in one of the containers and that's why we haven't reached them?'

'Not your problem, Quest,' from Jason.

'Oh! The pearls are long gone,' chuckled Malcolm. 'Nicely done and dusted without any problems!'

'Oh!' from a shocked Sam. 'I missed all the fun and excitement.'

'Yep!' laughed Jason. 'The pearls are now with the jeweller. It's too soon for you to be messing about with the pearls, Quest. Maybe next time. You're still on probation.'

Malcolm dropped a package, broke into spontaneous laughter, and replied, 'That'll be the day.'

Slightly confused, Sam challenged both men with, 'That'll be the day! I thought you trusted me. Have you forgotten that I dumped the drug delivery you gave me? If I'd been arrested with those drugs in my possession, I could have dropped you all in it. But no! I risked my life, my safety, and my freedom to save you guys from getting locked up. Now you tell me I'm on probation. Do me a favour!'

'Hey! Lighten up, Quest. It's been a long day and we're still going strong. We're pulling your leg.'

'So we've not yet hit the jackpot!' challenged Sam.

'All in good time. Don't you worry? You'll still get paid.'

A dozen different scenarios penetrated Sam's mind and sent his brain into turmoil before he eventually replied, 'Okay! I get your drift. Sorry, guys! Give me five. I need fresh air.'

'Don't be long,' voiced Jason. 'We've still much to do and you're one of the lucky ones. You're in the team. Now take five and remember you do as you're told when you're told by Jake, and not before. We're all in the same boat, Quest. It's just not our turn to row the boat this time out.'

'Okay! Okay!' remarked Sam as he made his way to the vessel's stern where he stood, placed his hands on the rails, and looked out across the Mersey.

'Jake! Bobby Banshee!' thought Sam. 'Oh, yes! They want my so-called network but not necessarily me. Where are they? No sign of them and yet I'm with Jason and Malcolm. Work all day, from dawn to night, but no sign of the main men. Why not? Where are they?'

Sam turned and looked the full length of the Ankara Queen, from stern to bow. His eyes caught sight of Captain Mikhail Jamilla who stood on the quarterdeck chatting with the Chief Mate.

'Misha!' thought Sam. 'If Mikhail Jamilla is Misha, like Rafferty and his bosses think, then why has he remained on the quarterdeck since the vessel docked? Unless I'm mistaken he's had no contact with any of us. Hardly the actions of a man in charge of illegal freight that is being unloaded. He's been on this ship for days on end from Colombia. With an illegal load of drugs, you'd expect him to be anxious to see the drugs being unloaded and off his ship. What's going on and why?'

Sam strolled along the deck, took a deep breath, and paused with his hands on the railings looking towards Misha docked next to the Ankara Queen.

'They want my network, but they don't trust me enough to put me where the drugs are,' thought Sam. 'They've put me with Jason and Malcolm because Jake and Banshee are… where? They're on the Misha,' decided Sam. 'And that's where the drugs are. On the yacht called Misha.'

'You joining us, Quest?' shouted Jason from afar.

'Yes!' replied Sam. 'I'll be along in a second.'

Jason turned away but then suddenly realised Sam was watching the Misha yacht. He turned back, studied Sam, and then shouted for Malcolm.

With one hand on the rail, Sam took his first casual steps towards Jason and Malcolm. That was the moment Sam glanced sideways at the yacht and saw Jake and Banshee appear on the deck of the Misha with two other men from the crew. They were each carrying dark blue leather suitcases.

Banshee saw Sam standing by the railings of the Ankara Queen's deck. Banshee used his free hand to make a call on his mobile.

Situated at the entrance to the terminal, the driver of a white Transit van set down his mobile phone and fired the engine. He set off for the dock with a wave to a forklift truck driver who reversed his vehicle away from the line.

The barricade was open. A vehicle was making for the dock. Jake and his crew lugged the suitcases along Misha's deck towards the gangplank.

Banshee made another call.

'The drugs are moving,' thought Sam. 'I need to be on that yacht. I must be near the drugs to give the signal.'

'Quest!' shouted Jason closing his mobile phone. 'That was Banshee on the phone! Come here!'

Sam glanced at Jason, looked again at the white Transit van appearing at the dockside and sensed the drugs were being moved. He looked skywards, searched for a dot in the blue above that was an aerial drone under the command of Bernard Rafferty, and saw nothing.

'Coming!' replied Sam. But he wasn't coming and had no intention of coming. In that split second of seeing four men carrying suitcases, he knew the drugs were moving.

A BMW saloon car parked close to the entrance to the docks moved towards the entrance. A forklift truck reversed, allowed the car to enter, and then closed the gap.

And a ginger-haired Irishman by the name of Sean O'Leary pricked his ears up at the sound of the name Quest. He glanced towards a proportionately built man whom he recognised from the Rope and Anchor. Revenge filled his mind, dominated his thinking, and confirmed to his innermost soul that he needed to even the score.

Sean O'Leary handed over his package to the next man before casually sauntering towards the location of Sam Quest and company.

In a high-rise building, a pair of binoculars panned to the white Transit, then the BMW, and then back along the docks to the Misha yacht. Confused and unsure, the hands that guided the binoculars swung the device back to the Ankara Queen and then sought Sam Quest.

Simultaneously, Rafferty's team adjusted the flight of the drone, guided the eye in the sky back to the action, and provided an overview of the activity.

The Transit stopped near the Ankara Queen. The BMW followed suit. A crane lifted a net containing boxes from the hold. There was a gentle silent swivel from the crane's platform and the boxes landed on the quayside. Eager hands stepped forward and moved the boxes into the back of the Transit van. Three men emerged from the van, helped to load the vehicle, and then loaded more boxes into the boot of the BMW.

'All units, I have control,' radioed Rafferty. 'Movement on the dock suggests the dealers have been called forward. A white Transit van and a grey BMW are queued at the gangplank of the Ankara Queen. They are being loaded with parcels. All units make ready to respond. Red Alpha One prepare to follow the Transit. Red Alpha Two take the BMW.'

Acknowledgements rattled across the airwaves with National Crime Agency callsigns joining in and arranging to take over from the Red Alpha teams once they had cleared the docks and central Liverpool.

The console burst into life on Rafferty's desk. It was the duo from Faversham Mews extending, 'The Ankara Queen! Excellent! Proceed as planned. Look out for a Russian visit soon. If one or more Russians arrive ensure they are arrested. We are aware they may or may not have diplomatic immunity depending on their status, but we need to identify them first. If diplomatic immunity is claimed, as we expect, we can move to declare them *persona non grata* and have them returned to their country once the politics of the case are determined.'

'What if Moscow is embarrassed at the capture, washes their hands of them, and denies any state involvement?'

'That might happen, Bernard, but we shall have demonstrated our ability long before that hurdle is reached. As a nation, we shall have the last say on the matter. Proceed as directed.'

'Understood,' from Rafferty. 'Do we need to inform senior command in Merseyside Constabulary? Surely you can concoct a form of words for their enlightenment.'

'Not until it is entirely necessary. No!'

On the Ankara Queen, Sam reached one of the gangplanks, leapt from the deck onto the dock, and strolled towards the Misha.

'Get back here!' yelled Jason.

'He's not responding,' remarked Malcolm. 'He's making for the yacht.'

'He's taken his balaclava off,' said Jason. 'Quest is in a world of his own. Look at him. What the hell is he doing?'

Sam reached the Misha with his balaclava in his hand. He wiped his brow with the balaclava.

'Get back on the Ankara Queen,' yelled Banshee. 'Not here! You're not wanted here.'

A pair of binoculars twitched in a high-rise building.

A flick of a switch adjusted the drone in Rafferty's command post.

'He's taken his hat off,' declared Rafferty. 'He's wiped his brow. That's the signal. He's making for the yacht, not the Ankara Queen. What the hell is going on?'

'Misha!' thought Sam. 'It's moored next to the Ankara Queen that's why the Transit and the BMW are here. The walkways almost join because of the proximity of the two vessels. They're linked but the drugs aren't on the Ankara Queen. They're on the Misha. Rafferty's team is going to follow all the vehicles that are called forward to the Ankara Queen. They'll be following the wrong targets. It's the yacht we want. Misha is the target.'

A suitcase hit the ground, was pulled into a safe position again, and was removed from the yacht and taken to Banshee's waiting Audi. It was the same silver Audi that Banshee had used when he followed Sam right at the beginning. It was a hire car. Sam recalled being told by Rafferty that Banshee's Audi was a hire car.

A remote signal from Banshee's key fob opened the car's boot. The first suitcase was loaded into the Audi. One of the men who had accompanied Jake and Banshee from the yacht loaded a second suitcase into the car boot and turned to wait for the third.

'We're on the wrong horse,' thought Sam. 'We've got the wrong ship and it's not even the Transit and the BMW. What a fiasco!'

Jumping onto Misha's deck, Sam waved his hat in the air for all his worth, knew his cover would be blown, and sensed the watchers thought it was all about the Ankara Queen when it wasn't. He waved with his hand high in the air and his balaclava fluttering in the wind as he rotated it.

Sean O'Leary boarded Misha, pointed at Sam, and shouted, 'Jake! Banshee! Hey boys! Look what you got here. Trouble! Trouble, so you have. Big trouble! Let me eat him.'

'The signal,' voiced from a high-rise office block. 'He's given the signal. He's waving his hat like hell.'

'Quest is waving his hat,' muttered Rafferty. 'What's he doing on the yacht?' He manoeuvred the drone controls and said, 'Oh no! It's the yacht. Suitcases! They're putting suitcases into that Audi of Banshees. Quest is telling us we should be geared up for the yacht, not the Ankara Queen.'

On the deck of the Misha, Sam wiped his brow again, wished he had a radio, hoped someone had seen him, and continued waving his balaclava in the air.

'Your hat!' yelled Jason. 'What are you doing with your hat?'

Sam stepped back, refused a reply, and continued to wave his hat frantically.

O'Leary began to make his way towards Sam.

Another crew member from the yacht appeared on the deck carrying a suitcase. He dragged it towards Jake and Banshee.

'Cop!' screamed Jason. 'The son of a bitch is a cop. He's signalling with his hat. I told you so. He's burning us.'

'He is that, so he is,' yelled O'Leary advancing at a fast pace now. 'He's mine!'

Jake pulled a gun from the back of his trouser belt and immediately panned the area looking for the police.

Banshee followed suit yelling, 'Where are they?'

'The bastard is signalling to them,' shouted Jake. 'They'll be watching from somewhere. Take him down!'

'With pleasure,' growled O'Leary.

In the control vehicle, Rafferty radioed, 'All units! Focus on the yacht. The yacht next to the Ankara Queen is the Misha. The drugs are on the Misha. It's in the suitcases. Ignore all those collecting from the Ankara Queen. It's the yacht. The yacht is the target.'

In Crosby, Logan still had his eyes on Malek's house, but he was monitoring the radio network. Seizing the moment, Logan radioed, 'Advise all units at the golf course to move towards the docks. Make haste, close the gap. It's the beginning. Take close order. Now! Move it!'

A dozen vehicles from the NCA fired up and drove from the golf course and made towards Crosby and Liverpool.

Two minutes later, Malek Osman switched off his computer, collected his wallet and mobile phone from the desk, and left home by the front door. He fired his Aston Martin and headed out of his driveway into the main thoroughfare.'

'Logan One has the eyeball. Subject Malek is out of the house and into his wheels. It's the Aston Martin. He's along the promenade route towards Crosby, right at the traffic lights and towards Liverpool. Logan Two report.'

Ten seconds later a voice reported, 'Logan Two has the eyeball. Following with three car cover at four zero miles an hour into Liverpool on the dock road.'

'Got that,' from Rafferty in the control vehicle. 'Osman on the move. Prepare to hit the target when Osman arrives. Keep a sharp look out for our Russian friends. They might be driving on diplomatic plates. More likely to be a hire car. Keep your eyes peeled.'

On the yacht, Sam turned, realised he'd blown the operation to kingdom come, but also knew he had no choice. The team had started following the wrong vehicles from the wrong ship. Now he was beginning to regret it.

Jason landed squarely on the deck of Misha. He rushed Sam and took him to the ground bundling him towards the side of the vessel with Malcolm following behind carrying a handgun and Sean O'Leary keen to get in on the action.

Sam rolled over, kicked out at Jason, and saw Malcolm aim the pistol at him. Launching himself from the ground like a cat, Sam slammed into Malcolm.

The pistol accidentally discharged. A gunshot ran out.

Sam seized the arm that held the gun and shook it trying to loosen the firearm from Malcolm's grip.

Another gunshot rang out.

O'Leary rushed the duo and bundled both men to the ground before dragging Malcolm out of the way and launching a frenzied attack on Sam.

The Irishman was insane. He was only interested in getting at Sam Quest. Everyone else was irrelevant.

Typing away merrily in an office on Regent Road, minutes from the dock, Jenny Higgins heard the gunfire, abandoned the keyboard, and rang 999.

'Emergency! Which service please?'

'Police! Quickly!'

'Merseyside Police! What is your emergency?'

'Gunfire! I can hear gunfire from the docks at Bootle. It's the Panamax docking facility,' gabbled Jenny. 'Someone is firing a gun.'

'Can you see them?'

'No! But I can bloody well hear them. Two shots so far! Sam is going to get killed.'

'Sam? Who is Sam?'

'He's an undercover cop!'

'What? An undercover cop! Are you sure?'

'Well, he's one of yours and he's on the dock where the shooting is. Come quickly!'

'Units are on the way,' from the emergency controller. 'Including an armed response unit. Now, the exact address please.'

Rafferty toyed with the drone coverage, saw the gun in Malcolm's hand, noticed a ginger-haired male wade into the fray like a madman, and remembered he had been instructed by his bosses that the asset was expendable. The important thing was to take out the Russians, and they were nowhere to be seen.

'Do I obey the bosses or try to save Sam?' thought Rafferty. 'Occasionally, he's been the most awkward independent character I have ever recruited. Do I follow the instruction to protect national security, or do I put my weight behind Sam Quest and potentially lose my job?'

Only a few seconds went by as Bernard Rafferty studied the screens in his control vehicle.

'We're blown,' thought Rafferty. 'They're attacking Quest because they've caught him signalling to us. He's done for. He's going to be killed.'

Rafferty flicked the radio network switch and radioed, 'All units! This is Jupiter. I say again, this is Jupiter. I have control. Trigger! Trigger! Trigger! Handguns in use on the Misha yacht next to the Ankara Queen. Prepare to lock down Bootle docks.' The alert message twisted through the air at record speed. Rafferty continued, 'Stand by! Stand by! Stand by!' He watched Jason and O'Leary repeatedly smash Quest in the face before kicking him to the ground. There was a fistfight in progress and Sam Quest knew he was losing when he slithered to the ground out of the game.

It was enough. Rafferty ordered, 'Strike! Strike! Strike!'

From Crosby to Liverpool the Security Service and the National Crime Agency roared into the fray. And a double-manned armed police response unit in a high-speed BMW responded to Jenny's 999 calls. The vehicle spun around in the centre of the road outside the Royal Albert Dock, activated its siren and blue lights, and pelted towards the scene. Other units were attending. It was the first indication of an operation involving an undercover cop in Liverpool that the local police had been made aware of.

Somewhat concussed from the fistfight, Sam rolled over onto his back, opened his eyes, and stared down the barrel of Malcolm's gun.

'Don't shoot him,' shouted Jake. 'No more gunfire. You'll have every cop in Christendom on top of us if you kill a cop. Chuck him in the river. Make it look like an accident. He fell over in the wind. Savvy?'

'Savvy!' acknowledged Malcolm.

'Out of the way,' snarled O'Leary tugging Malcolm to one side. 'Get hold of him.'

Sam tried to move, felt the rigidity of his back holding him down, and closed his eyes again. He knew he was hurting about the head and face and drifted into a black abyss.

Sean O'Leary took hold of Sam's legs. Malcolm grabbed the arms. The two men swung the lifeless body of Sam Quest counting, 'One! Two! Three!' There was a momentous splash when they threw Sam Quest into the Mersey from the yacht.

'He's a gonna,' declared O'Leary. 'Fish bait! He'll never get back from that. He's finished.'

'I could have put a bullet in his head,' voiced Malcolm.

'Too much noise. Enough! Come on!' ordered Jason. 'Let's get those suitcases loaded. You! Sean! Happy now?'

'No! I'd have strung the bastard up if we'd had time,' barked the Irishman.

Jake hit the digits on his mobile and said, 'One by one! Let them through. It's time to collect and deliver!'

Banshee turned to Jake and said, 'You'll be lucky! Quest signalled the cops. Were you deaf to the gunfire? The cops will be here soon.'

'Well, maybe he signalled and maybe he didn't, Banshee. I don't see any cop cars anywhere,' argued Jake. 'And we've got a hundred suitcases to move. Do it!'

Banshee shook his head in disbelief before waving towards the barricade of forklift trucks. That was when he saw Jenny Higgins running towards the dock shouting, 'Where's Sam?'

In the Mersey, Sam sank like a stone next to the anchor of the Ankara Queen.

'The anchor!' he thought. 'If only I could grab the anchor.' He reached out trying to grasp the iron links.

A snow plough appeared on Regent Road as Sam Quest sank towards the bottom of the river. Except it wasn't snowing and the security forces had snaffled the vehicle from the local council depot. The vehicle trundled along the highway bounced over the pavement and accelerated towards the line of forklift trucks.

The plough lowered its blade when a cloud of muck escaped the exhaust pipe at the rear. A line of saloon cars and vans followed the snow plough. There was a scream of shock followed by one of agony when the snowplough hit the first forklift truck and overturned it. Within seconds, the plough's blade had pierced the blockade. The make-shift barricade was down. The road into the docks was fully open. Security forces bundled into the docks with armed officers from the National Crime Agency in the lead vans.

All hell broke loose when the armed response unit from Merseyside police arrived at the scene to be met by an NCA officer who stepped into the road and waved them down.

The armed response unit braked to a halt. The driver lowered his window. The NCA officer stepped forward, spoke, gesticulated, and then jumped into the rear of the vehicle radioing, 'Zulu Zero One is now with the Merseyside police unit. I am the radio link. We're going in.'

Rafferty hit his keyboard, updated the Faversham Mews crew, and slammed his laptop closed.

'Me too,' thought Rafferty. 'I'm going in!'

At the stern of the Misha, only air bubbles from Sam could be seen gurgling to the surface. Down below, Sam was headed for the bottom with a thumping head and a dozen sores. Then his hand caught hold of the anchor and he held tight. He brought his other hand to the anchor and pulled.

'Get out of here!' screamed Jake. 'Banshee! Move it! They've scattered the forklift trucks. The cops are here.'

'Bring it on!' screamed O'Leary picking up a lump of abandoned piping.

Banshee glanced at the approaching snowplough, saw the line of vehicles behind it, and slammed the boot of the Audi down before jumping into the driver's seat.

'Wait for me,' yelled Jason as Malcolm backed towards the Audi whilst pointing the gun towards the approaching security forces.

Jenny reached the dock, shouted, 'Sam!' and then rushed to the quayside to see the Audi driving away. She tripped, fell to her knees, and lost a high-heel shoe when she regained her feet and made for the quayside. There was nothing to see other than air bubbles breaking the surface of the Mersey.

The first police vehicle arrived. Jenny pointed at the Audi and shouted, 'That way! It's them. They killed Sam.'

'Who's first?' yelled O'Leary charging like a mad bull at the police and wielding a long piece of pipe in the process.

Seconds later, the Irishman was stunned by the electrical current fired from a taser by an officer who meant business. Sean O'Leary crashed to the ground, shook, trembled, and surrendered his body to the arresting officers.

The snowplough came to a standstill. Two NCA cars hurtled through in pursuit of the Audi. Others engaged with the drivers of the forklift trucks. And on Regency Road, a score of security force personnel challenged the waiting dealers and began searching vehicles and making arrests for conspiracy and a variety of criminal offences.

Elsewhere, Operation Denial personnel, backed up by the NCA team from the golf course, closed the roads. Bootle was soon in lockdown.

Malek Osman's Aston Martin came to a stop at a red traffic light. Unaware of what had occurred, Osman let go of the steering wheel and held his hands up when Logan's team slid in front of the Aston Martin and rushed the car.

There was a shower of glass when the driver's window caved in, and officers reached inside to overpower their target.

Moments later, Malek Osman was in custody.

At the dock, Jenny shouted, 'Sam!'

She couldn't find him, couldn't see him, but then turned around and saw the air bubbles dwindling in ferocity from the surface of the Mersey. The frequency of the air bubbles was growing less visible. The source was weakening. What source?

Then she realised that the source was probably someone exhaling oxygen from their lungs. Removing her remaining high-heel shoe, Jenny threw her jacket onto the ground and dived into the Mersey.

Rafferty arrived with a team of officers. They stepped onto the yacht and swarmed the deck securing the crew and preventing the removal of any of the suitcases from the hold.

Underwater, Sam was holding the bottom of the chain that led to the anchorage trying to make sure he didn't submerge any further. It was murky in places and pitch black in others, but he became aware of a body diving towards him.

Jenny's arms thrashed their way through the water, grasped the weakened Sam around his chest, and pulled him beneath the keel and then out into the open water.

Almost out of breath, Sam clung to his saviour. He knew not who and felt his whole body being pulled to the surface by powerful arms.

They broke the surface. Sam took a huge breath, looked to find that Jenny had saved him, and then shook his head free when the same woman said, 'I told you we should go for a swim one day. Come on! Head for the rope ladder.'

Guiding him to the dock wall, Sam managed a few strokes, clung to the ladder, and then said, 'You told me you could swim, not dive! It's a good job you came. I was lost down there.'

'And you'll be lost down there again,' shouted Malcolm from above. Stood on the dock, an angry Malcolm pointed his gun towards Sam who was halfway up the rope ladder, and shouted, 'You bastard cop! We had it all until you arrived.'

Malcolm's fingers curled around the trigger.

A shot rang out.

Malcolm twitched, faltered, dropped the gun, and fell backwards onto the dockside.

Rafferty jumped from the deck of Misha, his handgun still outstretched before him, its muzzle hot from firing the bullet that had hit Malcolm and saved the life of Sam Quest.

Climbing the ladder to the quayside, Sam struggled to his feet to see Rafferty kneeling beside Malcolm, kicking the enemy's gun away from his reach, and then feeling for a pulse.

Malcolm had been shot dead by Rafferty.

'Twice in one day,' remarked Sam. 'I live this long and have my life saved twice in one day.'

'Give me a hand,' ventured Jenny.

Sam pulled her onto firm ground and hugged her. They were both wet, cold, and shaking.

Rafferty radioed for medical assistance and moments later a car arrived with blankets and a flask of hot tea.

There was more gunfire from the traffic lights where the road from the docks met the thoroughfare. Bootle docks had turned into a war zone with the area locked down, roads closed by NCA officers, surveillance officers with their vehicles, and armed officers engaging the enemy where necessary. The highway was strewn with the wreckage of vehicles that had tried to escape and failed.

Jake, Jason and Banshee were forced to a standstill by Logan's surveillance team who blocked the road and a squad from the National Crime Agency who challenged them.

All three men tried to escape, jumped from the Audi, and ran through the posse of men firing at will. One officer took a bullet in the shoulder before Logan dropped to one knee, fired in quick succession, and shot all three of the gang.

One of the NCA supervisors glanced at Logan in disbelief. He was mesmerised by Logan's bravery and accuracy.

Logan radioed, 'Contact! We have a man down plus three targets down. Ambulances and paramedics required Regent Road.' He holstered his weapon as if it were an everyday occurrence that he had just taken part in.

Blood and guts spread across the streets as all four men lived but did not die.

Ambulances attended and, under armed guard, wounded prisoners were escorted to the Royal Liverpool University Hospital

Emergency Department. In the hours that followed, NCA officers would attend, make formal arrests of the three detainees, and wait for their discharge in the days to come. The wounded officer would recover without further mishap.

A welcome silence descended on the streets when the gang were arrested and the dealers were searched, questioned, and arrested on suspicion of conspiring with others to supply controlled drugs. Some were found to be wanted on warrant for other criminal offences whilst others tried to evade arrest by offering false names and addresses.

In short, the police had to adhere to the legal definition of 'conspiracy to supply class A drugs'. Such an offence occurs when two or more people agree together to sell or supply class A drugs, such as cocaine or heroin. Prosecutions would follow where the police and NCA could prove that someone had driven a vehicle to collect a shipment of cocaine on behalf of another who was aware of the collection and the planned distribution. It is illegal to be involved in managing the delivery of cocaine. Charges would also follow where it could be proved that someone had been involved in planning the crime. This offence involved those who might not have taken part in the crime but had merely planned that the crime would take place. Others who had participated in the deal, including being a courier, financial manager, look-out, go-between, agent, link in the supply chain or involved in the division of bulk drugs, would also feel the weight of the law upon them. Other roles included being involved in the reduction of the purity, weighing and packaging or dividing drugs into smaller deals or advertising. There was no need to prove possession of the drugs if any of the above actions could be proved. Adding surveillance notes to telephone calls to meetings between the parties concerned and being in the location of the docks when an importation had occurred – and for which there was no reason for them to be lined up waiting to collect drugs – all added to the evidential elements of the cases that were to be dealt with in the coming months.

Rafferty was present when National Crime Agency officers searched the Misha, arrested the crew, and recovered three tons of cocaine with a street value of two hundred and forty million pounds. The drugs were packed in one hundred and twelve suitcases and that complimented the number of dealers arrested for being concerned with the supply of the drugs. It was the biggest-ever drug haul in the United Kingdom. Each suitcase contained twenty-five kilos of cocaine.

When the arrests went down in Bootle, officers across the UK carried out raids from Cumbria to Skelmersdale and throughout the Midlands. Both Turnbull and Caleb Cartwright were arrested in Skelmersdale and Carlisle respectively and the gradual process of breaking up their networks began. The enquiry would take many months to complete.

Rafferty's mobile sounded. It was Faversham Mews.

'We're listening and watching. How many Russians have been traced and who are they, Rafferty?'

'None!'

'Operation Denial is a successful failure by the sound of it. Were you so busy securing the drugs that you forgot to look out for the Russians?'

'That is not the case,' replied Rafferty.

'It seems to be from where we sit, Rafferty. We should have replaced you when we assessed that your fatigue might lead to incompetence.'

'Excuse me, gentlemen,' voiced Rafferty. 'I can't talk right now. I still have work to do. One or two things to clear up before the end of the day.' Rafferty closed the call and pocketed his mobile muttering to himself, 'Am I supervised by people who are themselves incompetent?'

Sam's arm curled around Jenny's shoulder when Rafferty approached him and said, 'Sorry to interrupt, Quest, I presume the young lady is the one I was wrong about?'

'That's right. Jenny, this is Rafferty: the man I report to.'

Rafferty nodded and smiled at Jenny before saying to Sam, 'Quest! We have work to do. I think you know what is outstanding. Are you up for this? Well enough to continue or would you rather throw the towel in now and rest easy? You've done your bit.'

Turning his head, Sam stared into Jenny's blue eyes, felt the softness of her skin, and touched the locks of her golden hair. She was gradually drying out from the unexpected swim and her temperature was returning to its normal level.

Jenny turned to Rafferty and said, 'Sam would like to help you finish the job, Mr Rafferty. Wouldn't you, Sam?'

'We've not known each other that long,' replied Sam. 'But you know me too well already.'

'Maybe we'll get that swim in later,' smiled Jenny. 'When we've more time and less to do.'

'Maybe a kayak too.'

'Maybe!'

'I don't have to go, Jenny. I've done my time.'

'No, you haven't. You told me you were a cop. Now go and do what cops do before they get a day off.'

Sam squeezed Jenny's hand and said to Rafferty, 'You heard the lady. Let's go.'

In the telephone intercept department of the Security Service in London, a light flashed on Becca's console causing her to immediately listen to the live conversation whilst confirming the automatic recording thereof. She made a note and waited until the call had ended before shouting, 'Janice! Operation Europa! One of the subjects has just gone off the radar. The case officer needs to know now. Check the recipient's number out. That's a jackpot call.'

'Let me see,' replied Becca's supervisor.

Examining the call details, Janice stated, 'All agreed! Priority One. Send to Jupiter right away and insist upon an acknowledgement. That call has just blown the puzzle into a thousand pieces. Execute!'

Becca chuckled, worked her keyboard, and replied, 'Execute! Execute! Execute! Don't I know it? What will happen next?'

~

Chapter Fifteen

~

A Short time later
Hope Quarter
Liverpool

'Jupiter to Red Alpha Six Eyeball, status update.'

'Eyeball Red Alpha Six! The team has the premises surrounded. We have an audio-visual on the subject who is in his apartment at the target address in Hope Quarter. The audio indicates he's listening to local radio coverage. He will be aware of the operation taking place at Bootle docks. The visual shows the target packing a suitcase in a hurry. All exits covered, Jupiter over.'

'Wheels?' probed Rafferty.

'Incapacitated by Red Alpha Six Charlie at the rear of premises where Bravo and Delta are currently situated.'

'I am attending,' from Rafferty. 'Is the subject armed?'

'Not known! No visible sign of a firearm in possession of the subject. He's presently wearing a pair of dark blue denim jeans and a white vest. Looks like he's packing before he gets fully dressed.'

'Understood!'

'Logan! Permission?' across the network.

'Go ahead, Logan.'

'Logan to Jupiter, I'm travelling with armed support to your location. E.T.A. ten minutes.'

'I have that,' replied Rafferty.

'Jupiter!' from Eyeball, Red Alpha Six. 'Your target seems to be ready to fly off somewhere. Visual reveals he has pocketed one passport in the inside pocket of his jacket which he has hung over the back of a chair. The other two passports are in the suitcase. Three in total suggests false passports, false identity, other documents not yet seen.'

'Can you see what colour the passports are?'

'One is dark blue! UK issue! Not sure about the other two. Eyeball over.'

'Understood! Jupiter to stand by.'

Rafferty holstered the encrypted radio and glided his car through a set of traffic lights into the city centre.

'How long?' queried Sam.

'Five minutes!' replied Rafferty. 'Doyle lives close to the Royal Liverpool University Hospital. You know what you've been doing of late, Quest, and we are very grateful. To fill you in on other elements of the operation is to tell you that we've been listening to Doyle's phone conversations as well as watching his apartment since he began to figure prominently in the investigation. I wondered if he might have a Russian visitor or two but that has proved not to be the case.'

'And he hasn't moved from the apartment since Operation Denial began?' queried Sam.

'Just to a public phone box earlier this morning. The Red Alpha Six team fitted all the public phone boxes with intercept devices in a two-mile area of his address and got lucky. Another one hundred yards diameter and they would have missed out. Anyways, Sam, Doyle rang a non-geographic smart number earlier today.'

'Interesting,' replied Sam. 'What the hell does that mean?'

'He rang a smart number,' explained Rafferty. 'That means he used a public phone box to contact an individual who has a device that allows him to answer instantly wherever they are on the globe. It's a whole new ball game, Quest, and one we've been anxious to join since the beginning. Such numbers are used by our military to turn out individuals at a moment's notice when a crisis happens. Doyle called someone who can route that call to the device of their choice. It might be a desk phone, a mobile handset, or a computer base. It even latches onto voicemail wherever they are and often goes

- 217 -

through an administrator's procedure wherein the call is encrypted and forwarded to anywhere in the world. We don't know what Doyle said but he made an encrypted call to a non-UK military unit. Pound to a penny says he spoke to his Russian contact today.'

'Wow!' said Sam. 'He's on the run and he's talking his controller.'

'He's packing to go,' declared Rafferty. 'What do you think, Quest? Is he running because he thinks Osman, Jake and the boys will shop him to the first detective that shows up? Or is he running because he's not sure of what is happening and wants to make a break to be on the safe side?'

'With three passports, one of which might be kosher and the other two false?' queried Sam. 'Maybe all three are duds, I don't know. I'd guess he's worked out that they've dropped him right in it with the police. Or if they haven't now, they soon will do to save their skins. People like Jake and company will do anything to reduce their prison sentence and if that means shopping their best friend, they won't hesitate. Doyle might be running scared. Either way, if he gets out of town, he can lie low and find out what has happened. It's an interesting one, Rafferty. If you are the main clown in the circus, you're usually on show to everyone but if you're a ringmaster like Doyle, who doesn't want his hands dirty, then you keep out of the way when the job goes down. That call he made suggests he has a guardian angel who might choose to save him from the legal onslaught heading his way.'

'So you can run and hide when it all goes wrong,' replied Rafferty. 'That hasn't worked for him today. Our problem is the call wasn't made to either the Russian Embassy or the travel agent in Piccadilly. It hit an unknown number somewhere. It looks like we may have another Russian in play, or I've worked it out all wrong.'

'Time will tell, Rafferty. But we're running out of time if he's one step ahead of us?'

'Come on,' remarked Rafferty. 'We're here. Let's do the approach. Logan won't be far behind us.'

'We need to keep some form of normality whilst keeping an eye on the other side of the coin,' remarked Doyle.

'Which is?'

'Russian!' replied Sam.

Rafferty pulled into a car park near a block of flats, parked the car, and radioed, 'Jupiter to Eyeball, Jupiter plus Europa are both on the plot. Status?'

'No change! Repeat no change! Progress!'

'I have that,' replied Rafferty.

The two men entered the building and took a lift to the second floor where Rafferty radioed, 'Jupiter at the front door. Status!'

'He's coming towards you.'

'Any firearm?'

'None! Progress!'

The door opened and Rafferty pushed his way inside with one hand whilst thrusting an identity card into Doyle's face with the other.

'We are officers from the Security Service. You are Brian Doyle, a detective sergeant in Merseyside Constabulary and we need to speak with you, Mr Doyle.'

Doyle stepped back, nearly fell back with the weight of Rafferty's hand, and then stepped away towards the table saying, 'MI5? What do you want?'

'You know what we want, Mr Doyle. We've been all over you and your drug-dealing gang for many weeks now.'

'Don't know what you're talking about,' offered Doyle weakly as he tried to step around the two men and assert his presence.

'Allow me to introduce myself,' said Sam who barred his way. 'I'm Sam Quest. The man you thought might be an undercover cop. You know who I am and where I'm from. I'm the thorn in your side from Carlisle that you just had to find out about. Guess what? You were right all along. Your problem is that you've just never seen me before, have you?'

'Never heard of you!'

'Except that time when you arranged for me to deliver two kilos of cocaine to an address in Bolton and then tried to have me arrested en route.'

Doyle eyed the two men, glanced at the door, and took hold of the suitcase handle.

'You won't make the ground floor, never mind the car park,' remarked Rafferty as he casually laid his hand on top of Doyle's.

'Not in socks, jeans and a vest,' teased Sam. 'You'll catch your death out there, one way or another.'

Doyle paused, relented, and let go of the suitcase.

'You are surrounded, Doyle,' declared Rafferty. 'Your car has been immobilised. You're going nowhere. Sit down and listen to what I have to say.'

'Can I finish dressing?' voiced Doyle.

'Of course,' replied Rafferty. 'Nice and easy. Keep your hands in view at all times.'

Opening a wardrobe with an index finger, Doyle said, 'How am I doing so far?'

'Never mind the theatricals, Mr Doyle. Get dressed.'

Doyle selected a shirt saying, 'I'm listening.'

'We have enough evidence to charge you with conspiracy to import Class A drugs, Doyle,' explained Sam.

'Is that all?' replied the Merseyside officer who grew in confidence as he buttoned his shirt and added, 'I'm famous in Liverpool as a thief-taker. Every barrister in the city and beyond knows me, and I know them. I know how the legal system works inside out. You've just pulled the wrong man.'

'The wrong man! How is that?'

'By the time I've convinced the jury that I was forced into helping the gang on the docks, I'll walk free. I'm sure you guys have an interesting story, but I've played cop all my life. I know how to walk away from stuff like that. I'm one cop frightened by an intimidating gang of thugs from the docks. I was scared stiff of them. Frightened to the core, so I was. I had no choice but to follow their orders or fear the consequences. I just need to prove an element of doubt. Now if that's all you've got then I suggest you walk away while I chuckle at your incompetence and marvel at my wisdom. No one takes me down. Not even M15.'

Rafferty produced a handheld recorder, pressed a button, and replayed the conversation they had just had.

Doyle's jaw dropped.

Allowing time for the message to sink in, Rafferty continued, 'You're listening to one of many recordings we've made of you talking to Malek Osman, Jake, Banshee and the rest of them. I have no element of doubt about that. I don't think you've quite assessed how much we know about your involvement. Mr Doyle,' remarked Rafferty. 'You're not used to playing second fiddle. Well, today we're taking your fiddle away because your time is up. What do you think about prisons? Ever been in a prison cell?'

Looking into space, Doyle did not reply.

'If you don't listen to us, Doyle,' voiced Sam. 'We'll go one better and charge you with conspiracy to murder.'

'Murder!' from a shocked voice. 'What murder?'

'The importation of drugs on the scale planned amounts to a plot to destroy people, Doyle. People are likely to die earlier than normal because of drug addiction. We can throw the book at you,' revealed Rafferty. 'Oh! Did I mention the Russian connection? Not forgetting the travel agent in Piccadilly, and a list of drug dealers you've put together that will distribute the drugs nationwide for the Russians? Did you know Malek Osman kept the list in a briefcase in his safe? A notebook in which you are repeatedly named as the person who has recruited the dealer into the nationwide network you

- 221 -

have put together. Your plan is to make lots of money. The Russian plan is to make more people drug addicts. Put the two together and you are conspirators involved in the same circumstances. Some will die and you know it. Conspiracy is obvious, even you know that.'

Doyle finished buttoning his shirt, tightened his trouser belt, and delved into the wardrobe saying, 'Shoes!'

'Take your time. You're going to have all the time in the world.'

Kneeling for his shoes, Doyle quickly diverted his hands and reached for his ankle holster. He snatched a Ruger handgun before spinning around to face the two investigators.

'Back away!' growled Doyle.

Both Rafferty and Sam held up their hands and stepped back as Doyle tried to squeeze his foot into a slip-on shoe.

'The gun is pointless,' suggested Rafferty. 'You're surrounded.'

'I haven't started running yet and you need to catch me.'

'You won't get far, Doyle. I can assure you of that.'

Doyle reached for the other shoe, grabbed it, lost his balance as he tried to put it on, and felt the full force of Sam's body when the undercover detective launched himself at the Merseyside cop.

The Ruger discharged. A shot was fired.

Sam wrenched the gun from Doyle's grip, elbowed him in the face, and then placed him on the ground ordering, 'Hands on the head! Now!'

'Shots fired!' rattled across the radio net from the Red Alpha team with Logan adding, 'At the scene. Making contact!'

Composed, Rafferty radioed, 'Hold positions! Target disarmed!'

As calm descended on the Hope Quarter apartment, Sam added, 'You can add half a dozen more charges regarding the possession and use of the Ruger if you want, Doyle. I'm sure your barrister friends in the city will advise you on the possible charges that can be laid against you. Up to you!'

Fidgeting, Doyle glanced around as if he were looking for another way out, but he couldn't find a route.

Sam manhandled Doyle so that he had his back to the wall and his hands on his head before saying, 'There's only one way out.'

Head down, Doyle remarked, 'A way out? Do you mean a deal of some kind? How?'

'How, indeed?' replied Rafferty rummaging through the suitcase until he found two passports. He spread them out on the table before reaching into Doyle's jacket hanging on a chair. Finding the third passport, he read the names out. 'Brian Doyle! Eamonn Murphy! Dmitri Ivanovich Kuznetsov!'

'A mouthful!' replied Sam.

'One British, one Irish, and one Russian,' remarked Rafferty. 'Which one are you, Mr Doyle?'

'The British one, of course.'

'Really?' replied Rafferty leafing through the pages of the Russian document. 'To obtain a Russian passport, you must prove to the Russian authorities that you have lived in Russia for at least five years and have a permanent residency there. What is your father's name.'

'I was born in Liverpool,' argued Doyle. 'My father died years ago. He was called Billy. We lived in Kirkby then.'

'Interesting,' nodded Rafferty. 'Did you know that all Russians have three names? Males always have the same middle name as their fathers. If you were born in Russia then, according to your passport, your father was called Ivan.'

'As I said, I wasn't born in Russia. I was born in Liverpool.'

'That means you are lying, and it was given to you by the Russians, or you were born in Russia.'

'I'm not lying.'

'Quest!' gestured Rafferty. 'Use his Ruger. Make it look like he's committed suicide. One shot only in the spy's head.'

Sam took hold of the Ruger and knelt beside Doyle who was now sweating with his heartbeat racing and his eyes dancing in his head as he tried to figure a way out of his dilemma.

'I'm not a spy,' yelled a fever-pitch Doyle.

'Enough here to put you away for spying though,' smiled Sam moving the gun closer to Doyle's head. 'You threatened us with a firearm and tried to make a run for it. It's complicated, but I'll happily pull the trigger and terminate someone who had no scruples when plotting my arrest and incarceration. If I had been killed that day, you wouldn't have batted an eyelid, Doyle. You'd have danced back to Liverpool. Now then, do you want this in the temple or through the throat?'

'No! No! I've done wrong but I'm not a spy, for God's sake!'

'The passports are only a small part of it,' remarked Rafferty. 'We'll sort them out at the laboratory later. You've been working with the Russians, Doyle. It's as simple as that so don't try to hide it. The travel agent in Piccadilly is called Novikov. It means newcomer in English. You were a newcomer to Novikov once, but that was over a year ago, wasn't it? You became a regular, Doyle. A cop turned spy for the Russians. But don't you worry, Mr Quest here will end it quickly for you now.'

'No! No! You've got it wrong! The Russians just paid me to set it all up. I'm not a spy. Don't kill me! I just made them a huge network. That's all!'

'Sorry! Don't believe you!'

The Ruger brushed Doyle's skin.

'How can I prove I'm not a spy? What do you want?'

'The names of all the Russians you have been talking to about this operation from the beginning,' ordered Sam. 'Who controls you? Who pays you? Where does the money come from? How does the money arrive in England? Which bank is used? The name of the Russian who got you into this? You have ten seconds, Doyle. I'm tired you see, Doyle. Very tired! Ten seconds! Nine! Eight!'

'I don't know any of the names. Just the faces. I met a different face every time.'

'What made you go to the travel agent in the first place?' probed Rafferty.

'No one controlled me. I went when they said, met who they said where they said, gave them a copy of the list of dealers, took the money, and that was it.'

'Who persuaded you to go to the travel agent?'

'I can't remember.'

'What was his name?'

'No name! No! There was no name!'

'Are you telling us this global masterpiece of a plan was all your idea?'

'No! Never me! Not me!'

Rafferty noticed an air of nervousness invade Doyle's voice and persisted with, 'Then who? Where did the idea come from?'

'I can't remember.'

'The name, Doyle. 'All the names! Seven! Six! Five!'

'I told you! I have no names to give you, just faces to remember.'

Rafferty and Sam glanced at each other.

'Stop counting my life down! I'm no use to you dead,' continued Doyle. 'What do I get in return?'

'A reduced prison sentence,' replied Sam withdrawing the Ruger to a safer position. 'I can guarantee that. Maybe! Maybe not! It depends entirely on what you give us. Nothing given by you equals nothing given by us. Understand?'

Almost panic-stricken now, Doyle replied, 'I can't tell you everything. I don't know it all. It's everything to do with that travel agent in Piccadilly.'

Relaxing for a moment, Rafferty flapped the Russian passport in front of Doyle's eyes and said, 'Why do you have a Russian passport?'

There was no reply from Doyle.

'I'll tell you why. It's so that you can get into Russia if you flee this country, isn't it? Ireland first, is it? Or straight out of Heathrow to Moscow? There's a travel connection, isn't there, Doyle?' proposed Rafferty.

'I can't tell you. They'll kill me.'

'Probably! You've got a better chance here with us,' proposed Sam intervening. 'They'll kill you, but we might give you a reduced sentence. Easy choice, Doyle. Live or die!'

Doyle's mind wandered to the edge. He paused, realised the danger he was in, and replied, 'I have to be at Carlisle airport this evening.'

'Why?'

'To meet my contact.'

'The name?' probed Rafferty. 'I want the name.'

Almost weeping, mentally defeated, Doyle whispered, 'Yurov!'

'Yurov?'

'Yes! That's the name. He calls himself Yurov. Yurov something. I don't know his full name.'

'Where did you meet him?' probed Rafferty.

'Here in Liverpool. He bumped into me outside my apartment. He made me an offer.'

'That you couldn't refuse?'

'They'd been watching me for I don't know how long, knew all about me, knew I had a good handle on the drugs world, the works! They had me sewn up so tight that they threatened to expose me as a corrupt cop.'

'They'd be right about that,' remarked Sam. 'I'll guess they knew you had used your position to force some of your prisoners to pay you to look the other way when they were caught drug dealing? You were running what I would call a mini-protection racket on the side, weren't you, Doyle? Work for me and I'll guarantee you will be untouchable on my patch. Is that it? Is that how it worked and how they caught you?'

Doyle threw an idle defeated look at Sam who continued, 'I thought so. You said earlier that you knew every barrister on the block and how to get out of the kind of situation we're talking about. What was the tipping point that made you comply with their approach?'

'They gave me a wedge of cash to go over to their side.'

'And in so doing confirmed you were corrupt. You could have refused, Doyle.'

'I took the money.'

'How much was the first payment?' queried Sam.

'Twenty-five grand! I was greedy and I needed it. I had to go to the travel agent to collect it. I regret it now.'

'Only because you've been caught.'

'Okay! Okay! There's no need to rub it in.'

'Sorry!' replied Sam. 'I say it like it is. I'm not famous for diplomacy. Tell me how you make contact with Yurov, Doyle.'

'He rings me. Yurov gives me a phone number for next time, but the number always changes. When he wants me, he rings me.'

'What does he say?'

'He fixes a meeting. I go and see him.'

'Face to face?' challenged Sam.

'Yes! I hand over the updated list and get paid.'

'Thousands of pounds? How much?'

Doyle reluctantly nodded in agreement and continued, 'Anything between five and fifty grand! It depended on how long the list was, the population area, and how well he thinks I'd done. They used money as an incentive to drive me. The more I produced; the more they paid me.'

'Bit like being means tested then?'

'I suppose you could say that. Sometimes I had to go to the travel agent to collect the money. I think Yurov didn't always have enough cash with him and never knew what I had.'

'Did you take a holdall to carry the money away in?'

'Yes! How did you know that?'

'Just a guess,' lied Sam recollecting a briefing that had originated from Faversham Mews following one of the first CCTV sightings of Doyle at Novikov. 'It's obvious really. Tell me, did they ever check the lists you gave them?'

'Not that I'm aware of. I can't answer that because I don't know. But like I said before, they knew me inside out. I never tried to double-cross them. Wouldn't dare. He's a mean-looking critter with an evil eye that kind of puts you in your place within a second or two, and that's without him saying a word.'

'Hardman?'

'Yes! Whenever I met Yurov I always got the impression that he was not alone. I presumed there was someone else with him. What we call in the cops a 'back up'. He wore a pistol in a shoulder holster. Never worried him if his coat flapped open and the gun came into view.'

'Do you remember anything else about those meetings?'

'He had a driver. Must have had a driver when I think about it. We met on the docks, at a supermarket car park, down an alley beside a café. He was a walking map. Knew Liverpool as well as me, maybe even better.'

'A professional!' remarked Sam. 'A foreigner of note unless he was born here of a Russian family. Do you know?'

'Never mentioned,' replied Doyle.

'The other thing that occurs to me is that money seems to be no problem to your newfound friends. Are any electronic transfers involved? Their bank to yours, for example?'

'None at all. It was always cash! Always used notes! And nearly always from the money he had with him.'

'When did you last contact him?' questioned Rafferty.

'I rang him today from a public phone box. It's the only way I contact him; the way I tell him that I have another list ready. This morning I told Yurov it had all gone pear-shaped. He wants me out of the country pronto. Yurov told me he wanted to spirit me away before the police got their hands on me. He told me the police would make me spill the beans. I agreed with him. I'm a detective, for God's sake. That's exactly what the cops would do.'

Rafferty and Sam exchanged worried glances before Rafferty said, 'Did he mention us: MI5, 6, British Intelligence, anything like that?'

'No! Just the police.'

Breathing an almost audible sigh of relief, Rafferty accepted Doyle's answer in the fervent hope that the Russians knew nothing of how he, Quest, and his commanders at Faversham Mews, had penetrated their operation. Rafferty continued, 'Did he use the words, 'Spill the beans' or were they your words?'

'His words! Why?'

'Your Russian friend has an advanced understanding of the English language if he uses a phrase like that. It shows he understands the lingo, the slang, and possibly the culture of the English people.'

'Never thought of it like that,' replied Doyle.

'Why would you?' remarked Rafferty. 'It occurs to me that Yurov has you worked out as a man who would do a deal with us to get a reduced sentence. Yurov isn't wrong. That's the way you are. He reads you like a man who reads a book that he can't let go of until the final page is turned. I think he may be something of a professional.'

'Yeah! I suppose so. But we're talking about a deal now, aren't we?'

'Did you ever meet Yurov in the Piccadilly travel agents?' probed Rafferty.

'No! Never! I went there to collect my cash and pass over the bigger lists. I met the manager or his deputy.'

'What were their names?'

'I don't know. I never asked. They never told me, but they knew who I was as soon as I walked in and gave them my name. They read the list, nodded, opened the safe, counted out the money and that was it. No coffee, not even a handshake. In and out without so much as a smile.'

'Not even a vodka?' posed Sam.

'It was just a bank as far as I was concerned,' replied Doyle. 'I'll guess someone in the system told them about me. Presumably Yurov! I never got orders, questions, or anything there. It was a money collection point, as simple as that.'

'Has it ever occurred to you that Yurov and his Russian mates might be coming for you? If they don't want you talking to us, they'll terminate you.'

'They wouldn't! They couldn't. He's in Dublin. That's what he told me.'

'They might be coming to rescue you, but I doubt it,' intervened Sam. 'They've no reason to protect you once the operation is finished and it is. Their dream of turning the country into a land full of drug-addicted zombies failed. It failed because you failed them. With so much police activity in Liverpool, Yurov will probably want you out of the country or dead. They don't need you anymore.'

There was no reply from Doyle.

'Now then, Carlisle airport! Tell us what the arrangements are.'

Doyle dropped his head and studied his feet for a moment. He was lost in the complexity of a mind used to continually winning, mastering the rules of the game, and then suddenly ripped apart by the law enforcement intruders who were now wrecking his mindset as no other had ever done before. 'I've to meet him tonight at Carlisle airport,' remarked Doyle. 'Then we go to Dublin for a flight to Amsterdam and then to Moscow or somewhere they've sorted out for me.'

'Is that so? Why?'

'They want me out of the country. He said it was an emergency extraction. They've promised me a new life somewhere else. I've to be at the airport to get a flight to Dublin. It's a private flight. I just turn up and board the plane. I've got to meet them in the café in the departures lounge. I think they'll refuel the plane before we take off.'

'That's what he told you?'

'More or less! Yeah!'

'It's more likely that you'll be shot and dumped in the Irish Sea on your way back to Dublin, Doyle,' suggested Rafferty. 'The Russian operation is dead in the water, and so might you be. All the drugs have been recovered and scores of dealers arrested. The Russians have no further use for you. You failed them. They want you out of the way permanently. You're a walking talking danger to them at this moment in time.'

'And Yurov will probably pull the trigger,' added Sam.

'Carlisle Airport?' queried Rafferty. 'When?'

Doyle checked the time and replied, 'Three hours from now!'

'Good! Get your shoes on! Let's go and meet Yurov.'

~

Chapter Sixteen

~

Continuous, That night
Carlisle Airport
Cumbria

They were out of the apartment in Hope Quarter and into a blacked-out minibus arranged by the Red Alpha team and driven by Logan. With a plain saloon car in front and one at the rear, Logan drove the vehicle with an ankle holster carrying one weapon, a shoulder harness carrying another weapon, a pistol in a trouser holster, and a semi-automatic beneath the driver's seat for rapid deployment. And he wasn't the only armed escort since Rafferty was worried that the Russians might mount an attack on Doyle if they knew of his whereabouts.

'One thing was for sure,' thought Rafferty. 'The Russians wanted Doyle dead. The corrupt cop had served his purpose. To allow him to live jeopardised the political stability that Russia sought to enjoy in the global arena. The Russians might not be the most popular country in the western world, but they always sought to maintain a certain level of diplomacy that allowed them access to others. Allowing Doyle freedom, and the operation he alone could prove to the rest of the world, was tantamount to shooting themselves in the foot. The Russians would do anything to keep that mouth closed to provide themselves with a coherent strategy that was reluctantly acceptable on the global stage. Many in the west despised Russia. But many in the east relied upon Russia for oodles of support. It's a historic feature of Russian geopolitics, and the culture derived therefrom, that they never allowed themselves to fall into a bear pit where the whole world – east and west – disowned them.'

It was a world of politics that Rafferty understood and accepted. And the reason why he updated his managers at Faversham Mews as they travelled north on the M6 motorway. With that out of the way, Rafferty rang his office to set in motion a range of enquiries to be undertaken as a matter of urgency.

In the rear of the vehicle, Sam broke into conversation with Doyle asking, 'Thinking back to the start of all this, what makes you think the Russians picked you and not someone else?'

'I suppose it was because I was the greediest,' replied Doyle.

'Was it just greed that drove you to it or was there something else going on that you haven't told us about? You said they threatened you. What did you mean by that?'

'I let it slip that I could do with the money,' explained Doyle. 'Who wouldn't these days? It's ten years since we had a proper pay rise and things are tough for most of us. They transformed me from a low paid struggling middle-class public servant into a nigh-on millionaire in the space of a year. From counting the pennies to pay the gas bill to buying shares in energy companies and counting the profits that make me even richer. That's how my life changed.'

'I'd say that all the money you've made will be seized under the Proceeds of Crime Act. Ever thought of that?'

'No! But if the money goes it'll only be because I told you. I'll be broke again. No doubt! Still, I won't need any money in prison.'

'What about the threats?'

'After a while, I got a lot wiser when I realised there was just me involved in the operation and if it ever went wrong, I would be the one carrying the can. I tried to back out, told them I would return the money, and tried to walk away.'

'And it didn't work?'

'No! They played a two-horse game.'

'How do you mean?'

'Firstly, they told me they would disfigure me, then kill me, then throw me in the Mersey. Then they told me they would pay me more and set me up with a new life wherever I wanted. Your choice, they said. They even gave me a travel brochure one day when I was at the Novikov travel agents in Piccadilly. God, I was a fool. I've destroyed my life rather than made it better. I've nothing to look forward to anymore?'

'Except living,' said Sam. 'Did Yurov give you the brochure?"

'No! One of the managers gave me it.'

'What was his name?'

'No idea!'

'Have you still got the brochure?'

'It's in the drawer over there,' pointed Doyle. 'Why do you ask?'

'Forensic examination!' replied Sam. 'DNA, fingerprints, smudges, and fibres! I'm not an expert but I know people who are. They might be able to identify who gave you the brochure following a scientific examination of the document.'

'Which country did you pick?' added Rafferty as Sam seized the travel brochure.

'I didn't pick anywhere,' replied Doyle. 'The man told me they would select it along with a new identity. Probably Russian but I'm hoping for a Spanish passport and some sunshine.'

'I wouldn't count on it.'

Rafferty's mobile sounded and he answered it.

'And not once did you stop to think that what you were doing had the likelihood to change the face of our country?' continued Sam.

'Not really! I never gave it a thought, to be honest,' replied Doyle. 'Why do you ask?'

'Just thinking of what a judge might ask you if we ever went down the path of a reduced sentence for you in return for helping us to expose the wickedness of the Russian Intelligence Service. That's all.'

'How did I do?'

'Crap!' stated Sam. 'One fat zero out of a possible one hundred. I'd sling you in the cells and throw the key away but then I'm not a judge.'

'Yurov Bogdanovich Dimochka!' declared Rafferty suddenly from his seat close by. Closing his phone, he remarked, 'That's the man who took off from Dublin in a private four-seater plane. On take-off, he squawked, 'Cessna Skyhawk 0254'.

'Squawked?' queried Sam.

'That's his transponder code,' explained Rafferty. 'The pilot has to enter his squawk code into the transponder to speak to flight control. We've got him on flight operations and we're monitoring his progress. Looks like he's headed for the northwest of England.'

'Should be Carlisle.'

'He's filed flight plans for Carlisle airport and has one passenger. Flight arrival is as you said, and the purpose of the flight is leisure.'

'Any history?' queried Sam.

'None!'

'But there are two of them.'

'Correct! One to fly, one to do the business.'

'Probably both Russians.'

'I'd say so.'

'Is Yurov a known FSB man?' posed Sam.

'No! But the pilot is. The pilot goes by the name of Igor Mihajlovich Sokolov. Igor has a track record as an FSB officer working in Prague, Lisbon, Paris and Dublin. Our friends in Ireland have an interest in him. As far as Yurov is concerned, we have his ports movement recorded on automated passport readers that detail Yurov Bogdanovich Dimochka visiting Heathrow, London from Moscow, as well as flights to and from Dublin, Manchester and Liverpool. There is no previous history of him in either MI5 or the sister service at MI6, but we have his photograph courtesy of the automated passport system. We're on the right track. The office is sending me their photos to my mobile. I'll show you them when the phone pings.'

'Good!'

'Quest! You up for the next part?'

'I want to be there when the curtain closes,' replied Sam. 'Have you any idea how we will take the Russians down?'

'I'm giving it some thought,' replied Rafferty.

'I have a plan,' chuckled Sam. 'It goes like this…'

The convoy continued their journey into Cumbria at high speed as Sam explained his proposal and Rafferty used his mobile to make the necessary arrangements.

As Logan approached the city in the minibus, Sam's plan went into action causing the convoy to peel off at the end of the M6 motorway and pull into a lay-by near the Greymoorhill Interchange.

The escort vehicles, front and rear, drove off leaving the minibus and a taxi parked on the lay-by.

'You sure you know what to do?' queried Sam.

'Yes!' replied Doyle. 'I think so.'

'You think so!'

'Okay! Yes! It's my ticket out of the game. The deal! Deliver the two Russians and you'll put a word in for me with the attorney general and the presiding judge. Am I right?'

'You got it,' replied Rafferty. 'Nice and simple! Nice and easy. Just like Sam says.'

Logan twisted around from the driver's seat, opened his top coat to reveal a shoulder holster, and added, 'And no funny business, Mr Doyle. I wouldn't want you to get hurt in any way after such a journey. Don't even think about running away. Understood?'

Eyeing the man and the holstered gun, Doyle replied, 'Oh yes! I hear you loud and clear. It's too late to run. I've lost my freedom, everything I've ever worked for. Just as well I'm single with no family to worry about. I hear you loud and clear, pal. I want the deal. I'm taking the deal. Is that understood?'

Relaxing, Logan closed his jacket and slid from the driver's seat onto the tarmac where he stretched his legs. He walked around the vehicle until Rafferty lowered a window and accepted a package from him.

Logan stepped away, stretched his legs, and waited.

Turning to Doyle, Rafferty said, 'Unbutton your shirt.' Then he reached across and fitted a small appliance to Doyle's kidney area. He secured it with transparent tape and then ran a thin wire from the device up the inside of Doyle's shirt. Nimbly, he pinned the opposite end of the filament to the inside of Doyle's shirt collar. It was hidden from view, couldn't be seen, and signified the main part of the operation that Rafferty needed to accomplish. Rafferty adjusted his earpiece and said, 'You're wired. Speak normally.'

'What do you want me to say?'

'Turn your head to the right and then the left and talk to me.'

'Okay! Should I say something about the weather?'

'That'll do,' replied Rafferty. 'The pin in your shirt collar is a microphone that picks up speech from three to four yards away. Try to talk directly to the other person when you are face-to-face with them. The product sounds better that way. Okay! That's enough. It's all we need. The wire is working correctly.'

'I presume you are recording everything I say?' queried Doyle.

'Yes! That's right,' replied Rafferty. 'The sound is transmitted to a control vehicle where it's recorded and saved.'

Nodding, Doyle hitched his shirt collar slightly and said, 'Okay! I'm ready to go when you are.'

'The taxi!' indicated Sam. 'Get in the back. The driver knows where you are going. Just follow the orders given to you by Yurov when you get there.'

'Will do!' replied Doyle adjusting his clothing.

Rafferty stepped out of the minibus allowing Doyle to step onto the tarmac and climb into the rear of the taxi.

Moments later, the taxi burst into life. The driver squeezed the accelerator, and the vehicle took off towards Carlisle airport with Doyle installed in the rear passenger seat.

Logan sat patiently as Rafferty and Sam took their seats in the minibus. He checked his wristwatch and eventually said, 'One minute! Let's go. We don't want to be late for the party.' He fired the engine and the minibus set off for the airport following the taxi at a respectable distance. 'Just a couple of things,' continued Logan.

'Such as?' queried Rafferty.

'While you were busy, I took a call for you from the Chief Constable of Merseyside. Following a conversation with the Director General, she's now taken over responsibility for the ongoing criminal investigation.'

'Good! Any problems?'

'None! The cops are still arresting people and recovering drugs and stuff. Almost three hundred arrests countrywide so far.'

'Excellent!' beamed Rafferty. 'The police now have formal control over the drug and crime side of things, and we remain in control of the national security arena. Just what we wanted.'

Shaking his head, Logan replied, 'Maybe so, but she wants to know the whereabouts of Detective Sergeant Doyle. He's implicated in the enquiry and Merseyside police want to talk to him pronto.'

'I bet they do. What did you tell her about Doyle?'

'That he was helping you with your enquiries and when you were free you would ring the Director General to confirm the primacy of the investigation now lies with Merseyside police. I told her that was the agreed protocol between the two services. She agreed and then I said you would ring her with an update once the protocol had been cleared with the DG.'

'Helping with enquiries,' chuckled Rafferty. 'You bought us some time, Logan. Thank you.'

'It also leaves a door open,' intervened Sam.

'Yes! I see it ajar too,' replied Rafferty. 'Are you thinking what I'm thinking?'

'Probably! If the Merseyside Chief bought the line that Doyle was helping us with our enquiries, she just might be thinking that Doyle has been on our side all the time.'

'Unlikely!' suggested Logan. 'By the time they've got through interviewing Osman and his cronies, as well as a few hundred drug dealers, they'll have a mountain of evidence to contradict that assumption and stick Doyle behind bars for the rest of his life. If you ask me, he deserves it. No disrespect to you two but why are you talking about arranging a reduction in Doyle's sentence when he was close to helping the Russians destroy society with cheap drugs and a move towards drug addiction? He's an evil bastard who should be hung, drawn, and quartered for what he's done.'

'Thank you for replying to the Chief the way you did, Logan,' replied Rafferty returning to an earlier part of the conversation. 'You bought us time and put a spanner in the works.'

'That doesn't answer my question,' argued Logan.

Biting his lip, Rafferty sat contemplating for a moment as the minibus travelled past Houghton Hall Garden Centre. As the vehicle began its approach to Linstock roundabout, Rafferty replied, 'I don't suppose the police would accept the proposition that Doyle was working undercover for us. There's too much evidence to contradict that. On the other hand, Doyle has agreed to help us mount a counter-attack against the Russian Intelligence machine operating in this country. I can't miss out on the opportunity to challenge the Russian state.'

'Why not?' debated Logan. 'Doyle is bent. Stick him where he belongs. In jail! When this job hits the national media, they'll join me in shouting for Doyle to be hung, drawn and quartered. What is so important about putting Russian intelligence down?'

Sam Quest looked Logan in the eye and said, 'You told me way back in Moray Firth that Jupiter was the biggest planet in the solar system, and that in ancient Roman religion Jupiter was the God of the sky and thunder. He was the king of the gods in ancient Rome. Logan, I'd cut my right arm off for you, but if Mr Rafferty, who you guys call Jupiter, tells me the sky is green, not blue, then I'll walk with him because the sky must be green and he's right. He's got the whole picture. Not just part of it. Isn't that right, Jupiter?'

'It's a world in which I am used to both winning and losing,' replied Rafferty. 'In this one, there is no win for us in the media either way we play the game.'

'You mean it's a draw?' probed Logan.

'Yes! If we're lucky!'

'Well, I for one don't understand. Explain!' demanded Logan. 'I train your team in physical and mental capabilities so that they might succeed. I don't train them to lose or draw.'

'I should have trained you in the politics of the intelligence world,' revealed Rafferty. 'Do you want me to tell you where we are going with this, and why we have taken Doyle to the brink?'

'Yes! Absolutely! Yes!' demanded Logan.

'Doyle is a prisoner of his own making. He'll go to prison either way this works out. In my mind, he is no longer important. He's finished. I look upon him as an asset although he does not realise it.'

'An asset!' challenged Sam. 'That's what the powers that be call me, is it not?'

'It's about the politics of a nation,' explained Rafferty. 'We cannot let the Russians win. If we allow them to walk away unscathed, they'll be back again in a couple of years and they'll do precisely the same thing without a care in the world. They might even do it to one of our allies. We need to show them, and the rest of the world, that British Intelligence is better than they are. We want the Russians to fear us, not walk all over us as if we were a doormat. We've got to be so hard on them that they think twice before they return with such mind-boggling stupid ideas that, if they were successful, would be catastrophic to our way of life. We must make them frightened of us, wary of us, to the extent that they think twice about attacking us in case we counter-attack and defeat them in a way that they cannot imagine.'

'It sounds like a complicated chess game,' remarked Logan.

'It is,' admitted Rafferty. 'Except I don't care how we win the game. I'll upset the table, tip over the pieces, and cheat if I have to. Any which way we can!'

'And Doyle?'

'Doyle is a pawn in the big picture,' explained Rafferty. 'If he gets us the evidence then we'll do him a deal of some kind and he'll go to prison for ten years instead of twenty.'

'I thought you had enough against the Russians?' challenged Logan.

'No, not yet! We've no names to shout other than Yurov and his pilot friend and we haven't captured them yet. We've got two nameless managers in a dubious travel agent in Piccadilly, a cash trail, and Doyle's word for it. Some CCTV footage shows Doyle in Novikov but he has their travel brochure in his apartment which is the reason his solicitor will say that he repeatedly went there. He'll tell the court his client was planning a holiday.'

'But that's all wrong,' said Logan. 'We know better.'

'Agreed! It's not watertight. I need it to be one hundred per cent correct not just suspicious.'

'The cops might not play the game with you if they don't get what they want,' suggested Logan.

'So what!' continued Rafferty. 'The police will get it in the neck for months and every cop in the country will be tarnished because of Doyle. That said if we got lucky and were able to convince everyone that he's been on an undercover assignment for the last three years then he'd be written up as a hero and the media might not be so keen to cover the story. You know what journalists are like. A page-one headline article can soon be shuffled onto the inside pages if something bigger and more interesting comes along. Even better, Doyle would walk free with a pat on the back, a handshake, and a medal or two.'

'I could make that happen for you,' replied Logan. 'All I need is an access code into the computer framework of Merseyside Constabulary and the Police National Computer. I can soon drop a false story into the digital files somewhere. That might help if you go down that route.'

'I know you can do it,' nodded Rafferty with a smile. He clasped his hand on Logan's back and continued, 'You did it for Quest here. But so far, the bosses at Faversham Mews haven't sanctioned that course of action but I wouldn't be surprised if they were thinking about it. People like the heads of MI5 and MI6 don't reach the top because their club membership is fully paid. No! They get there because they see the bigger picture and understand it. The thing is, Logan, in the bigger picture, it's more important to beat the Russians than it is to imprison Doyle. Do you understand my position?'

'Perfectly, now that it's out in the open,' replied Logan. 'It's my army upbringing, Mr Rafferty. I'll take soldiers up a hill to defeat the enemy because the Colonel tells me. That doesn't mean I know what we're going to do when we've taken the hill. The bigger picture! Yes, I see it now.'

Sam coughed and intervened with, 'When you two are quite ready, can we kindly cut the idle chatter and watch what happens next? We're almost at the airport. That chess game is up and running and your problem, Mr Rafferty, is that it's too late to cheat. It's down to Doyle. It's as simple as that.'

'I'll get the teams into position,' remarked Logan. 'Richardson can take look out in the control tower. Laidlaw is a dab hand covering the wire recording in the control vehicle and the rest of the team is armed and dangerous. Looking at the map, I'm going to deploy some of them at the rear entrance to the airport near the Solway Aviation Museum. Another unit will occupy near the Carlisle Flight Training Centre and the remainder can provide vehicle support when we strike. Sounds like an army but there are less than a dozen of us. Just pray there's no gunfight with the Russians. It's the last thing we need.'

'Okay!' nodded Sam. We've no time for an Ok Corral fight!'

Logan rattled out his instructions on the radio system and then turned into Carlisle airport. He found a parking place close enough to watch the runway entrance, and switched off the engine with, 'No sign of Doyle. He should be in the café in the departures lounge by now.'

In the control tower, the duty air traffic controller noted the position of an inbound Cessna Skyhawk from Dublin, acknowledged its radio signal, welcomed the pilot to the airport's airspace, and waited for the private plane to descend from its current altitude towards the runway.

Standing close to the air traffic controller, Richardson, from Logan's team, put away his identity card and gave the controller a thumbs up saying, 'Once he's landed bring him in close to the fence by the entrance to the apron for all the service vehicles.'

'He's going straight to the fuel bowsers at the refuelling point,' revealed the air traffic controller. 'That's what he radioed permission for earlier and I granted it. That's not unusual. I expect he's either returning right away or hopping over to Europe for the rest of the flight. Our man will refuel for him, and he'll pay before he leaves. If he stays for a while, we might even receive an amended flight plan.'

'Thanks! Any more flights due today?'

'A couple of private flights and a few learners are waiting for the Cessna Skyhawk to land. Once he's down, they'll bring them out of the hangars, taxi out onto the runway, and take off. Touch and go practice tonight. All learners! Don't worry! No one will take off until the Skyhawk is refuelled and I'm happy with its bearing.'

'Hopefully, it will be the end of his journey,' stated Richardson. 'I'll watch if I may. You have a great view here.'

'Be my guest,' gestured the air traffic controller. 'You'll find a pot of coffee on the boil behind you. Help yourself but pour two.'

In the skies above the city, Igor Sokolov guided the Cessna Skyhawk and gradually descended towards the airport. Crossing the plain of the River Eden, the Cessna's altitude quickly lowered when the land suddenly rose from the river bed and caused the altimeter to recalculate.

'I see it,' radioed Richardson to the team. 'Prepare for the landing. It's on its way.'

As the team acknowledged on the radio net, Doyle sat in the departures lounge café. Gazing through the window he took in a panoramic view and watched as a dot appeared in the sky. The dot grew and became an aeroplane as Doyle sugared his coffee and unwrapped a chocolate biscuit. By the time he had eaten the biscuit, the unmistakable shape of the Cessna Skyhawk continued to descend towards the runway.

Moments later, the Cessna touched down and taxied towards its allotted stand and out of Doyle's sight.

'We have an arrival,' radioed Richardson across the net from the control tower. 'To the stand at the rear of the building near the flight school.'

'I have that,' radioed Rafferty. 'In fact, I have an eyeball on the plane now. Hold all positions as arranged.'

The Cessna engine cut out allowing the passenger in the front seat to unbuckle his belt and drop to the ground from the plane's wing. The pilot followed suit and the pair walked towards the airport building.'

A lean-looking man dressed in overalls was sweeping the pathway close to the rear entrance. Placing the brush to one side, he pressed a button on his overalls and radioed, 'Alpha

Nine has eyeball. From the photographs provided, I can confirm the pilot is Igor Mihajlovich Sokolov. The passenger wearing the ushanka is Yurov Bogdanovich Dimochka. Apart from the traditional furry hat, he's wearing a long dark overcoat. I'm out of here. They are coming towards me.'

'I have that,' from Rafferty.

Alpha Nine collected his brush and moved further along the building line working his way towards the maintenance hut where a quad bike was situated. Slinging the brush on the back, he mounted the quad bike and set off out of sight of the two visitors entering the departure lounge café.

Doyle remained seated, glanced at his visitors, and took another drink of coffee. He gestured for the pair to join him.

Yurov held his ground, looked around, and realised there was no one else in the café. Standing at least six feet tall, the Russian was also leanly built, and clean-shaven, but with a tanned complexion suggesting he was a well-travelled man. Removing his gloves and ushanka, he placed them on Doyle's table and sat down.

'Coffee?' queried Igor engaging Doyle.

'From the machine over there,' pointed Doyle.

As Igor went for coffee, Yurov fidgeted with his hat before pushing it to one side and asking, 'How long have you been here?'

'Long enough to get a coffee and relax from the rigours of Liverpool. Did you bring me money as usual?'

'Money!' exclaimed Yurov.

'Yes! I have a new list of drug dealers for you. They'll help in any plans you might have in the future, but some cash now would be nice to keep me going. I couldn't get to the bank you see. I'm broke.'

'You won't need money where you're going,' replied Yurov. 'How did you get here? I didn't see your car.'

'I left my motor outside the flat so that anyone calling will think I'm still in Liverpool. I bought some time that way, don't you think?'

'You haven't answered the question,' persuaded the Russian. 'How did you get here?'

'By train direct from Liverpool. How do you think I got here, Yurov? It's too far to walk.'

'Funny man today,' replied Yurov scanning the landscape through the window and then checking to see if anyone had entered the café. 'You're alone then?'

'Of course!'

'What happened in Liverpool?'

'It went tits up,' said Doyle. 'All that time and money wasted. Doesn't it break your heart?'

'I asked you what happened in Liverpool,' demanded Yurov suddenly adopting a mean streak and banging his fist on the table. 'Stop playing stupid games.'

Doyle paled and feebly replied, 'I just wanted my coffee before we go. It'll be a long trip I suspect, and that plane you came on will rattle and wobble anywhere. It won't have a coffee machine hidden in the back seat, will it?'

Wringing his hands, Yurov replied, 'Drink your coffee, Doyle. We'll be taking off soon once the plane has been refuelled. Tell me what happened at the docks. Why did it all go wrong?'

Igor returned, placed a coffee in front of Yurov, and sat down next to him.

'We ran out of luck,' declared Doyle. 'I've spent a lot of time raking through the world of drug dealers to find the ones that would work for you. I made lists and gave you their details, phone numbers, and all kinds. In return, you paid me huge amounts of cash which I either got from you or collected from the Novikov travel agent in Piccadilly. The point is, Yurov, the word on the street is that one of the drug dealers shopped us. The police moved in en masse with Customs and Excise and searched all the ships at Bootle docks. There were hundreds of cops. They hit Misha first and turned us over. The boys ran for it. I think they must have been caught because I've not heard anything from them. The dealers in their vans got locked up.

The cops got the drugs, and I made a run for it. I thought it best to get out of the way until I knew what was going on.'

'It's not quite like that on the television news,' revealed Yurov.

'I don't know about that,' replied Doyle. 'I wasn't at the docks. As you know, I never go near the docks. I leave it to Malek Osman, Jake and the boys. Not my scene, Yurov. I keep out of the way when the drugs are offloaded. The first proper news I heard of it all was when I phoned you at the agreed time and you told me to get out of town as quickly as possible. Yes, I've heard bits since on the radio and the train but I don't know everything. You told me to come pronto. I did. Here I am.'

Yurov glanced at Igor who raised his eyebrows and set down his coffee before saying, 'Now listen, Doyle. You know Yurov here but you don't know me. I'm gonna eat you alive because you failed us. You stupid man!'

'Yurov said to come here as quickly as I could,' replied Doyle hurriedly. 'If you know more than me then that's good. I'm only telling you the way I know it. I've been on a train for a couple of hours. Then I got a taxi to get here on time. All I know is that one of the dealers shopped us to the police. Who else could it be? I know you paid me to get some guys able to sell a couple of tons of cocaine and heroin to make the country into addicts, but I never let you down. Never!'

'Who was the dealer?'

'No idea! I thought you knew. Was it mentioned on the news?'

There was no reply from the Russian pair. Just a puzzled look between them.

'Come on, guys,' pleaded Doyle. 'Whatever happened down there is done. The job is blown by the sound of it all. You wanted me out before the cops got to me. I'm here. I'm as free as a bird just waiting to fly anywhere you care to take me. I didn't shop you or anyone else. Do you see an airport full of cops waiting for you?'

In the control vehicle, Rafferty listened to the conversation courtesy of the wire Doyle was wearing. He turned to Sam and said, 'He's gone far enough. He's put the operation to the Russians, mentioned they paid him for the list of drug dealers, and a whole lot more. What do you think, Quest? Pull him now or let him run on for a while?'

'Those two Russians haven't admitted a thing,' interrupted Logan.

'True!' replied Sam. 'But they haven't denied it either and for Jupiter's purpose that's what we want. We've got a lot of evidence about the operation but not the Russian involvement. Doyle is putting everything on a plate for us and they aren't arguing. Tell me, Logan, if they were innocent what are they doing miles from home at Carlisle airport having flown from Dublin to listen to a man about a drugs operation in Liverpool? Remember, he's saying they are involved in that operation, and they aren't denying it. He's making the case for us.'

'He's followed your briefing well,' declared Rafferty.

'Bit of international law and politics, if you ask me,' suggested Logan with a slight shuffle of his body. 'All above me, but then I get you. They'd have trouble explaining their way out of that conversation.'

'I think we'll take them when they all board the plane,' decided Rafferty. 'Doyle told us that's why he had to come here. To meet Yurov and be taken away by him to another place. A place of safety! A place where he could live out the rest of his life under a false identity created for him by the Russian State. The very least we can do is prove Doyle is right about the getaway clause he had with Yurov. All agreed?'

Logan nodded and Sam replied, 'You're the boss, but we all think they are going to take him away and kill him. They'll probably dump his body in the Irish Sea as they fly back to Dublin. Let him run a while. I'd like him to cover Novikov a bit more but… Wait…Listen in. I think they're coming out now.'

'What about Novikov?' queried Doyle.
'The travel agents? Why mention them?' replied Yurov.
'Oh! I just thought they might be closing down,' explained Doyle. 'I presumed that if you're ending the operation then you'll be pulling the two managers and taking them home to Moscow. What were their names again?'

'Too far,' remarked Rafferty listening to Doyle's wiretap. 'He never knew the names, was never told them. Too direct!'
'You're right there,' added Sam. 'Teams to stand by. Tell me where you want me, Logan.'
'Right here,' replied Logan. 'Next to me. Let's see what their reaction is.'
Rafferty radioed, 'This is Jupiter! All call signs, I have control. Stand by! We have progress. Move to forward positions only.'

'Names!' blurted Yurov. 'What names? You were never given names. Why all the questions, Doyle?'
'Get him to the plane,' ordered Igor. 'It'll be refuelled by now. Let's get him out of here. That's what we came for.'
Yurov grabbed Doyle by the lapel and pulled him onto his feet with, 'Come on! It's time to go.'
The wire inside Doyle's clothing dislodged itself.
'No need to pull me,' snapped Doyle. 'I came here so that you and the bosses in the Kremlin could harbour me somewhere safe. I'll walk. No need to manhandle me.'
'Just move it,' snarled Igor. 'Yurov! Get in the back seat with him. Keep him company. I'll start the plane.'
Igor strode ahead and climbed into the cockpit. There was a sharp hacking sound from the engine before the propeller burst into life and began its never-ending spin.

'The Kremlin!' snapped Yurov. 'What kind of remark is that, Doyle? What's got into you?'

'Spying!' replied Doyle. 'Me! I was more or less spying on behalf of the Russian State via you. You are my handler.'

'Handler!' growled Yurov. 'What are you up to? Come here.'

Doyle took a step back only to be grabbed again by the lapel and pulled forward.

The wire tumbled out of the front of Doyle's shirt. The recording device was ripped from the small of his back and joined the thin wire now clearly exposed for Yurov to see.

'Wired!' screamed Yurov. 'Igor! It's a set-up! He's wired.'

In the control vehicle, Sam remarked, 'Oh, no! That's done it, boys.'

Rafferty snatched the handset and radioed, 'This is Jupiter. I have control. All call signs! Strike! Strike! Strike!'

Igor pushed the throttle forward, opened the passenger door, and shouted, 'Get him in here. Now! It's a one-way ticket. Jump in!'

Yurov dragged Doyle towards the plane, pulled a handgun from his shoulder holster, and pointed it at his prisoner shouting, 'Get in, Doyle. Now! If anyone comes near you then you'll get it first. Move it!'

There was a growl of rage and a squeal of brakes when two high-powered saloon cars hurtled through the rear entrance and slewed to a standstill on the tarmac close to the plane. Jumping from both cars, balaclava-clad men from Logan's team took cover behind the car doors, pointed their weapons at the Cessna Skyhawk, and heard Logan shouting on a megaphone, 'You are surrounded! Put down your weapons! Place your hands on your head.'

A team of a dozen men leapt from the maintenance shed, the flight school, and the rear of the café. They charged towards the Cessna, guns drawn and making ground as fast as they could.

Sam Quest led the way, unarmed, his body thrusting forward at speed as he raced towards the Cessna.

Igor gradually moved the plane forward as Yurov wrestled with Doyle hauling him onto the plane's wing and then hitting him with the butt of his pistol trying to weaken his resolve.

Logan appeared, crept from behind the plane, and grasped the pilot's door handle. He pulled the door open and shoved his semi-automatic into Igor's face shouting, 'Off! Switch the engine off! You're going nowhere, pal!'

Igor glanced at Logan, saw the gun in his face, and reached out to help Yurov pull Doyle into the cabin shouting, 'You'll never shoot me. You can't. Get him in here, Yurov! Get the bastard in here!'

Logan twitched and wanted to pull the trigger but knew they were ahead of the game. Pulling the trigger would strengthen the Russians and weaken the British case. 'I'll shoot!' he lied.

Igor accelerated. The aircraft began to surge forward. The propellor moved into overdrive.

Yurov was inside the cabin with Doyle's legs dangling outside, trying to find purchase on the wing. Doyle was half in and half out.

A gunshot rang out.

Sam glimpsed at Yurov, saw a gun pointed skywards, knew it was a warning shot from Logan, and promptly rugby-tackled Doyle grasping him around the waist.

The two men crashed to the tarmac and rolled over with Sam covering Doyle's body to protect him from any Russian bullets. A glance revealed Yurov twisting his body into a shooting position. The Russian aimed at Doyle.

The Cessna gathered speed lengthening the distance between Yurov and his target with Logan shouting, 'The tyres! Shoot the tyres!'

A barrage of gunfire followed with Logan's team blowing out the plane tyres and moving closer to the Cessna.

The gun toppled from Yurov's hands, landed on the tarmac, and was kicked away by a balaclava-clad lawman.

'Stay where you are,' boomed from a loudspeaker when Rafferty hit the tarmac and bellowed directly at the pilot.

In the control tower, Richardson's mouth dropped. The traffic controller hit the deck thinking the bullets were headed his way as pandemonium invaded the airport and the screams of legitimate visitors and staff rent the air.

Sam rolled across the ground again clutching Doyle as Igor laughed aloud and screamed, 'You're not taking us!'

Guiding the plane towards the two saloon cars, Yurov yelled, 'What the hell are you doing?'

'Battering ram!' growled Igor.

The Cessna moved forward, collided with the first saloon car, made Logan's team jump out of the way, and then careered towards the second car with Logan still drilling the Cessna's tyres with bullets.

Doyle rolled away from Sam and said, 'Thank you. You saved my life!'

'All in a day's work,' returned Sam.

'My last day of work,' replied Doyle. 'Save yourself! My life is over!'

As Sam reached out to stop Doyle, the Merseyside detective scrambled to his feet, raised his arms, and shouted, 'Sorry!'

Doyle broke into a sprint and threw himself into the plane's propellor.

There was a falter in the fast-moving rotation when Doyle's head slammed into the propellor shaft. Then the innards of the shaft twisted, contorted, and then exploded from the sheer size of Doyle's shoulders penetrating the system. The blast promptly decimated Doyle's skull into a dozen separate pieces. Blood and body parts splattered into the air, dowsed Sam, Logan, and others, and left the headless torso wobbling on its feet before the legs crumbled and the body collapsed in a heap of blood and mucus.

The Cessna was done, out of the game, finished, with the awestruck Igor frozen in the cockpit unable to pilot the aircraft any further.

Yurov climbed fully into the plane, shook some blood from his clothes, and then glanced at the windscreen. It was as if an abstract painting had been splashed across the window, daubed in dark red, bloodied beyond comprehension, and compliant with the needs of a deceased artist.

Logan regained his composure and pulled Igor from the cockpit. Others dragged Yurov from the other side of the aircraft and took both men to the ground where they were searched and handcuffed. Two handguns were found, bagged, tagged, and secured.

Rafferty stood over the two Russians and said, 'We are officers from the British Security Service. You are both detained in connection with a conspiracy to commit a hostile enemy action in this country. You will be taken into custody and transported separately to a secure location of our choosing.'

'We have diplomatic immunity,' snarled Igor. 'Let us go now or there will be trouble for you.'

'You may well have diplomatic immunity,' replied Rafferty. 'But until you are formally identified and that is confirmed I have every right to arrest you both and seize your firearms. Logan! Arrange their detention.'

'With pleasure,' voiced Logan as he moved in with his team and organised transport.

Sam lay on the ground motionless, his eyes staring at Doyle's lifeless body. There was a sudden unexpected twitch from the lower leg of the torso. Perhaps no more than the final act of a nervous system destroyed. Blood and mucus, of a bodily kind, ran from Sam's forehead, dribbled down the bridge of his nose, and then dripped onto his top lip. He ignored the procession of blood, the horrific scene of a body torn to pieces by an aircraft propellor, and just held the memory in his brain. Dumbstruck, Sam Quest was transfixed by the horror of it all.

'Quest!' from Rafferty. 'Quest! It's all over. We got the prize.'

'And Doyle lost,' whispered Sam almost inaudibly.

Rafferty watched the two Russians being taken away. He knelt by Sam and said, 'You did what you could. You probably saved his life but then he decided enough was enough.'

'He didn't have to do that,' from Sam.

'He chose to,' replied Rafferty. 'We'll tell it like it was, Quest. We'll let the others decide if he was trying to stop the Russians from escaping or did he deliberately throw himself into the propeller to commit suicide.'

'We'll never know now,' replied Sam. 'But I'm going to remember him shouting, 'sorry', for the rest of my life.'

'No, you're not,' declared Rafferty. 'You're going to replace it with happier memories. Now get on your feet, get cleaned up, and get some coffee on in the café over there.'

'You coming?' asked Sam.

'Not yet! I have a phone call to make,' explained Rafferty.

As Sam walked towards the airport building, Rafferty stepped away and hit the digits of his mobile phone. It was answered almost immediately, and Rafferty said, 'This is Jupiter. You have control. Strike! Strike! Strike!'

Rafferty listened, heard the reply, and closed the phone.

Instantaneously, the Police Commander in Piccadilly closed his phone, lifted his handset, and radioed, 'All callsigns, this is Boss car. I have control! Stand by! Strike! Strike! Strike!'

Four liveried patrol cars scorched into Piccadilly. Two from one direction and two from the opposite direction. The first two vehicles stopped outside the Novikov travel agents whilst the other two vehicles slewed broadside across the road blocking the highway.

Accompanied by a blaze of flashing blue lights and a cacophony of wailing sirens, the four units were supported by two police minibuses that also pulled in outside the travel agent.

A score of uniform officers rushed into the building whilst, simultaneously, another unit entered by the rear door. The premises were secured in minutes and a search began.

The manager, his deputy, and all the staff were rounded up and the Commander introduced himself and read out the search warrant in his possession. He explained they were looking for evidence relative to an alleged conspiracy to engage in hostile enemy action in the United Kingdom. They were looking for money that had been laundered, lists of drug dealers and criminal entrepreneurs that were involved in the said conspiracy, and any other evidence deemed relative to the enquiry underway.

Within a short time, the search revealed a hidden banking system inside the travel agent, lists of drug dealers from across the United Kingdom, and a treasure trove of computerised activity that would eventually lead to the conclusion that Novikov was merely a front for the covert operations of the Russian Intelligence Agency: the FSB.

In another part of London, a telephone was answered in Faversham Mews. The recipient smiled and phoned the Foreign Secretary to inform and persuade action against those working for the Russian Intelligence system whilst resident in London.

A phone call was made from the Minister summoning the Russian Ambassador from his embassy in Kensington Palace Gardens asking him to explain the actions of so-called Russians either residents in the UK or serving as diplomats in the embassy and various trade delegations.

The matter would dominate the headlines for weeks to come, enthral the readers and followers of the story, and condemn the tale of a corrupt cop to the inside pages of the national tabloids with the headline, 'Courageous cop or corrupt cop? Will we ever know the truth?'

Days later, in an old castle on the Moray Firth, Logan poured three brandies and said, 'Thanks for joining me on my last day. You all know I have reached the age where I need to rest both my body and my mind. I need to relax and refresh. These last few weeks have made me think I may be past my sell-by date.'

'You will never be passed your sell-by date, Logan,' announced Rafferty. 'We need men like you. Even when your body and mind tire you have a wealth of knowledge and wisdom to impart to others. No one who has ever done this job at your level retires. They are always on the books, and they know it. But I congratulate you on your worthy service and wish you a well-earned rest. Here's to you.'

The trio raised their glasses and drank a toast to Logan.

'Thank you,' came the reply. 'Time for you to step up now, Sam. It's your job if you want it. Am I right, Jupiter? Is it time for Europa to take over?'

'Why not?' answered Rafferty. 'Yours if you want it to be, Quest. No question about that.'

'Do I have the credentials? That's the question. I'm not a teacher and have never learnt anything about how to be an instructor.'

'You certainly do have the credentials,' replied Rafferty. If it wasn't for you, Quest, we'd have raided the wrong ship and the Russians would have laughed their socks off all the way back to Moscow. You have the credentials. You've done a great job for your country. Do you want Logan's job?'

'I don't know about that,' replied Sam. 'When do you want to know?'

'Soon but take your time. I'll understand if you walk away,' revealed Rafferty. 'The money is there waiting for me to push a button and it's yours. Just say the word. There's a bonus in there too. You'll never need to work again. On the other hand, it's up to you, Sam. Only you can decide, and you're used to making your own decisions.'

'Funny that,' replied Sam. 'That's the first time you've ever called me Sam. That might mean I am no longer an asset.'

There was a trio of chuckles before Rafferty replied, 'Doyle became an asset, Sam. And we ran him well even if the unexpected occurred. Apart from that, well! We can't be too close to the troops you know. That would never do.'

'Thinking back,' replied Sam, 'It all went wrong when he ran into that plane. I wish we'd taken him straight to the nick. No deals, no Russians, nothing.'

'It helped in a way,' replied Rafferty. 'No one truly knows how bad a cop Doyle was. His corruption will not become well known in police circles. Maybe the bosses at Faversham Mews will talk to the Home Secretary and the Merseyside Chief and construct a form of words that reveals Doyle was always on our side.'

'Another undercover cop, you mean?' smiled Sam. 'A man who set the Russians up when they approached him. A man you guys ran against the Russians so that you could score heavily in the political climate.'

'Something like that,' nodded Rafferty. 'Faversham Mews would be interested in your response to that scenario.'

'Tell them I'm an asset, Jupiter. I have no decision-making abilities. Never been granted any such skills since the start. Just did it my way with a little help from my friends. You two.'

'Anything else they should know?'

'I am Europa: an asset without a voice at the table of political squabbling. I don't need this. Jupiter. Sorry!'

'But we need you and people like you.'

'Assets! That's all we are. Tools to be used by those above who see us as no more than that. Assets for the use thereof. The sell-by date is short and the quality of manufacture questionable.'

'I can change things for you.'

'I'll let you know. I have someone to see and things to do. I'm planning a holiday in the sun.'

~

Chapter Seventeen
~

Four weeks later.
Praia do Paraiso, Carvoeiro,
The Algarve, Portugal

Sam's paddle penetrated the Atlantic Ocean forcing the blade through the water like a knife sliding through butter. Droplets of sweat trickled down his arms and dribbled into the sea when the cave came into view. One last pull through the water; one last mighty heave and his kayak surged forward.

Daylight paled. Growing darker, the heat of the sun faded on Sam's body. Only the beach ahead and the cave's darkness beckoned.

There was a sudden jolt when the kayak's bow glided into the soft sand and embedded itself. The vessel wobbled from side to side until Sam used the paddle to steady the balance. The waves broke on the beach, pushed forward a yard or two, and then retreated to the quiet waters of the Algarve.

Loosening himself from the kayak, Sam waded into the water and made the beach before turning to look back towards Carvoeiro.

Alone for a moment, in the isolated splendour of one of the caves that frequented this part of the coastline, Sam asked himself the questions that had rattled inside his head since touching down at Faro airport a couple of weeks earlier.

'Five years? Should I go again? Or should I settle and find someone who cares, someone to become part of my life forever? If I told anyone that I am alone in this stupid life of mine, what would they think? No one would believe my story. What do I do? What would she have me do? Yes, I want her. But does she want me? How do I ask a woman so beautiful that I want her to be part of me? I love the way she walks, the way she talks, and the times we have shared. How do I tell her that I was close to distrusting her, walking away, shunning her for the rest of my days because she was one of them, not someone I wanted in my life? How things have changed.'

Splashing water nudged Sam into the present. He looked up to see Jenny approaching in her kayak. Her blonde hair was longer now, blowing behind her before resting on her shoulders when the kayak made the cave and beached alongside his.

She waved, untangled the damp ends of her golden tresses, and allowed them to cascade across her shoulders. 'Made it!' she laughed.

'Beautiful,' he thought. Smiling, waving, just beautiful. 'I'm going to miss her when she's gone.'

'That was some pull.'

'She's smiling and waving,' thought Sam. 'I can see how happy she is.'

Jenny back paddled and moved slightly away from the beach.

'Can I talk to you about something?' queried Sam.

'You certainly can,' replied Jenny. 'You can apologise to me for cheating.' She laughed. 'You said it would be a fair race and then set off like a man possessed leaving me on the beach at Carvoeiro pushing the kayak out. You, Sam Quest, stole ten yards or more. You are a cheat.'

'Yes! I am. I tell lies for a living. You caught me out again.'

'An easy thing to do when I know you.'

'Are you coming onto the beach?'

'No way. I'm turning around ready for the race back. I'm ready and raring to go. You need to climb in and turn around. You're not the only one who can cheat.'

Sam knelt and splashed water at Jenny who reacted by sticking a paddle into the water and turning the kayak around in record time.

'There's something been on my mind for a while, Jenny. Can I ask you something?'

'No! You're repeating yourself and you need to make up your mind.'

'But I haven't told you what I want to talk to you about.'

'You don't have to. I know you. I know what you do, why you do it, and what kind of life you lead.'

'I can have a better life with you,' posed Sam biting his lip.

'Maybe,' she replied.

'Your favourite word!'

'Maybe I can have a better life with you when you've finished doing whatever it is they want you for this time. I don't know. You'll know better than me.'

'There's a vacancy if I want it,' explained Sam. 'It's in Scotland. The Moray Firth and I'll have lodgings up there and some weekends off. It's not full-time. Well, maybe for three to six months of the year and then I'll be home again.'

'Just like Liverpool then?'

'It's a training post. Flexible! The man who trained me is retiring soon. Rafferty wants me to take the job and...'

'Take it!'

'Will you wait for me?'

'Maybe!'

'That's not enough.'

'It is for me, Sam. You know where to find me.'

'By my side is where I want you,' persuaded Sam.

'Maybe!'

'I love you, Jenny.'

'At last! I thought you'd never say it.' Jenny chuckled and continued, 'I know I love you. I could come to Scotland with you.'

'Maybe!'

'That's my line, Sam. There's no maybe about it. It's yes or no. Make your mind up, Sam Quest.'

'It's a yes!'

'Come on!' beamed Jenny. 'Time to celebrate then. You and me together kind of permanently, I mean.'

Sam smiled. He had no more words.

Jenny returned the splash, stuck the paddle into the ocean, and shouted, 'Let's go around the point to the beach at Carvoeiro. It's ice cream time. Race you back or paddle together, which?'

'Together! Always. No maybe's about it.'

Jenny guided her kayak until it was pointed out of the cave and towards the daylight that glorified the Algarve coast. She waited.

Sam shook the sand from his feet and climbed into his kayak.

They rowed into the Atlantic, forever together.

Until the next time…

The End.

Reviews

~

'One of the best thrillers and mystery writers in the United Kingdom today'....

Caleb Pirtle 111, International Bestselling Author of over 60 novels, journalist, travel writer, screenplay writer, and Founder and Editorial Director at Venture Galleries.

*

'Paul Anthony is one of the best Thriller Mystery Writers of our times!'...

Dennis Sheehan, International Bestselling Author of 'Purchased Power', former United States Marine Corps.

*

'When it comes to fiction and poetry you will want to check out this outstanding author. Paul has travelled the journey of publication and is now a proud writer who is well worth discovering.' ... Janet Beasley, Epic Fantasy Author, theatre producer and director - Scenic Nature Photographer, JLB Creatives. Also, Founder/co-author at Journey to Publication

*

'Paul Anthony is a brilliant writer and an outstanding gentleman who goes out of his way to help and look out for others. In his writing, Paul does a wonderful job of portraying the era in which we live with its known and unknown fears. I highly recommend this intelligent and kind gentleman to all.' ...

Jeannie Walker, author of the True Crime Story 'Fighting the Devil', 2011 National Indie Excellence Awards (True Crime Finalist) and 2010 winner of the Silver Medal for Book of the Year True Crime Awards.

*

'To put it simply, Paul tells a bloody good tale. I have all his works and particularly enjoy his narrative style. His characters are totally believable and draw you in. Read. Enjoy'....

John White, Reader and Director at Baldwins Restructuring and Insolvency.

*

'Paul Anthony's skills as a writer are paramount. His novels are well-balanced throughout, all of which hold the reader with both dynamic and creative plots and edge-of-your-seat action alike.

His ability to create realistic and true-to-life characters are a strength lacking in many novelists who pen stories based on true events or real-life experience. He is a fantastic novelist that will have you craving for more! Get his books now...a must-have for all serious readers!'

Nicolas Gordon, Screenwriter - 'Hunted: The enemy within'.

*

'Paul Anthony has been working with the Dyslexia Foundation to develop a digital audio Library, he has been very generous in giving his time and expertise for free. As a long-time fan of Paul's work, it was very altruistic of Paul to allow us to use one of his excellent books. We have recently turned 'The Fragile Peace' into our first audiobook, to be used in an exciting project to engage non-readers in the world of literacy. The foundation has an audiobook club that will be running in Liverpool and Manchester and Paul again has been very generous with his time in agreeing to come and talk to the audiobook club about his book The Fragile Peace. The Foundation, and clients, are very appreciative of the support of the author Paul Anthony.

Steve O'Brien, C.E.O. Dyslexia Foundation,

*

This guy not only walks the talk, but he also writes it as well. Thrillers don't get any better than this...

Paul Tobin, Author, novelist, and poet.

*

Printed in Great Britain
by Amazon